MW00939792

ENGULFED

a novel by

KATHLEEN COSGROVE

Copyright © 2012 Kathleen Cosgrove
All rights reserved.

ISBN-13: 978-1478160359

DEDICATION

To my best buddy, Steve "Zig" Sebeckis.

He made me laugh every day, and that's not nothin'.

The Gulf of Mexico

It is a place of life, beauty, and wonder.

It is not a giant gas station.

ACKNOWLEDGMENTS

Many thanks go out to,

My mother for the writing gene.

To Jan Dynes, my friend since seventh grade who said, "You should write a book."

To The Nashville Writers Meetup Group, who made me a better writer, and especially Lily Wilson who polished this thing until it shone.

To Billy Howard @ Billy Howard Photography for my beautiful photograph; he is indeed magical.

To my son, the talented Charlie Wetherington, for designing this awesome cover.

To my nearest and dearest friend,Shelby Malmstrom, who went through this with a fine tooth comb.

And to all my family and friends who believed in me, encouraged me and endured me throughout this process, especially my son, Tony Wetherington, who has been my constant cheerleader.

ENGULFED
CHAPTER ONE

When you're a divorced woman from an Irish Catholic home you sort of expect God to punish you once in a while. It's his benevolent way of making you pay here so you don't have to burn in hell later; at least that's how I look it. Therefore, I was not really surprised when Hurricane Fanny, who was supposed to ramble on over to Mexico, changed her trajectory and decided to head toward southwest Florida the moment my plane touched down at the Fort Myers, Florida airport.

Now granted, I had come down to Florida to be a good daughter and help my folks move from their first retirement home in Bonita Springs to the super fancy assisted living apartments they had rented in the same town. That good deed only earned me enough points to have God downgrade Fanny from a category three to a one.

And, because my parents were a good Irish-Catholic still-married couple of sixty-five years, they themselves were not here to weather the hurricane but were instead enjoying Disney World with my brother and his grandchildren.

Such is my relationship with The Almighty and my reason for being in what I consider to be a place only slightly more livable than the sun.

The drive from my parent's *soon to be ex*-home to Shell Harbor Assisted living took me ten minutes and two bottled waters to get to.

The *Welcome Home to Shell Harbor* sign was flanked on either side by palm trees of assorted shapes and sizes, and hibiscus bushes with their pink, orange and yellow petals reminding everyone that this was the tropics. The architecture of the building, however, was like most of the newer buildings in S.W Florida, rounded, beige and uninteresting.

"Hello. Oh, is it raining?" asked the young woman at the reception desk, looking at my rather damp hair and blouse.

"No, no it's not" I told her, it's just really humid out there, huh?"

"Oh, sorry," she said, backing up on her rolling office chair in some involuntary attempt to distance herself from me,

1

Before I could say something I'd later regret, the sound of high heels clicking down the hall stopped me. I turned to see a young, attractive woman making her way to me at a near gallop speed. Her brown, shoulder length hair bounced and glistened like in a shampoo commercial. The closer she got the more beautiful I could see she was, like a Miss America contestant.

I'll bet she doesn't look like she got caught in the rain even when she gets caught in the rain, I thought. I decided right then and there I wasn't going to like her. She breathlessly reached her hand to me, bracelets banging about on petite wrists.

"Mrs. Finn? I'm so glad you could come. I'm Brandy," she said, a bit out of breath, "I'm the director here. I met your folks, lovely couple; we're super excited they'll be living here. I know we promised you a tour this morning but since the hurricane tomorrow…well, this may not be the best time."

"I know," I said, "I think I have to go buy a flashlight or something but I thought I'd just take a quick peek if you don't mind. Just in case, well you know, I could be dead tomorrow," I joked, "killed by a flying coconut to the head or something."

She looked at me like she didn't understand then said, "Oh my! Alright, well, just a quick peek. Then she put her arm through mine like we were on a date, smiled, glanced at my hair and asked," Is it raining?"

Our tour took us outdoors and we walked toward a lake that was about the size of a football field. In the center was a fountain that sprayed water out *Old Faithful* style. Brandy pointed out a wooden fishing pier and a tiki-hut structure that she identified as a tackle shop.

"There, on the other side of the lake is our Arnold Palmer designed golf course," she waved her arm toward the expanse of green with its adjoining parking lot full of golf carts designed to look like antique cars.

"This is really nice," I said, taking it all in. "I was feeling kind of bad about my parents moving to a…well, a…that they're getting old. So many great memories…" I drifted off in a bit of reverie.

"I understand completely," said Brandy, "and our hope is that your family will begin building new memories here. Grandchildren are always welcome of course, but we do have a few rules regarding their visits here."

"Oh, their grandchildren, *my* children are grown now, but they will want to bring their own little ones to visit."

"How many children do you have?" Brandy asked, sneaking a peek at her watch. "You certainly don't look old enough to have grown children."

I was certain she has to say that frequently here, but in my case it seemed especially ludicrous. The makeup I wasted my time putting on this morning had long since slid off of my face in the tsunami of sweat coming out of my pores, my hair was damp and limp, and I was certain I smelled like a gym locker. She was probably more amazed that there was a man out there desperate enough to have fathered *any* children for me. But, instead of high five'ing me for getting a man to have sex with me, she just smiled her little Brandy smile, politely awaiting my response.

"I have four children," I told her, "two sons and two daughters," certain that would rate another high five in her mind.

"Wow," she said, "four?" sounding truly incredulous.

"Yes," I said, "and three grandchildren. Do you have children Brandy?"

"Oh no, no children," she said in the same way you would have expected her to deny having lice or anthrax. Then she smiled her beauty pageant smile, put her arm back through mine, and resumed her spiel which included something about cigar smoking areas and, I think, *dating* activities for the single residents. Pushing that mental image to the back of my mind I began looking around for a water fountain or an ice cream stand.

We had completed our abbreviated tour of *The Shell*, as the locals here call it, and were making our way back to the front of the building when I saw a group of *the greatest generation* gathered in the reception area.

"What's going on here?" I asked.

"Oh," she said, "the radio station is here today to do a live broadcast from nine to eleven. It's always so much fun when they come out we decided not to cancel. They give out prizes and the D.J. they send out is so funny, Ziggy he calls himself. They all love him here, they never miss his show. I can introduce you if you'd like."

"Gee thanks, but I think I'll pass," I said. "I've still got lots of stuff to get ready at my parents' home." I raised my voice attempting to be heard over the sound of a dozen people speaking to each other at the same level you would if you were standing in front of a jet engine.

We were in the lobby now and I could see a van parked in the circular drive just outside the front door. It had a satellite dish attached to the side and a painted mural of a beach that included crabs, seagulls and a leaping dolphin all with images of people where the animal head should be. I assumed these were the radio personalities and I recognized the *crab man* as the one seated at the long table in the center of the lobby. The call letters for the station were painted on the sides of the van in large green letters…WWTF.

"The radio station is WWTF?" I asked Brandy.

"Yes, it stands for Waving Through Florida."

"But, surely they must get kid…"

Brandy interrupted me, "Oh Ziggy!" she waved to the crab man.

Ziggy stood up and made his way toward us. He appeared to be about my age, was tall, thin and nice looking. He was wearing shorts that went to his mid calf, a long sleeve *Tommy Bahama* shirt, and a leather necklace with an Indian head nickel dangling from it. I suddenly felt a little self conscious of my appearance and reached up to tame my hair, instantly regretting it; it looked so obvious.

"Brandy! Long time no see. How've you been darlin'?" he asked with a large smile and an arm around her shoulder.

"Hi Ziggy," Brandy gushed. "It's really great you're here. Everyone's been asking when you were coming back."

He looked at me and smiled.

"Ziggy, this is Mrs. Finn." Brandy said. "Her parents are moving in the beginning of the month."

"Maggie," I said as I shook his hand, "nice to meet you."

"Nice to meet you Maggie," he said. "This joint is pretty nice huh? If I weren't so young, I'd be looking at moving in myself."

"Well, it's very nice to meet you too," I said. "Brandy says you're quite a hit here at The Shell."

"Ah, yeah, they love me here, they're my best audience. All the markets I've worked in, this is definitely my favorite."

He looked around and waved at a couple of elderly women who giggled and waved back.

"I really lucked out getting this gig," he continued, "great folks down here. Yep, I love it."

He stopped himself, probably aware that he was going too far out of his way to sound convincing, but I think Brandy, at least, was buying it. From the tattoos and long hair I'm certain he more used to playing Pearl Jam than String of Pearls

"You gonna stick around and watch the show?" he asked me. "We have a lot of fun and some company's comin' out later to demo a new mobility device."

"Gee, that does sound fun," I said, more sarcastically than I had wanted, "but I've got an appointment."

"Suit yourself," he said, and looked at his audience. "I gotta get back to work." He sauntered back to his table in long, easy strides and began talking to one of the set up crew.

"I think I insulted him," I told Brandy, "I didn't really mean it like that."

"Oh, I'm sure he wasn't insulted, he says crazy things himself all the time."

"Well, thank you so much for taking the time to show me around today," I said to Brandy. "I really like it here and I can tell my parents will love being here too."

"I'm so glad you could come by. I hope we get to see lots more of each other. When do you have to fly back to....Albuquerque is it?"

"Yes, Albuquerque, and I don't have to be back for a couple of weeks. I'm sure we'll see each other again."

She began talking to a small group of elderly gentlemen and I headed for the front door.

The crowd had begun to gather around the WWTF table. Cables ran from the front door to the van outside, and someone was taping them down and putting bright orange hazard placards around them.

Ziggy was seated at one of the two large tables, the one with all the audio equipment. The other table was festooned with balloons, drink cozies, mugs and T-shirts all emblazoned with the WWTF logo. He was speaking into the microphone giving the weather.

"....and batten down the hatches, so skip the back nine and head straight for the clubhouse."

Over Frank Sinatra's *The Lady is a Tramp* he called out to me, "Nice to meet you Maggie."

"Nice to meet you too, good luck with the show," I said as I walked quickly away. Not quickly enough though.

"Hey Maggie," he said, "you get caught in the sprinklers?"

I turned around to say something, something witty I'm sure, when I heard the scream.

****

Old people are simply cool under pressure. Once the initial shock of the scream had passed, the majority of the residents moved, as one, to the back patio, the origin of the shriek. By the time I maneuvered around the WWTF tables, slow moving people with walkers, and a janitor cleaning up something I didn't want to look at, I made it out to the back patio. A small group hovered around a woman who had apparently fainted. She was being revived by one of the cleaning staff who was waving a bottle of Windex under her nose like smelling salts.

An even larger group was gathered near a buffet table bent over and looking at something on the ground. The tops of their heads were all I could see from where I stood. I tried to move to the table but they were shoulder to shoulder and oblivious to me. I took a step forward and heard. "Ouch! That's my foot," and "Excuse me, but I was here first."

I was moving in and out of the crowd, trying unsuccessfully to jockey for position amongst them, but since they all spoke to each other at the sound level of a cattle auctioneer, I had no trouble *hearing* what had happened.

Apparently the woman I had seen being revived with window cleaner, Gladys, was walking her dog near the lake when the animal brought something out of the bushes and dropped it on the floor here.

"Is it real?" asked one of the women bent in half.

"Sure it is," said one of the men "who would make a fake one so little and ugly?"

"In my opinion, they're all ugly," said a woman with a reverse skunk stripe in her hair, "and let's face it, at our age they're all little."

"Yes," said her companion, a round, sweet faced lady who smelled like arthritis cream, "and shriveled. But I've never seen one chewed up."

"Stop saying chewed up," whispered another woman, "you're going to make Gladys faint again."

I finally got behind a woman short enough to see over; well, not over, but more *through* her teased up, yet very thin hair.

"Is that a finger?" I asked her. "It looks like someone's pinky."

"I don't have a hanky," she answered.

"No, is that a…?"

Just then Brandy came in sounding frantic, "Everyone, please move away," she said, and the crowd parted for her. She looked at the floor, stood there motionless for a minute like someone had hit the pause button on the remote, and then fainted.

"Someone call a doctor!" I yelled, and the cleaning lady came over with the Windex, this time waving it under Brandy's nose.

"Who lost a finger? Is anyone bleeding?" I asked, though I didn't see any blood. "Has anyone called 9-1-1?" I went on pleading to the group."

"Honey," a woman said to me as I bent over it, "that's not a finger, that's a…"

"Oh my God," I said, "that's *not* a finger, that's a…"

Someone tapped me on the shoulder. I jumped, and turned to see one of the landscapers holding a leaf bag out to me. He said something in Spanish that sounded like a question.

"Does anyone here speak Spanish?" I asked the crowd.

One of the women from the kitchen staff came over and said something to him in Spanish, he replied in the same language. She turned to me and said, "He wants to know what he should do with this."

The man held up the bag.

"What's in it?" I asked.

"A leg," she said, dramatically in her heavy Cuban accent.

"Si, leg," the man said.

I looked in the bag, felt woozy and yelled, "Someone bring me the Windex!"

ENGULFED
CHAPTER TWO

The crowd of residents were milling around the patio chatting and drinking juice discussing the events like it was intermission at the theater. I walked to the lobby to ask the receptionist if she had called the police and at that moment saw a virtual parade of police cars, an ambulance, a van, and a couple of white sedans with blue lights on their dashes making their way up the drive. Some of the vehicles parked in front while the white sedan, the van and two squad cars drove across the lawn toward the back.

I grabbed a WWTF pen from the radio station's table, a couple of Shell Harbor pamphlets off the reception desk, and walked over toward an open closet pretending to take inventory.

From behind me, a man's voice asked, "Are you the person in charge here?"

I turned around to see a tall man that I could make out only in silhouette because of the bright window light behind him. I opened my mouth waiting for words to come out when I spotted Brandy charging into the lobby from the back door, the sound of a cavalry bugle playing in my head. I went back to my pretend inventorying and eavesdropped.

"Are you the police?" asked Brandy. "I'm Brandy Saint-Pierre, the director here."

I wrote *Saint Pierre* on my brochure followed by, *that's got to be a made up name.*

"Thank you for not turning on the sirens," she said, "our guests are very...uhm...fragile."

Is she kidding, I wondered? Not *these* people, these people are having a ball. It's the highlight of their day, year probably. I never realized older people were so tough.

"I'm detective Gonzales. You're going to have to try to keep them inside," he told her. "My men are taping off a crime scene area. "

"Crime?" Brandy shrieked. "You think there was a crime committed here?" she asked, her voice breaking.

I was imagining the detective looking at her incredulously and started to snicker at that image. I quickly made a kind of cough, sneeze sound to cover it and started writing the words *pens, paper, tape,* on my brochure.

Their voices began trailing off as they walked away from me toward the back doors and I followed as stealthily as I could. Brandy went to her office so I followed the detective outside.

This was all becoming a fabulous show for the residents and the ones lucky enough to have rooms facing the lake were already sitting out on their balconies leaving the rest scrambling for the few bench seats and lawn chairs outside. The ones in wheelchairs were jockeying for the best position and the more limber ones actually spread blankets on the ground picnic style. They wore clothing in varying shades of white, most with broad brimmed hats, and nearly all were wearing sunglasses that seemed to have been made for viewing A- bomb tests. The heat and humidity were bad enough to make Tarzan pass out but these people appeared impervious to it, even to luxuriate in it.

"Excuse me dear," an orange haired woman stopped me. "Would you mind going to my room and getting me my hat? The sun is very bright today and I have this spot," she pointed to something near her temple.

"I'm sorry," I told her, "I don't work here but I'll find someone to help you."

"Oh Miss!" A woman in a lawn chair tugged at the hem of my blouse. "Can you please be a dear and get me some water, not tap water, that stuff is terrible for my kidney, I like the..."

I looked over, saw a bottled water near a man that had dozed off on a bench, and handed it to her.

Nearly sprinting, I was closing in on the detective who now had a large group around him to whom he appeared to be delegating tasks to.

So far my attempt at looking like I belonged there in some capacity seemed to be working; no one stopped me from tagging along. The uniformed officers were busy putting yellow crime scene tape around the entire lake area and pier while others were poking in the bushes.

"Have the divers gotten here yet?" I heard Detective Gonzales ask someone, but before he got his answer, a man at the other side of the pier called to him.

"Walk with me," he directed the group, which now included me. I kept my brochures with me, writing notes to myself. My feet kept sinking into the ground where it had become rain soaked and muddy, and I felt myself slip a couple of times in my flimsy sandals but managed to keep up with the group.

We approached a young man who was not wearing a uniform but rather one of those bright greenish-yellow vests you see construction workers wear.

"What have you got?" the detective asked him.

"Arm Index and ring fingers are missing. Looks like a gator got him."

I gasped involuntarily. The detective looked at me and then turned around when someone else started speaking.

"Well, that's not gonna make our dive team happy," said one of the plain clothes officers. "It's hard enough to pull up a body when it's not in pieces."

"Call for whoever that guy is we get when there's a gator problem," said Detective Gonzales.

A rotund man I remembered meeting on my tour was making his way toward us from the building. His name was Ralph I recalled from the shell-shaped name tags everyone wore. He was the security guard for The Shell. The walk from the building to the lake was only about 100 yards but Ralph looked to be carrying 40 years worth of burgers and beer around his middle. He was out of breath, beet red, and sweating profusely.

"Brandy says Max Coffman is missing," he told the detective, panting but excited.

"Is she certain?" Gonzales asked him. "It seems like no one is in their rooms right now," and he gestured to where the spectators had gathered.

"Well, everyone is still lookin' but Mad Max wouldn't miss somethin' like this for nothin'" said Ralph, who has bent over, wheezing.

"Mad Max?" the detective asked.

"Oh yeah, everyone calls him that on account of he's a crazy old bastard, and mean too." Ralph righted himself up and tugged at the waist band of his pants. "If it *is* him dead, those folks back there will be throwin' a party," he gestured to the gathering behind them, then suddenly looked around nervously and lowered his voice. "I hope that don't sound too disrespectful but he was, *is*, one mean son of a bitch."

"Well Ralph," said Detective Gonzales, "If that *is* Mr. Coffman's dead body; you might want to consider the implication of your statement."

"Oh shit, I didn't mean I *wanted* him dead. No way! You can't think…"

"Relax Ralph, I'm not accusing you of anything," said the detective in a voice that sounded like he was accusing him of *everything*. "Now, please return and see what more you can learn about Mr. Coffman. I'm sending Officer Dwyer with you."

"Oh yeah, sure, of course, whatever you need." Ralph had gone from nervous to eager. "Sure, come on," he said to officer Dwyer who was staring daggers at the detective, "we'll go up there right now."

Detective Gonzales smiled at his remaining team, "you won't see him anywhere near here again."

The men laughed and I giggled and snorted which made all the heads turn to me.

"And you are?" Gonzales asked me.

"I'm helping out Brandy," I lied, "making sure none of the guests…"

He interrupted me, "I have officers in charge of that."

"Of course, but she…Brandy that is, she…she wants to make sure none of them get too upset and make one of your officers have to…uhmmm…"

His cell rang, thank God, and he began walking away as he answered.

I realized how nervous I had felt, tingling armpits, dry mouth, racing heartbeat, hands shaking. I wasn't sure why, it's not like he would have arrested me or anything, but I was shaken and had to take a minute to clear my head. *Focus Maggie*, I told myself, *focus*.

I leaned up against a van, then realized it belonged to the coroner and felt a shudder go through me. I moved away a few feet but still close enough to watch Detective Gonzales.

He was crouched, sitting on his heels, looking at something on the ground.

"Who's here from forensics?" he asked the uniformed officer next to him.

"Chase, she's over with the dive team."

"Go get her, I'll wait," he said, pulling a latex glove from his coat pocket.

While he was engrossed in whatever he was looking at on the ground, I moved closer and stood behind a tree, like a character in a cartoon.

Gonzales' phone rang, "*Bobeshi*, are you well?" he said, followed by silence, then, "Good, good…glad to hear it. I'm working on a case right now so I can't talk." More silence followed, then "No, I can't call the rabbi right now, I have to work. Well, I'm sure it will be fine for you to go to the supper, just tell them you keep Kosher, they'll know. And don't call them *goys*, that's not nice. Call me after your date. Ok, I love you too. *Agutentog*."

I peeked from around my hiding tree and saw the woman I assumed was from forensics, Chase, standing over him. "Your daughter?" she asked.

"My grandmother," he answered distractedly, pulling something from the ground and putting it in a plastic bag.

"Your grandmother's going on a date? How old is she?" asked Chase.

"Eighty-six and I don't want to talk about it," he handed her the bag. "It's marked," he said as she took it from him.

"Oh we ARE talking about this later, I mean, your grandmother dates and you don't?" She peered at the plastic bag.

"Miranda, can we please focus?" he sounded annoyed.

"Sure, I'll lift these scooter tracks," she was saying, crouched down beside him "but you need to go see Mosley, I think they have some more body parts."

"You're sure these are from a scooter?" he asked her, pointing to the ground again.

She glared at him as though he'd asked if she knew her own name. "Go!" she waved him off, "they're waiting for you over at Gatorland."

She started taking things from the bag she had with her, but I kept my eye on the detective who glanced at the crowd of spectators and shook his head. It sounded like he said *meshuggah*.

The crowd was, in fact, yelling out advice to the investigators like, "Hey! You should get one of them German Sheppard dogs that sniff out bodies and drugs."

And, "You want me to get pictures for you? I got a camera."

Then there were the offers of nice cold glasses of tea or cookies. Some of them shouted that they couldn't see and could everyone please move over a little.

I managed to get close enough to the edge of the lake to hear most of what was being said but to see only a little bit of what was going on.

"So, you're certain this is *the* gator?" Gonzales asked the tanned and long-haired man standing near what I think was a large cage.

"Croc, and yeah, it's him," the tall man answered.

Then Gonzales said something more, but I couldn't tell what it was since he was now facing away from me.

I couldn't get closer without being obvious, but one of the officers who was standing a few yards away yelled over to them.

"I got a woman's high heeled shoe and some earrings." The officer held up a plastic bag in his gloved hands and waved them at the group standing near the gator.

I could hear Gonzales say, "Ok, destroy the croc and take him to the coroner,"

Then Gonzales, and half the entourage, walked over to the *shoe* man.

"It's a big one, a size 12," the man holding the bag yelled.

"That's gotta be one big woman," said another officer.

Gonzales held the bag, examining it, when his phone rang again. He walked in my direction, looked at me curiously and turned his back. I thought I could make out most of what he was saying though, but I couldn't be sure since some of it sounded Spanish.

"Abuela, I cannot talk now I am working. You'll have to ask Papa that, I'm too busy. Si, yes, a flush beats a straight..." followed by more Spanish.

I watched the woman, Chase, from forensics walk toward him. I turned my back to them and pretended to be counting the old people.

"Let me guess, your other grandmother?" she asked him. "You got one messed up family."

"I've only been gone a month," he told her, "this is their way of checking up on me, they worry. Can we stop talking about it now?"

Before she could answer him, another officer made his way toward Gonzales.

"There's no sign of the guy they call Mad Max, Maxwell Coffman," he said, reading from his notepad. "Eighty-six year old male, Caucasian, widowed, two sons living in state. He was last seen last night, 10 p.m. in his room watching TV. They're going over the surveillance camera tape now.

"They're just *now* watching the tape?" asked Gonzales

."Yeah, it's pretty old school," said the officer. "For a place this expensive you'd think they'd have a more up to date one, but they're running it now."

"How many cameras?" asked Gonzales

"Just the one in the lobby."

"A place this size has one camera?"

Yep," answered the uniformed officer. "I think it's one of those first ones, like from the eighties."

"Alright," said Gonzales, "have someone call me as soon as they read it, then go make a copy. Is that lady who runs the place looking at it?"

"Yes, her and the guard," said the uniformed officer.

Gonzales started walking away.

"Ah Detective," the officer stopped him, "one more thing, there's some people from a company called Charley Davidson wanting to get in here. They say they've got some of their equipment in here and they want to make sure it's ok."

"What kind of equipment?" asked Gonzales.

"One of those scooters that old people ride on."

"Yes," said Gonzales, "I'll see them." He started toward the building,

"Charley Davidson," he mumbled to himself, "meshuggah."

****

Once they had started pulling the remains of Mad Max out of the lake, and the coroner was filling her van with whatever parts were not in the digestive system of a large alligator, or crocodile, (I'm certain poor old Max was not splitting hairs on this point from whatever after- life he found himself in), the party was over. At least for me it was.

The residents were forced to go inside and all non essentials, like the unknown lady who put herself in charge of counting old people and office supplies, were summarily dismissed, and quickly so, since a hurricane was on its way and we needed to *take shelter.*

ENGULFED
CHAPTER THREE

Edison invented the electric lamp in 1879. He also invented the talking doll in 1886, but that's beside the point. The point is, if we've had electric lamps for 130 years and had wind and rain for at least that long, it should stand to reason we would have come up with a way to make electricity work even when it's windy and rainy.

I knew these Edisonian tidbits from the little Thomas Edison brochure I found lying on the kitchen counter in my parents' home. It seemed Thomas Edison lived and worked, and thought about talking dolls just a few miles north of here in Ft. Myers.

There were all kinds of little touristy brochures my mother left for me, which I was reading, by candle light, to remind myself that this is a nice state, a friendly state, a happy state, a state that tourists pay lots of money to come visit. It's a place that's just fine for my parents to live out their golden years. I had to remind myself of these things because right then it felt as though I were living in one of the nine circles of hell.

Hurricane Fanny. What a stupid name for a hurricane. If you wore a T-shirt that said *I Survived Hurricane Fanny*, people would think you'd won it in a mud wrestling contest.

I was surrounded by all the supplies the helpful man at Home Depot advised I get. There was duct tape, bleach, batteries, canned food, bottled water, first aid kit, candles, flashlight, and a bottle of wine. Ok, the wine was actually my idea.

Cut off from the world save my little battery operated TV, I was second guessing my decision to stay here instead of going to one of those hurricane shelters. After convincing myself earlier that one could be just as easily blown away there as at home, that logic now no longer appeared as sound and the idea of cots and port-a-potties didn't seem so bad after all.

Three hours after the storm started Fanny was in her full glory. The wind made roaring, window rattling sounds, hail was hitting the windows and there was lots of lightning. By lots, I mean the sky was almost continually lit. In fact, it was the only illumination I could see besides an occasional flashlight beam from the house behind mine. There was one exception though, and that was the intermittent large blast of greenish blue brilliant light, with its accompanying ear splitting crack and boom. These were, in fact, Mr. Edison's great-grand children exploding as wires came lose and hit the ground. I was not quite sure if one of those monsters of power was outside my parents' home. That's not one of those things you look for when you're negotiating a sales price from your crooked real estate agent and simultaneously toying with the idea of feeding her to an alligator.

I had learned from the lawn guy that the alligators here were free to wander around Florida hunting our poodles and de-clawed cats and took it upon himself to warn me about all the creatures lurking just outside my door waiting to bite, chew, claw, and sting or eat me.

"Great," I'd said, "my parents are living in a jungle, isn't that swell?"

The power went out after the first eight raindrops fell so there was no air-conditioning and the house had become a 1,500 square foot sauna. I was sweating profusely and at some point, regardless of what would happen, I cracked open a window.

I wandered from room to room, unconsciously turning on light switches and wishing I had bought unscented candles; the house smelled like a new age shop.

Staring at the patio doors, I was afraid something, or God forbid, some*one* would come crashing through them. The very concerned man on the TV was talking about how I should have boarded those up, as if he could see into my home. "A little late for that now," I yelled at the TV. "Thanks for the heads up Home Depot guy."

Going back out for boards now was out of the question so I emptied and flattened packing boxes, taped them to the doors and windows, and stood guard. I was reminded of a scene from a Winnie the Pooh book I read to my granddaughter. Pooh stayed up all night marching back and forth, in his little Pooh house, with his little pop gun, protecting hearth and home from Heffalumps and Woozles. That was me. "Stay away you Heffalumps and Woozles, I've got duct tape and I'm not afraid to use it."

The sustained wind speed, according to the news reports, was 85 miles per hour, but occasional gusts were much stronger, tearing tiles from roofs and uprooting trees, one of which went down in the neighbor's yard and put a hole in their roof. I was very glad they were away in a regular state that God was *not* smiting, instead of being pinned under a large coconut palm in their bed.

With every sound, I'd held my breath, imagining a tree falling into the living room and somehow impaling me into my mother's pink sofa. There would be blood stains that I'm sure even she, the self proclaimed Queen of Laundry, would be unable to remove. The first aid kit looked ridiculous in the face of tree impalement, but at least I had the wine. It was good it was a Pinot Grigio, even warm, those goes down well.

Another flash of lightning and I could see how many screens there were left on the patio; just one, holding on by three molecules, flapping in the wind.

The little TV was my only company, and I was fascinated watching this poor weatherman in his bright yellow parka, standing out in the storm, warning us to stay indoors. Street lights were whipping wildly around him attached by only one cable, and he kept listing to the right. The rain was hitting his little baby face with such a force that I was sure he'd be pock marked for life. A large black garbage can went flying over his head and nearly hit him. He should go back inside, I thought, and wondered how much he was getting paid to stand out there. I was guessing it was not a lot and hoped he had a flask stashed inside that parka.

I kept pacing through the house, which was nothing like the home in Brooklyn that I grew up in. First of all, this place was much bigger with a lot more windows. Everything was decorated in pastel pinks and blues and there were pictures of the ocean and sail boats and pelicans on the walls.

"Who are these people who live here?" I said out loud to no one, "And what have they done to my parents; my born and raised two blocks from Prospect Park parents?"

Along the entire back of the house large sliding glass doors opened from the living room to the patio.

In Brooklyn, everyone sits out front; in Florida, everyone sits out back. Patios are big here and the stores make a killing selling people all kinds of furniture to go in them. Umbrellas for tables are more plentiful than cannolis in Italy. If I lived here though, and had this swimming pool; I'm certain it would be no time at all before I too join the tanned and unsociable set and put furniture in the back of my house.

I got a pad and paper and amused myself thinking of creative curse words and derogatory anagrams I could make with the name Florida, and also to come up with equally creative excuses I could use to *not* visit my folks here in the future. I loved them, and wanted to see them, just not here.

"Do your worst Florida!" I hollered, "I can take it. Hurricane shermicane, you're not so tough, but sweet Jesus it's hot. It's soooooo damned hot!"

I got a helping of semi- liquid ice cream from the freezer and held the bowl to my forehead for a minute before eating, or more accurately drinking it down.

The worst of the storm appeared to finally be over and Fanny was making her soggy way out of here, leaving us all to locate our missing patio furniture and stray pets.

I had sweat away twelve pounds and immediately put them back on by eating all the ice cream in the freezer. I used up all the batteries in my little TV and burned down all the fragrant candles, and was, fortunately, not killed by either flying bodies or tree limbs.

I figured I'd try to sleep a bit, and in the morning, when this chapter out of the Old Testament was over, maybe I'd be lucky and wake up in Oz or Kansas, or even Jersey, anywhere but here.

ENGULFED
CHAPTER FOUR
TWO DAYS BEFORE THE HURRICANE

The two octogenarians sat in the rec room of The Shell Harbor Skilled Nursing Residence inches from the television set.

"Gosh Max, I don't know. Grace wouldn't like this at all," the thin man in the plaid robe said.

"Why the hell not?" answered his companion, a bare-chested man wearing boxer shorts and slippers. "They say you get all your money back from those stiffs at Medicare. It's just a goddamned deposit for Christ's sake."

"I, I know, but Grace says…"

"For crying out loud Frank, don't be such a whiner. You're eighty seven goddamn years old; you gotta ask your wife's permission to take a shit? Oh, wait, I forgot, you haven't taken a shit for eight years now, ain't that right Bernie?" Max bellowed across the recreation room to the nurse's station.

"Bout time for an enema for ol' Frank here, right? Cause if ever there was a man in need of a good dump, its ol' Frank."

"Awww, geeze Max, will you hold it down?" pleaded Frank.

"Holy crap Frank! You think any of the rest of these geezers in here gonna hear a thing I say? Christ, I could hire a brass band led by one of them fat dago opera singers screamin' her tits off and no one would even look the hell up. I ain't livin' here for free and the goddamned Hebes that own this place don't ask if I like it here in this crap hole. They don't gotta like me and I sure don't give a flying fu… "

"Max! Watch it!" said one of the attendants from his desk in the corner of the room.

The staff was used to Max, and had bets on which one of the other residents would come in at night and smother him in his sleep. One of Max's sons had money, tipped the staff well, and gave generous donations to Shell Harbor or he'd have been kicked out long ago. The only good part of Max was his wife Shirley, and when she died, he turned all his blather to his only friend at The Shell, Frank Stubbins. They were the kind of pair you've known your whole life; the bully and the bullied. The bullied too meek to stand up, the bully too self absorbed to notice the other was around only out of intimidation, not friendship.

"Gosh Max, you better watch it," said Frank. "Your son's already threatened to send you over to Miami to one of those nursing homes where no one even speaks English."

"Shit, Frank, I don't give a good goddamn. I'm just sick to death of being stuck in this place. Alls I'm saying is, we get us one of those new bad ass bikes and we can get outta here in style once in a while. You walk around with that dumb lookin' shit walker thing with goddamn tennis balls on the bottom. I ain't goin' nowhere with one of them, makes me look like some old fart. So we're stuck in here like a couple of old shriveled up geezers. My useless prick of a son won't give me any money or I'd...oh shut up will ya? The ad for it's comin' on right now."

****

"Heyyyyyy, it's me, the Fonz, on my Big Dog, from Charley Davidson. You never have to leave the house looking like a square again. Not when you can ride one of these beauties. This bike, I mean mobility device, does more than just look cool, it is cool. With its leather seats, leather saddlebags and custom chrome details, The Big Dog makes a great looking ride. But its coolness goes way beyond that. How about this? A GPS navigation system, with my voice programmed in, to tell you how to find all the swingin' places you're gonna want go to now that you can get there in style. Your Big Dog comes with an anti theft device and alarm. And speaking of safety, we keep your medical needs in mind with a blood pressure device, a pill dispenser with water bottle, and a medic alert all on the handle bar. There is a cell phone holder and charger so you can stay in touch anywhere, anytime. And if you get the optional power package for extra speed, we even install an airbag.

Heyyyyyy, see you guys and ladies later, gonna go cruisin on my "Dog" with my built in sound. That's one juke box that's always playin' my favorite tune. Heyyyyyy"

****

Max was watching Manny, the attendant at the front desk, doze off and on for thirty minutes. Manny's head would drop to his chest and startle him awake, but only for a moment or two. Then his head would fall back and a loud snore would make him jerk his head back upright. With each cycle, he'd glance around nervously to see if anyone noticed, then the whole process would repeat.

The other two attendants on duty were watching TV in Hazel Schwartz's room. Hazel had been asleep for about seven months so her room was a favorite hiding place for the night shift at The Shell.

Max would normally wander down there to tell them some complaint he had about his dinner, or the temperature in his room, or an off color joke. But tonight he wanted to stay far away from the staff hideout; tonight, he was hatching a plan.

What Max really had his eye on was just outside the reception area, in the front courtyard of the Shell. It was the Big Dog rider and to Max it was a black and chrome wet dream. The Charley Davidson folks had left it there for the radio show the next day. They had some sales people coming around in the morning to let some of the residents test drive it around the courtyard and he knew a lot of the men were going to order one. He was not one of them. He didn't have the cash to lay out on one while he waited for the Medicare reimbursement. He'd call his son and ask for a loan, but his son wasn't speaking to him. Max had called his daughter- in- law a whore last month and surprisingly enough, his son resented it.

Just as well, they're pains in the asses the both of them, he thought.

The moon was full and the light from it was shining on the *bike* leading him to it like the Bethlehem star. In fact, Max was actually talking himself into believing just that; that it was a gift to him from God, with the heavens lighting the way. He figured it was God's way of making it up to him for killing his wife.

"OK God, I forgive you. You givin' me this bike makes us square," he said to his ceiling.

It was early September, still summer in South Florida so the air conditioner was humming loudly.

Max turned his TV up to add some more background noise. He had it tuned to Fox News; the only news channel he knew wasn't controlled by New York liberal Jew fags. Bill O'Rielley was on and Max paused a moment on his way out of the door to growl some obscenity at Bill's guest, a Hispanic Congresswoman.

Then he poked his head out of the door, made sure he wouldn't be seen, and walked out.

ENGULFED
CHAPTER FIVE

The power was restored just as I had given up hope of a hot shower and bathed myself in the pool,
I was able to plug the portable television in, but could find only the briefest mention of the earlier events at Shell Harbor. There was some stock footage of the exterior of the building and a voice- over that said, *"Police were called to Shell Harbor Living yesterday to investigate what may have been an attack by an animal, possibly an alligator. No other facts are known at this point but we will keep you updated as soon as more information becomes available."*
The next story was about the disappearance of one Doctor Bruce Haney. According to the reporter, Doctor Haney was on the board of nearly everything in Florida; The State Medical Board, The State Medical Insurance Commission, The Medicare Advisory Committee, a bunch of other things and, Shell Harbor Living.
The report said that he was last seen leaving his office yesterday at 6pm by his secretary and then I couldn't remember anything else except that the police were suspecting foul play.
I always thought *foul play* a stupid phrase for a possible murder. It sounded more like something you'd say if someone committed an error in one of those British sports where all the players dress in white. It seems a poor phrase to imply kidnapping, stabbing or dismembering.
Oh God! It had just hit me. What if the body parts in the lake were not of that old guy, but the missing Doctor Haney? If I were a *real* reporter, I'd be investigating the hell out of that possibility.
But, I'm not a *real* reporter. Oh, I wanted to be one when I majored in journalism in college. I'd imagined myself a great investigative reporter. My first news job was at the Brooklyn News Herald, working as assistant to the food editor. It was just to get my foot in the door I'd told myself. I'd uncover some illegal activity at a fancy, no prices on the menu restaurant and, zoom, big career boost and a rocket to the top. That, of course, never happened. I never did make it as an investigative reporter. It's been mostly columnist work for me, like, *What's Happening Atlanta,* or *About Town Cleveland.*

Since I had now succeeded in completely depressing myself, I got showered, dressed in something pretty, and went for a drive. I headed north because I thought I might run out of dry land too soon if I headed south.

The sign in front of me said I was entering Ft Myers Beach. I hadn't planned on driving this far north, but going back to an empty house didn't appeal to me either. I stopped at a traffic light, heard music coming from the hotel bar on my left and thought, *that's what I'll do, I'll get a drink, listen to some music, watch people dancing, all with a nice view of the Gulf.*

The public lot was across the street. I gave the man five dollars, dodged the slow moving cars to get to the hotel, and walked around back to the beach entrance. The surf was moving in gently and a full moon was casting a beautiful light on the water. A few couples were dancing awkwardly to *Margaritaville* and I maneuvered around them to the bar, found a stool and pondered what I should order.

"Hi. What can I get for you?" asked the bartender, a Baywatch looking blonde in a floral top with a name tag that read *Staicee.* Her smile was big and so were her boobs, which I'm sure wouldn't move if she were doing jumping jacks.

"I'll have a Pina Colada please. And can you girly it up for me with fruit and one of those little paper umbrellas? I'd like to feel vacationy tonight."

"You got it hon," she said in southern roadside diner style.

I spun my chair back around to look at the band and the dancers. There was only one couple on the dance floor now. The band had slowed the pace down and was playing Unchained Melody. The middle aged couple on the dance floor was obviously very drunk and it was hard to tell if he was groping her or just passed out on her. He was balding and wearing a golf shirt and khaki pants, her hair was colored coal black and she was wearing capri pants and a very low cut stretch top. They were both overweight and their fat feet hung over the sides of their sandals.

All the members in the band looked forties to fiftyish. Their hair was gray or graying and I was sure they had day jobs as accountants, or lawyers or boat repairmen, but tonight they were part of a band and they weren't bad.

Staicee came back with my drink and it was a sight to behold. It *screamed* tourist with its oranges and cherries pierced through a green plastic sword, coupled with a tiny paper parasol, both sitting on the rim of a Marilyn Monroe shaped souvenir glass with the hotel name printed on the side. A straw peeked out of the rum laced whipped cream giving me a come- hither look that made me smile. I took the first sip and thanked God I lived in a world where such delights as these existed.

"Thank you," I said, "this is fabulous."

"Glad you like it," she answered in her thick southern accent. "Where you from?"

Just down the road, Bonita Springs." I didn't feel like sharing my life's story with her.

"What about you Staicee?" I asked, "where you from?"

"Tennessee, Sevierville, near Dollywood. You heard of it?"

"Sure. I bet it's pretty there, up in the Smokey Mountains, right?"

"It is, it's real pretty, I miss it sometimes, the mountains and all," she said, gazing out with more of a blank stare than a reminiscent one

"What brought you down here?" I asked.

She came back from whatever void she had entered, "My boyfriend and I come down here for a vacation and we liked it so much we just picked up and moved here. He got a job doin' construction and I got this. We broke up though, and he's back in Sevierville. I can't go back yet 'cause my folks won't let me live with them no more so I'm tryin' to save enough for a place of my own."

She picked up a wet rag and started wiping down something under the bar and I turned to look at the signs on the wall to avoid her cleavage. She straightened up, emptied an ashtray, picked up a nearly empty beer bottle, tossed it in the trash, and squirted diet Coke into a glass from a nozzle, all while continuing her saga.

"I found me a second job working at the Baja Burrito over on the boardwalk during the day. I'll be makin' enough to get my own place soon; I'm staying with friends now, sleepin' on their sofa. Then I'll maybe go to school too." She took a drink of the diet coke, burped quietly and smiled. "I think I want to be a doctor's assistant. My sister does that back home. She works for a plastic surgeon. He gave me a really big discount on my boob-job on account of she's been workin' for him for over a year. That was before I moved down here with my ex though. He even paid for them for me. Wasn't that nice?" She arched her back to extend her boobs forward. "Anyway, usually it's a lot more crowded in here and the tips are pretty good.

It's just lots of people left 'cause of the hurricane. It'll pick back up real quick I'm sure. That's what Jeff, the manager, says."

"Well, I'm sure it will too," I said, as I slurped the last of my drink.

"You want another?" she asked eagerly.

"Sure, why not," I handed her the glass.

"You better watch it, those things'll knock you on your ass you're not careful," came a voice from the other end of the bar.

A tall figure was approaching and as it passed under the *Foster's Beer* sign I could make out the face. It was Ziggy, from the radio remote at The Shell. Was he even better looking than I remembered or was that the Pina Colada haze over my eyes?

"Hey there," I said, in a voice that sounded way too eager. I gave myself a mental ass kick and toned it down. "What brings you up here?"

"I met with some friends, they just took off," he said. "I was just getting ready to go myself when I spotted you over here. Maggie, right?"

"Yes, it's Maggie, and your name is Ziggy?"

"Well, the senior set calls me that," he leaned his elbow on the bar and faced me, "everyone else just calls me Zig."

"That was a lot of excitement at The Shell the other day, huh?" I said realizing immediately how stupid that sounded.

"I saw you out there mixing it up with the cops, you a reporter or something?" he asked, then signaled to Staicee who nodded and went to settle his bill. I didn't see a ring on his left hand or a tan line where one would be and felt self conscious for looking.

"Yes, I am actually," I said. "Well, not *actually.*"

"You wanna try that one again?" he asked.

Before I could answer, Staicee came back with his bill. He pulled a credit card from his wallet, laid it on the bar and glanced at my drink.

"You got any alcohol under all that shit on the side of your glass?" he asked.

I laughed, "Staiceeeeee and I have an arrangement. Can I buy you a drink?"

"Nah, I'm driving. That's my bike out there." He pointed toward the front door. "So, you were telling me how you simultaneously are and are *not* a reporter."

"Oh yeah, well, I'm a journalist." I told him. "I love saying that." I sipped my drink. "It's impressive to have a title, don't you think? I'm a journalist, you're a D.J., it's way better than saying I work at this place or for that company, you know?" I took a large gulp of my drink and wiped my mouth.

"Ok sure. So, what do you write? Let me guess, fashion, travel?"

"Of course, I'm a woman, what else would I write?" I said in my most sarcastic tone. "You forgot to mention a food column."

"Well excuse me," he answered, heavy on the *excuse*, "so you write a food column?"

"No," I said and slumped a few inches down on my bar stool. "I write a gossip column now, I used to write food." I picked my head up and looked him squarely in the eye, more angry than I should have been. It was the argument I just had with myself earlier, only now, saying it out loud, it made me angry at myself and I was taking it out on him. I knew this but I inexplicably went on

"It just pisses me off that no one ever thinks of a woman as an investigative, or political, or even sports reporter."

"Hey, back up there Chuck. No need to get all *women's lib* on me. I just asked a question to be polite. I really don't give a damn honestly."

Staicee put his card and receipt on the bar and quickly walked away.

"Oh, so now you admit you don't even care what I do? You were just making small talk till I get sufficiently lubed up to go back to your place and have sex with you?" My voice had gotten loud enough to attract some stares.

"Well, that was kind of my plan, yeah. But now that you're all pissed off, that idea's not lookin' so attractive anymore." He grabbed his card off the bar and stood up.

"Urggghhhh, Forget it!" I said, why don't you go ride your big boy bike off in the rain and cool off?"

With that, I promptly got up off of the bar stool and in what I hoped would be a grand indignant exit, fell to the floor. On the way down, I hit my head on the metal foot rest of the bar stool. I was too humiliated to feel any pain. I thought, *if I just lay here, no one will notice me and when the bar closes for the night, I'll sneak out.*

"Maggie, you ok?" Zig was over me with his hand stretched out to help me up.

I closed my eyes hoping he'd go away. I could sense him crouched down next to me.

"Maggie?" he asked in a more concerned tone, tinged with a small amount of panic.

"Go away, I'm fine," I told him.

My head was pounding, the floor felt sticky against my face and smelled of so many different nauseating things that I held my breath and hoped I would pass out.

"Well, you can't lay there all night. Besides, I saw a guy puke in that exact spot earlier tonight."

"All right, but I can get up by myself. Just leave ok?"

I reached for the leg of the bar stool to pull myself up and it started to come down on me. Zig caught it and reached out his other hand to pull me up.

"Thanks," I told him, getting to my feet. "I guess I shouldn't have had those drinks on an empty stomach."

The room was spinning and I was definitely feeling that rum. Everyone in the place was staring at me. Staicee was looking at me in horror.

"It's ok," Zig told her, "I've got this."

"And what is it you think you have?" I asked, wiping God only knew what off of my face.

"I just mean I'll take you home."

"I'm not one of your little radio groupies, I can take care of myself." I said looking down at my dress and wondering if my backside had hung out when I was on the floor.

"Little radio groupies? Lady, that ship sailed a long time ago, did you see my audience today?"

I was pulling seeds or sand or something from my mouth, "Whatever, I just meant I'm not some helpless female."

"Yeah, I can see that. You're Wonder Woman," he said.

I didn't say anything, just stood frozen in my humiliation.

"Fine then, stay here all night if you want," he said turning to walk away.

"Oh no!" Staicee shrieked, "She can't stay here. I gotta get everyone out of here by two. No one's allowed to stay no matter how drunk they get."

"See?" said Zig, "no lushes after two."

Ignoring that I turned to Staicee, "Don't worry, just give me the name of a cab service, ok?"

"There isn't a cab that's gonna take you from here to Bonita at this time of night, this is just a dinky little beach town."

"Then who can I see about getting a room here?" I asked Staicee who was staring at a point just beyond my right ear. I put my hand in my hair there and pulled out something that I couldn't bear to look at, and threw it on the floor.

"Jeeze", said Zig, "you're a stubborn little drunk."

"I'm not a drunk," I said.

He grinned and almost laughed before I interrupted. "Ok, maybe right now I am drunk, but that's just because I haven't eaten today and the heat and the extra rum on the top…"

Now he *was* laughing

"Oh God! I'm slurring my words aren't I?"

"Yeah, c'mon Miss Priss. Hop on the bike and I'll take your drunken ass home."

"The bike? You have to be kidding. Can't we go in my car?"

"Now *you* have to be kidding. I'm not leaving my Indian on this street alone."

"What? Who's your Indian?" I asked, looking around the bar.

"My bike, it's an Indian, Christ, where'd you grow up, Sesame Street?"

"I can't ride a motorcycle. I'm wearing a dress. I don't have a helmet. Do you have insurance?"

He laughed again, "Quit your whinnin' and come on, you'll be fine, I'll go slow. Just let me know if you have to stop and puke or anything, OK?"

He put his arm around my back and walked me over to *The Chief.* I had to admit, it was pretty nice. It was pure sex in all its black leather and chrome. It screamed power and high energy and it scared the shit out of me.

"If I had a bungee cord I'd strap you on," he gave me his helmet, "but instead you're just gonna have to hold on to me. Where do you live?"

"Rio Rancho, just near Corrales." I answered attempting to put the helmet on.

"Sweetie, I ain't driving you to New Mexico," He grabbed the helmet, turned it around, and plopped it on my head.

"Oh shit, yeah, I forgot. Just drive down this," I indicated the road outside the bar, "till you get to Bonita Beach Road, my folks' house is just a block over from there."

"No kidding? I live just down the street from there myself."

I wrapped my arms around his middle and hung on for dear life. We pulled slowly out of the lot with slight tilts to the right and left as we weaved in-between parked cars. Once we got onto the main road we just cruised. The street was lined with hotels and bars and surf shops. Further down the road the buildings became fewer and fewer until there was no more light pollution and I had a nearly unobstructed view of the gulf. The full moon was brilliant and reflected off the surface making the water appear to glow from the bottom. The white tips of the rolling surf were as bright as the moon itself and the entire scene gave the impression of being unreal.

I was still feeling light headed but the exhilaration of sitting on that big engine was clearing it up quickly. My terror left me and what I was feeling now was pure excitement. The cool wind was blowing all around me and sent my hair flying out into the night from under the helmet. I held tighter onto Zig and smelled his cologne and instantly got a rush I hadn't felt in ages.

Wait, I told myself, *this guy is not only a total stranger but he's an arrogant, chauvinistic jerk. It's just the alcohol and the Indian. Was that a stereotype or a cliché I pondered?* I didn't care. I hadn't thought about sex much in, well, in quite a while, but I damn sure was thinking about it right now.

We were getting close to the house now.

"Ok, turn here," I yelled into Zig's left ear and we pulled into my parent's drive.

He turned off the bike, put the stand down and waited for me to get off.

I reached into my bag and felt that combination of panic and frustration you get when you've done something stupid and have no one to blame but yourself. "Damnit, I go in and out through the garage," I said, "the opener's in my car."

"So," Zig said, "you got two choices. You can come back to my place, which is just over on the next street, and sleep on my sofa, or you can come back to my place, and sleep in the bed with me."

"Taking me back to my car is out of the question then?"

"Look Maggie, I'm really tired. I've been up since five to get ready for that remote today. I'm too tired to drive back and forth to your car, and I'm probably too tired to jump your bones. Besides, you hair smells like the floor at the bar and you have orange seeds stuck to your face. Right now, believe me, the safest place in the world for you is on my sofa."

Well so much for feeling all sexy, now I just felt like the bottom of my shoe.

"Doesn't sound like I have much choice in the matter," I said.

We rode the Indian to Zig's place. It was a small community of manufactured homes, all nicely kept with little tiny front lawns, tiny palm trees and tiny hibiscus bushes, kind of like Munchkin Land.

I jumped off the bike like a pro now. My head was all clear and I hoped the wind blowing on me helped to clean me up a bit more too, like sand blasting the side of a house.

A frog was attached to his screen door and a three legged cat greeted us. I bent over to pet the cat and my brains slid down toward my eyes and my stomach sent up a small geyser of old rum to the back of my throat. When I recovered, I glanced around and was startled to find feminine, antique looking furnishings. I guess Zig saw my surprise, or else he was just used to people wondering but he said, "This is mom's place. She moved into the Shell and asked me to move in here to be closer to her, I'm an only child."

"Where were you living before then?" I asked, "I mean...did you *want* to move here?"

He shrugged one shoulder and bent over his computer to look at his e-mail. "Chicago. I had a really great gig there, morning drive on rock and roll."

Wow, I thought, *he isn't an ass, I am.*

ENGULFED

CHAPTER SIX

I ended up sleeping in Zig's room...alone. He slept on the couch. I think if he could have locked my door from the outside, he would have.

The smell of coffee roused me at eight, according to the clock next to me. I managed to sneak to the bathroom unseen and groom myself with the few contents of my purse available for the job; lip gloss, and Tic Tacs. I was running fingers through my hair to comb it when Zig shouted through the door.

"We gotta' run, I need to get back to Mom's'"

"The Shell? I asked walking out to the kitchen. "Is everything ok? They didn't find any more bodies or parts or anything, did they?"

By way of an answer, he handed me a *to-go* mug, opened the front door and waved me out. We walked past the motorcycle, thank God, and he opened the passenger side door of a black sports car.

"You're gonna have to go with me," he said, "I'll take you to get your car when I'm done."

"Black car with black interior," I said, lifting my butt cheeks off the seat, "bet you don't see a lot of that down here."

He looked over with a halfway suppressed grin that faded just as fast, "I got a call from mom saying I needed to come over, said she couldn't talk now."

"Did she sound sick?"

"No, she sounded fine, just in a hurry."

He looked focused so I didn't try to talk. We drove the rest of the way in silence.

We entered The Shell through a side door, took the stairs to the second floor and didn't see a soul anywhere along the way.

We walked into Zig's Mom's apartment; him calling for her and knocking on bedroom and bathroom doors and me taking in the place. It was exquisitely decorated; very retro and had the feel of a Doris Day movie. Then I noticed that, in fact, there was a snap shot photo of Doris Day on a shelf in the living room. Glancing around the room I noticed lots of black and white photos in various style frames sitting on end tables, coffee tables and some larger ones on the walls.

"This is Doris Day," I said, "and Rock Hudson and...is that your mom standing between them? Wait!" I said excitedly, looking at the photo next to it. "This is Bing Crosby and...your mom again?" My head was pivoting around, trying to take them all in at once. They were faces I recognized from 40's, 50's and 60's movies and all with the same woman.

"Is that your mom?" I asked trying to replace the photo on the table as he was grabbing my arm and walking me out the door.

"Yeah," he said, "that's mom. She must be downstairs, let's go."

"She's an actress?" I asked rather breathlessly as we sprinted down the stairs.

"Yeah," said Zig, and he pushed the stairwell door open.

Once we got outside I could see why the interior had been deserted. The back lawn was as overrun with spectators as before and then some. Added to the mix today, however, were T.V. news vans and reporters.

I had to jog to keep up with Zig, weaving in and out of lawn chairs and golf carts, until we came to an elegant looking woman who was apparently his mother. She was sitting next to an equally dapper looking older gentleman on one of the few shaded benches. They were laughing and sipping drinks from martini glasses, her companion grabbing a bottle of champagne from a basket to his right and pouring a small amount into what looked to be her orange juice.

"Really, Mom?" Zig said, sounding both annoyed and winded. "I was worried something was wrong so I rush over and find you here throwing back Mimosas and having a gay old time."

"I'm sorry darling, I didn't mean to alarm you, but as you can see," she said, gesturing to the growing assemblage near the lake, "We are in the midst of a situation here."

"Now what's happened?" Zig asked, looking to the crowd of reporters in front of the lake, "more bodies?"

Before she could answer her companion asked, "Do people still say *gay old time?* I thought that word meant something altogether different now."

Zig ignored him and looked at his mother, "Mom?"

Her companion shrugged and sipped his drink.

"They've identified the body that they fished out of here." She said, sipping her drink and taking a grape from the plate on her lap. "Have you tasted these yet Roger?" she asked her companion. "The ones yesterday were sour but these are delicious."

She looked at me, "Roger used to be ambassador to France, the man knows his grapes,"

"Mom, you're killing me here." Zig said. "You're doing this on purpose."

"Nonsense darling, do you think I'd stoop to such a thing?" she asked, reaching for another grape, "just because you were rude to my friend Rosemary yesterday?"

I saw her grin and it made me smile.

"Mom, I have someone with me that needs to get to her car, will you please just…"

His mother eyed me over her sunglasses, looked back to smile at Roger and then looked at me again. "My dear, you look much too smart to be taken in by my son's…"

"Oh no," I protested, "It's not like that. Your son gave me ride when…"

"Maggie," Zig interrupted and looked at me, "you don't have to explain anything," He turned to glare at his mother, "*You* on the other hand…"

His mother reached her hand to me, "Hello darling, I'm Dorothy. I'm sorry my son hasn't properly introduced us. I raised him better but…" she made a shrug of resignation.

I shook her hand, "I'm pleased to meet you ma'am, my name is Maggie…Finn."

"Ahhh, I'm pleased to be knowin' ya Miss Maggie Finn,' she said in a perfect Irish brogue, "And how is it you've come to be tangled up with this heartbreaker?" she looked at Zig.

I laughed, "We just met… here… yesterday. I understand you're an actress Miss…Mrs…"

"Just call me Dorothy my dear," she dropped the brogue and turned to her companion, "Roger, this is Miss Maggie Finn."

Roger set his cocktail glass down and extended his hand to me. "Pleased to meet you Miss Finn. Can I interest you in…?"

Zig interrupted, "Oh for crying out loud, is anyone gonna tell me what's going on here?"

"Calm down Steven," Dorothy said, "I wish you'd sit, it's hurting my neck to keep looking up at you this way."

"Ma, I'm…"

"It's Bruce dear," she looked toward the lake and we all followed her gaze.

"Bruce?" I asked.

"Bruce Haney," said Dorothy, "*Doctor* Bruce Haney. My own personal physician and director of all this," she made a sweeping motion with her arm indicating The Shell and then raised her glass to the sky. "Well Bruce, at least you made an exciting exit. Here's to you," and she downed the rest of her Mimosa.

"You couldn't have told me that over the phone?" Zig asked, his eyes taking in the crowd of news people. Then he raised both hands and slapped the sides of his head. "Oh Christ on a bike...Mom...really?"

"I just thought you could ask her if there was something she knew that maybe they weren't tell…"

Zig interrupted her, "No. No, no, no, no, *hell* no.

"Her who?" I asked, squinting to see the faces of the reporters.

"Christine Elin, she's with CNN now," Dorothy said, "she and Steven used to be engaged."

"Who's Steven?" I asked, "Oh wait, never mind, I got that."

I looked at Zig, "You were engaged to Christine Elin? She's gorgeous and, well…she looks so…"

"Young, yeah, I know," he said. "Ok, well, we're all done here, "and turned his back. "There's no way I'm going to her to beg for information."

Dorothy grabbed my hand, "So my dear, do you live here in Fort Myers?"

"No, I live in Albuquerque, well, as of three weeks ago I do. I'm just here to help my parents, they're moving here to The Shell the end of this month."

"You'll have to jot their names down for me, I would love to meet them when they arrive. "

"I will, thank you, they'd love that I'm sure."

"And what do you do in Albuquerque Miss Finn?"

"I'm a journalist," I told her.

"Yeah Mom, you'll love her, she writes the society column." Zig said.

"Society column? In Albuquerque?" she asked, "Imagine that. Well," she smiled graciously," I've always had a soft spot for gossip columnists. My career would never have taken off as it had without them." She patted my hand. "I think Steven is ready to go. It was a pleasure to meet you Maggie Finn."

"You too Mrs...Dorothy. It was a huge pleasure for me. Take care." I reached over and shook the hand of her companion, Roger, "Nice to meet you sir."

He stood up partway, grabbed his drink, raised it to me, and smiled.

"Bye Ma, I gotta' go. Nice seein' you again Roger," said Zig who then glanced toward the lovely Miss Elin, before walking back the way we came.

Once we were back in the car I asked, "You were engaged to Christine Elin? How long ago was that?"

He looked at me like he was going to say something sarcastic then turned his face toward the road and said, "A while ago. We both worked for the same station in Austin."

"She was a D.J.?" I asked incredulously.

"Nope, receptionist."

"Please tell me she's at least got her journalism degree."

"High school."

I sat pouting for a minute and then said, "Tell me something then, something I don't know that will make me feel better about all that."

"Her last name isn't Elin."

"Of course not," I said, "she's related to someone rich and powerful and that's how she got the job. Wait, the name isn't Turner is it?"

"No, it's an impossible to pronounce Swedish name with a bunch of Js and Ks. She's not related to anyone," he said, then added under his breath, "she's just good at using people."

We both sat in silence for a half a mile while. I, and probably Zig too, was remembering her there in front of the lake all beautiful and glowing with a hair and makeup woman on one side of her and another holding her Diet Coke.

"Well," I said, "we have one thing going for us."

"What's that?" he asked, not looking at me.

"I'm sure that lake's got more alligators."

ENGULFED
CHAPTER SEVEN

By the time Zig dropped me at my car and I drove back to my parents' it was late morning. There were too many facts to trust to my memory, but I wanted to be clean more than I wanted to be organized. Besides, I could more easily organize my thoughts under a stream of hot water, so I convinced myself I would actually be multi-tasking.

There was a missing mobility device that everyone felt sure was at the bottom of the lake behind The Shell. The police had identified the arm and man-part as belonging to Doctor Bruce Haney, but there was also a missing resident by the name of Max who was reputed to be the orneriest old fart on the planet. It was possible, I supposed, that pieces of both men could have been pulled from the lake, *and* out of the alligator, and the coroner was fitting them all together now, like a giant, really creepy, human jigsaw puzzle. There was that colossal size woman's shoe and the earring they had found at the scene, and I began to wonder just how many people could be in that lake of death.

I woke three hours later to the sound of a rabid dog at the foot of my bed and then realized it was actually my stomach alerting me it wanted food. My parents had graciously left me a bottle of ketchup, pickled beets, and Metamucil in the fridge, and the cabinets weren't much better.

The Pizza Hut guy arrived thirty minutes later. I had finished one slice and a bread stick and was swigging down my Diet Coke when my cell rang. I looked at the caller ID and decided to take it.

"Hi Jan," I asked, using my most upbeat voice. "How is almost married life?"

"Fabulous," she said, "I'm having sex three times a day. I've lost ten pounds."

"I'm having pizza and my underwear feel tight. How are things at the paper? Are you running retrospectives in my spot?"

"Yes," she said, with a tone of exasperation. "Honestly Maggie, with all the social events I send you on, it's really inconceivable that you haven't met a guy yet. You should be having loads of sex too before you forget how."

"How to what?" I asked

"How to..."

"I know Jan, it was a joke. I'm glad you're happy. To tell the truth, I am having a bit of fun myself."

"Oh?" she asked, her tone improving. "Who is he?"

"Either Bruce or Max, we haven't actually met, and I know for a fact he no longer has a penis, so sex is right out."

"Maggie, what in God's name are you talking about?"

"I've stumbled on what could be a murder," I told her. 'Well, it's probably an accidental drowning coupled with alligator mauling, but I'm hoping for murder. I'll let you know what I find out."

"Murder? Be careful sweetie. Do you know what you're doing?"

"It's ok," I said, "It's not like I'm going undercover or anything, I'm just snooping around. I've got my parents stuff pretty much all settled so I'm going to have a little fun."

"You know, most people would go to the beach."

"I love you, call you later, bye," I said, and hung up.

I had eaten a second slice of pizza, felt guilty about it and then ate the York peppermint patty I had picked up at the gas station. I answered email, called my daughter and checked on the babies, called my folks and let them know how things were going here, except for the dead body, and looked up the directions to the police station. It had been more than twenty-four hours since the police took the body away. I didn't know too much about autopsies, but twenty-four hours seemed like plenty of time to do one.

It was now four in the afternoon.

I threw the two suitcases filled with my father's Hawaiian style shirts in the trunk of my car, keeping the promise I had made to my mother to donate them somewhere. Well, she had told me to set fire to them, donating was my idea.

I set my G.P.S. for the Naples police department and pulled out of the garage.

It had been sunny and hot all day, but now some fairly ominous-looking clouds were building up. This happens all the time in Florida; it rains hard in the afternoons for about an hour and then that's it. I could wait until it blew over, I thought, but not knowing what time the detective left for the day and not even sure he'd see me when I got there, I took my chances and headed out.

The Naples police department is pink. Well, maybe it's a coral color, but the sun was low enough in the sky to cast a decidedly pink color on it. It was the boutique of police stations. I stepped out of the car, and then as if on cue, it poured down rain. I was drenched in less than twenty seconds, ran inside, slipped, and nearly fell on the puddle I had just made.

When you're in your twenties and get soaking wet, you look sexy. When you're in your fifties and get soaking wet, you look like you should be offering someone a poison apple.

I approached the man at the desk who was talking on the phone, but put his hand over the mouthpiece and looked at me questioningly.

"Hello. I wonder if I could have a moment with Detective Gonzales?" I asked, dripping water on his desk and trying to dry it off with my sleeve. Papers fell at my feet.

"I'm so terribly sorry," I said as I retrieved them. "They look like they got a little wet. That's some rain out there huh?"

He looked at me like I was a lunatic. "Detective Gonzales works out of the Fort Myers office."

"Do you know what hours he keeps?"

"No."

"Do you have a phone number for him?"

"I can give you the number for the station" he said as he wrote it on a post-it-note.

"Thank you so much. Could you give me the address too please?"

He glanced up at me and wrote the address too.

I was actually relieved. I would try to make a better first impression in Fort Myers. I chalked this up to a dry run. Well, not really a *dry* run.

Looking around the room on my way out, it was easy to see that there was obviously an underbelly to this city, way under. That reminded me of something I had meant to ask, and walked back to the man at the desk. "Is there a homeless shelter in town?"

"Are you homeless?"

God, I looked worse than I thought. "No, I have some things to donate."

"Yes, you want that address too?"

"Yes please."

He looked up the information on his computer and wrote it out for me.

I glanced at the paper, "Dharma House? Interesting name, huh?"

He looked over my shoulder and said, "Can I help you?"

A woman with piercings in her nose and eyebrows was standing behind me.

"Thanks for all your help," I told the officer and left.

By the time I walked out, the rain had stopped and the sun was back. The ground barely looked wet anymore.

"Jeeze, this is one weird state, huh?" I said to the couple getting out of the car next to mine. They walked away quickly without answering. They probably thought I was peddling poison apples.

ENGULFED
CHAPTER EIGHT

Dharma House was one of those old Florida style houses that were built in the forties and fifties to be vacation homes. It had wood siding painted a pastel blue with white shutters on the windows, and a mostly sand covered landscape with smatterings of pale green, either grass or weeds. The driveway was gravel and threw up a dust storm as I drove in with pieces hitting the underside of my rental car. It didn't appear to have gotten even a drop of the deluge that had soaked me just three miles from here.

The walkway leading to the front door was made of stepping stones that had verses painted on them, "*To the mind that is still, the whole universe surrenders*" and "*If you do not change direction, you may end up where you're headed.*"

Wind chimes and bird feeders hung from the smaller trees and an artificial waterfall that fed a small fish pond flowed under a very large shade tree. A couple of handmade wooden benches under the shade tree had verse painted on them as well, along with small paintings of birds and butterflies.

Hibiscus of every color climbed trellises and short fat palm trees made a type of hedge around the entire house.

The front door stood open with a screened door in place allowing the aroma of incense to drift outside of the home. Over the doorway a hand painted sign read, "*When I let go of what I am, I become what I might be.*"

I knocked on the screen door frame and hollered in. "Hello!"

"Hello," a voice came from behind me so suddenly I startled and made an unconscious gasp. I turned to see a man who appeared to be my age or perhaps a few years older. He was darkly tanned with deep lines and creases around his eyes and mouth. His thinning gray hair was pulled back into a ponytail and he was wearing tattered jeans and a tank top emblazoned with NYPD across the front. Leather sandals, a rope anklet, and his blue John Lennon style sunglasses completed the hippie persona. I would have taken him to be one of the homeless except that he looked like a man who works out a lot, and his teeth were perfect.

"The police department gave me the directions here. Is this a homeless shelter?" I asked.

"We are listed by the city as a halfway house. How can I help you?"

"I'm looking for whoever is in charge," I told him.

" My name is Rod." He reached his hand out, "and although I am founder of Dharma House, I feel my position here to be one of guide."

"Oh, Hi. I'm Maggie," I said and shook his hand. "This doesn't look like...well, I guess I was expecting..."

"I take in men who are temporarily in need of food, shelter and a little guidance to walk back into the world on their own. Would you like to sit down?" he motioned to one of the benches under the tree.

"Thank you," I said, "but I have some things in the car I wanted to give to you if you would like."

"That would be wonderful. Do you need some help getting them from your car?"

"Actually yes, that would be great, thanks."

As we walked to the car I asked him, "So why the name *Dharma House*? I've heard that name once; it was a TV show."

"Dharma is a Hindu or Buddhist word that implies walking a path to become in harmony with the natural world. To be in synch with yourself and all the creatures you travel this world with." He stopped and looked around. I looked around too. The neighborhood consisted of tiny homes in varied stages of disrepair, landscaped with forever-stationary cars. I wasn't sure I wanted to get in sync with this particular part of the world, but I understood what he was saying, sort of.

We got to my car where I opened the trunk and we each took a suitcase and started walking back to the house.

"Are you Buddhist?" I asked, looking down at the stepping stones.

"I do not subscribe to any organized religion. I have made a study of Buddhism though, as well as Taoism and Zen, and other philosophies that encourage inner peace and tranquility. I am endeavoring to live a more harmonious existence with the world around me."

"I see the NYPD on your shirt. Were you on the force?"

"Yes, I retired five years ago and came here to open this place. It was a vision of mine."

"Really?" I said. "Most people who retire down here envision buying a big fishing boat and running charter trips."

"Well, I hope this doesn't sound too cliché, but it was when I was recovering from an injury that I began to reexamine my life." He set the suitcase he was holding down by the front door and I followed suit.

"I'm sorry to cut this short," he said, "but I have a new resident I should check on. Can you wait a moment while I empty the suitcases? I can bring them right back out to you. May I bring you a glass of water?"

"No, thank you, and please, keep the suitcases as well."

"Thank you very much Maggie. Please come by again and say hello. We enjoy visitors here."

"I doubt I will," I said, "I live in Albuquerque. I'm just down here this week and next."

"I have family in Santa Fe," he said, "it's quite beautiful there, very sacred ground."

"Oh, well, I wouldn't know," I said, "I write society happenings for the Albuquerque Herald and they never send me to sacred ground, well, not unless there's a golf course there. Here's my card," I handed him that object, "you can tell your family in Santa Fe to call me sometime; occasionally I can wrangle tickets to something."

He thanked me again and went inside.

I stopped to look at some of the writings on the stepping stones and heard a voice speaking to Rod from inside.

"Who's the broad? How come you made her stay outside? You ain't one of them religions that wants their women to wear them beekeeper get-ups are ya'? A course, after seein' some of them broads I can see why those guys like it that way. Yeesh! Those dames got more mustaches than the Mexican Army."

ENGULFED
CHAPTER NINE

Back at my parents' home that evening, I was in bed with my laptop, going between reading about Doctor Haney and checking status updates on Facebook when Zig called.

"You wanna meet mom and me for lunch tomorrow?" he asked.

"Sure, but why?"

"She has some information about Haney she's not sure what to do with."

"I was just on line reading up on him" I said. "He's like the king of doctors down here. He sits, well, *sat* on all kinds of boards including the one for The Shell and is.....hmm, let me see what it says here, *resident physician for Well Life Government Services for the State of Florida*."

"Yeah, I know, I've met him," Zig said. "He still looked in on Shell residents sometimes and was mom's personal doc before he got too busy."

"I don't understand. Why are you asking me to come? Don't get me wrong, I want to, but you guys don't even know me." I set the laptop on its side of the bed and stretched my legs out.

"It's mom's idea. She likes that you're a reporter and thinks you'll be able to help."

"Yes, but I'm not a real report..."

"*We* both know that," he interrupted, "but Mom likes you and wants you to be there."

"Ok, where are we meeting?"

"I'm taking her to the Fish House. It's on Bonita Beach Road, west of forty-one, eleven o'clock."

"Alrighty then, I'll see you there," I said, "call me if anything changes."

Looking at Haney's picture and knowing he was now minus some of his parts was really creepy. Imagining him getting chomped on by the gator made me feel ill. I needed a break and decided to look at a YouTube video of a baby laughing at a kitten. *Ahhhhhh*, I thought, *much better*.

The next morning I actually prepared for my day and was feeling very clever about it. First step was going out to the car to turn the air conditioner on, then back inside to grab a bottle of water and an emergency backup blouse, a can of hairspray and a makeup bag.

Next, I put them all in a very large purse in which I also packed a note pad, several pens, business cards and a press-pass. The press-pass was from Atlanta and it was expired, but I thought it might come in handy anyway. In the car, I put a Beatles C.D. in and sang along with the boys up Tamiami Trail and into downtown Fort Myers and Martin Luther King Drive. It occurred to me that no one ever names the really posh parts of town after the civil rights legend and felt that to be unfair. I wanted to rename the streets here and have the one with the million dollar homes be called *M.L.K. The Hero Drive* and name the road the police station was on, *Beverly Hills Paradise Haven Gulfstream Road.* A bit long, but I'd find an acronym. .

This police department was more functional than pretty, no pastel pinks or sea shell paintings like in Naples, but it still had its share of palm trees and tropical flowers. I came away with an appointment with the police liaison officer for later in the afternoon. Not with the detective, but it was something.

I had some time before meeting Zig, so decided to drive to The Shell to see if I could learn anything new.

After driving past twenty-five handicapped spots, I came to one marked *visitors.*

This time the security guard, Ralph was at the front desk on the phone, "No, Mrs. Callahan isn't in right now. Yes, she has voice mail, hang on," he said and looked at the console in front of him, appeared confused, and then hung up the receiver.

"Hello," I extended my hand. "Ralph, isn't it?"

He looked at me warily and extended his hand in a pseudo handshake. "Yeah," he said. "Listen, if you want to wait over there," he indicated the lobby sofa, "Jessica will be back in a minute."

I ignored that, "Been really crazy around here the past couple of days huh?" I said.

He eyed me suspiciously then turned to look down the hall, probably for Jessica, whom I assumed was the receptionist.

"Yes," I continued, "I'm sure you really have your hands full right now. This place is very lucky to have you here. I know everyone feels safer knowing you're here to look after them." I gave Ralph my most flattering smile. Almost anyone else would have seen how disingenuous I was, but he appeared obtuse enough that I thought I could get away with it. I was right.

"Yeah". He grinned and hiked his pants up a bit. "Nothin' I coulda' done about the other night though. I mean, Haney didn't even tell me he was here or nothin."

"Did he do that often? Come by without telling anyone?"

"Well, if he did, I wouldn't know," he looked nervous again.

"Did he spend a lot of time here? He was a pretty busy man."

"No, no. I didn't hardly ever see him. He almost never came here, least not when I was here." His eyes were looking everywhere but at me and he was clearly agitated. The phone rang and he startled, "Sorry, gotta get this. Shell Harbor Living," he said into the phone. "No, Mrs. Callahan ain't here; you want me to connect you to her machine?"

He hung up on that person too.

"She sure does get a lot of calls," I said.

"Yeah, she's got lots of friends." He hiked up his pants again and began looking around. Jessica was coming back up the hall and he started to walk away.

"Ralph, before you go, did that man Max ever show up?" I asked.

Looking relieved to have changed the subject, he answered, "No, but we got a call from him sayin' he was stayin' with some friends."

"Oh, that's good. Glad he's all right. Thanks again Ralph. Have a good rest of your day."

"Yeah, you too," he said.

Ok, I thought, walking back to my car, he seems kind of creepy but maybe that's just because I was being nosey and somebody died here on his watch.

My cell vibrated in my pocket, causing me to drop my bag and see all of my stuff to spill out. I pulled the phone out of my pocket and answered, trying to pick my things up at the same time.

"Oh, Hi Jan," I said after hearing her voice.

"What are you doing?" she asked, "You sound weird."

"Picking my stuff off the ground, can I call you right back?"

"Of course, call me back." She hung up.

My lipstick rolled under the car and I was flat on my belly trying to get it when I heard a voice approaching and saw men's shoes walk to a car one spot over from mine. It was Ralph's voice.

"....I don't know who she is but she's way too nosey," a minute of silence then, "she's friends with that Callahan woman I think. I don't know...."

His voice trailed off and was replaced with the sound of a car starting and driving away.

The pavement was hot and I could feel my stomach and chest burning from it. My phone vibrated and scared me again, this time I jerked my head up and hit the side of my face on the wheel well.

"Shit!" I yelled out then answered the phone.

"Hello?" I said in a whisper.

"Mom?" It was my daughter.

"Hi Megan."

"How is Florida?" she asked.

"Oh fine," I said, "It's great."

"Are you ok?" her voiced sounded worried.

"Yes, I'm great. How are you?'

"Mom, why are we whispering?"

"I'm at the library; can I call you back in a minute?" I said, backing out on my belly from under the car.

"You sound kinda' weird, are you sure you're ok?"

"Oh yes, yes. I'm fine," I told her, "they don't allow you to talk in the libraries here."

"That's crazy even for Florida," she said, "all right, call me right back."

"Bye," I told her, finally extricating myself from under the car.

I was on my knees when I glanced over to my right and saw none other than the man himself, Detective Gonzales, and he was looking directly at me.

I stood up, brushed the gravel off of my knees, gave him a weak smile, held up my lipstick and unlocked my car and got in.

"Shit!" I yelled out loud when my butt touched the metal buckle on the seat belt.

He was still looking at me, so I smiled again, shut the door, turned the ignition, backed up, and drove away. Looking in the rear view mirror I could see him shaking his head slowly.

I make lousy first impressions, and second and third...

ENGULFED
CHAPTER TEN

.

The Fish House had wooden bench seats, wooden tables, and food served in red plastic baskets. Beer was served in cheap glasses and children in the booth across from us were barefoot. The back wall was windowed and looked out onto a narrow waterway lined with overgrown mangroves and sea grasses on the opposite shore. All in all, I found it charming.

Dorothy, however, looked as though she should be dining at the Ritz. She wore a perfectly pressed white cotton suit over a jade green silk blouse and somehow gave off the air that a spotlight was forever shining on her. She made broad gestures when she spoke that were accentuated by the dazzling assortment of jewels banded around her perfectly manicured fingers. She talked about her days on Broadway and in Hollywood and peppered her stories with lots of gossip and backstage intrigue.

After finishing off a plate of clams that had the addictive quality of heroin, and figuring I'd look like a glutton if I ordered more, I decided instead to just come back that night for dinner.

"Darling," Dorothy held her glass toward Zig, "be a dear and get me another spritzer will you? I fear our young waiter must have fallen into the marina."

She turned toward me and spoke in a stage whisper, "Marina; I wouldn't tie an old rubber inner tube up out there." Then she smiled broadly at her son.

I thought she was magnificent. I could not stop staring at her and she didn't seem to mind. On the contrary, I believed she not only enjoyed it but expected it.

Zig returned with her spritzer, "Well now that you two are such great friends, can we get down to the Doc Haney business?"

"Yes," I said, "I really appreciate you including me in on this. I'm not a *real* reporter though, just so you know. I mean, I used to be about a million years ago. Now I'm a columnist."

"You work for a newspaper" said Dorothy more as a statement than a question.

"Oh yes, like I told you, I write the *About Town* column for the Albuquerque Herald."

"Then you're reporter enough for me."

"Thank you for your confidence in me," I said, beaming.

"Well my dear, I have a very good friend whose name I will not give to you. Now please don't be offended. I haven't told Steven either."

"I'm not offended," I said, "but first, can I ask, how did Steven become Zig?"

"Actually that's a funny story," began Dorothy.

"No, actually, it's not funny, not funny at all," said Zig looking out the window and heaving a sigh.

"You see, my mother," Dorothy continued, ignoring Zig, "Steven's grandmother, was one of the original Ziegfeld girls. She thought Steven looked like Flo Ziegfeld when he was a child, so she started calling him Zig or Ziggy since he was....I'm not sure, how old were you son?"

"I don't know mom. Can we get back to Haney?" Zig said, turning back to us.

"Well, he was probably about three or four," Dorothy continued, "and it's just been his name ever since."

"It turns out to be a pretty cool radio name too, huh Zig?" I nudged his side with my elbow but he ignored that, stabbing at the fried clams on his plate with the little sword they had given me in my margarita.

"Anyway," Dorothy went on, "back to the business at hand. I was visiting this friend, whose name I shall not reveal, when I started feeling kind of woozy. I had finished a small glass of Chardonnay but that would not have accounted for what my friend said was some slurring of my speech. I have excellent diction you know, it is vital in my career." She cleared her throat and sipped her wine spritzer.

Zig held his empty beer glass up, waving it in the air attempting to get the attention of our server.

"Now, my friend is quite brilliant and noted immediately that I was having a stroke. It turned out to be quite mild fortunately, a T.I.A they called it. What does that stand for again Steven, do you remember?"

"Transient Ischemic Attack," Zig answered exasperatedly, still waving his glass in the air.

"Oh yes, that," said Dorothy. "So my friend called 911 of course and Bruce......"

"Bruce is Doctor Haney," Zig interrupted, paying attention again.

"Yes, Doctor Bruce Haney." Dorothy said. "He's been my doctor for ten...no...has it been...wait, he was my doctor when I had my glaucoma surgery and that was in ninety-one. I know it was ninety-one because that was when I turned sixty. I had the surgery just the day before my birthday and still went out and celebrated at The Turtle Inn." She sipped her drink. "Have you ever been there? The chef at the time was Italian and terribly full of himself....."

"Mom, can we get back to that night please?" Zig pleaded.

"I'm getting there," she told him.

"Yeah, she's getting there," I added smugly, then smiled at his mother. "Go on Dorothy."

"Well," she continued, "Bruce arrived just as the ambulance men were taking me out of my friend's apartment. Now, granted, I was a bit distracted at the time, but I'm certain I heard my friend and Bruce arguing about doctor-patient confidentiality and he, Bruce, was telling my friend that he wasn't *his* doctor, he was mine."

"*His?*" Zig asked, open mouthed. "Mom, you didn't tell me your friend was a man. Are you....you know.....*seeing* this guy?"

"Oh Ziggy, don't be ridiculous, he's your age," she said.

"Why would your friend need Doctor Haney to keep something confidential about *him*?" I asked.

"Well dear, I'm sorry but I can't tell you that either but, later, in the emergency room, I heard Bruce on the phone. I'm certain he didn't know I could hear him and he was telling someone that he just hit the jack pot and that; now these are his words not mine, that he's found one big f'ing goose that was gonna lay them some f'ing solid gold eggs, only he completed the f words."

Zig had gotten his beer midway to his open mouth and stopped, staring incredulously at his mother.

"Well, I *told* you, Steven," she said, "Those were *his* words. You know I never use profanity." She turned to me, "It is my opinion that profanity is merely a crutch for the unimaginative." She sipped her drink, wiped her hands with her napkin, took a deep breath and continued.

"Anyway, he said he might need some help in case the goose started causing problems. I know he was talking about my friend."

"This sounds pretty serious," I said. "Especially now that...you know..."

"Of course," she said emphatically, "that is why I'm asking for your help. I don't want my friend getting into trouble over this. He was just trying to make sure I was all right."

"Did you know any of this?" I asked Zig.

"No," he turned to me, his mouth still hanging open, "Mom just said she wanted to tell me something she knew about the Doctor." He turned toward his mother, "Mom, this is pretty serious. You need to talk to the police."

"I can't. I told you," she said adamantly. "I just need for you two to find out, somehow, if they are even looking at my friend."

"How will we know?" I asked. "We don't know your friend's name."

"Oh trust me, you'll know," said Dorothy, "you'll know."

"I really wish you felt you could confide in us," I said. "I promise it won't go any further than this table."

"I can't dear, I made a promise."

"You're wasting your time," Zig told me, "she refused to answer Joe McCarthy during his Communist witch hunt in fifty-three."

"That's right..." Dorothy began.

Zig interrupted her, "Yeah Ma, but we're not Senator McCarthy."

"I know that dear, but this way, if the police talk to you, you will have plausible deniability."

"Plausible deniability, Ma, where do you get this stuff?"

"Books my dear," she told him. She turned to me, "I never could get him to read."

"I don't need books, I've got a computer." Zig said.

"Don't argue with your mother Zig," I told him, then turned and smiled at her, "Don't worry Mrs. Callahan, I'm on this."

"Thank you dear. I knew I could count on you the very instant we met."

I'm pretty sure that last line was out of politeness but I accepted it graciously.

The rest of the lunch was a blur, my mind racing from fear of letting her down, to the thrill of doing something this exciting. Where do I even begin, I wondered. I know. I know just what I need to help me think.

I asked them, "Does this place have a dessert menu?"

ENGULFED
CHAPTER ELEVEN

It was late afternoon when I finished my disappointing interview with the Ft. Myers police public affairs officer. She didn't give me anymore than what I already knew. Every question was answered with the standard, "I can't release that information at this time since it is part of an ongoing investigation." She wouldn't even confirm that the dead man was Doctor Bruce Haney. What I did take away was the fact that it was most probably not an accidental drowning. I knew this because she kept saying it was an ongoing investigation. She did offer me a tour, which I took. I was more interested in seeing the place than hearing the stuff she was prattling on about like, the history of the department, how many officers they had and everything else you could find on Google. I thanked her and walked out.

In the parking lot I checked my cell. They were all calls from my mother and children except one number that I didn't recognize; I listened to my voice mail. "Hello Maggie, this is Rod from Dharma House. I wondered if you wouldn't mind calling me at your earliest convenience," and he left his number.

Oh God, I thought, I knew I should have checked the suitcases better before I gave them away. What if my mother left granny panties or a romance novel or, worse, what if my father takes Viagra and that's in there? I was almost afraid to return the call.

I decided I could probably ponder that at the beach as well as anywhere else and I had promised myself, as well as Jan, that I would go, so I put the coordinates in the G.P.S. and followed the sun.

The further west I got the more interesting the drive became. Waterways flowed behind seafood restaurants and bathing suit shops. Bait shops displayed wooden signs advertising boat and Jet Ski rentals, scenic water tours, and sunset sailing cruises. I rolled down the window and breathed in warm sea air. I was hit with the smell of bait mixed with boat diesel, heard the music of sea gulls overhead, and beheld a cloudless, bright, azure sky. It was sublime.

From the top of The Matanzas Pass Bridge that leads to the island, I glimpsed Fort Myers Beach laid out before me. Her shops, restaurants, and hotels were painted in bright blues, yellows and oranges haphazardly arranged in front of the waters of the Gulf, like pieces of junk jewelry around the neck of a goddess. I was having one of those, *it's great to be alive moments* and couldn't wait to walk on that sand and get my feet wet on that shore.

The exhilaration faded and was replaced with mild annoyance when I circled the public parking lot waiting for a spot like a vulture. I watched for people walking toward their cars with armloads of towels, coolers and beach chairs, then jockeyed to get to them first, which I did at last, and waited while they packed everything in their car before I could replace them in the coveted spot.

The walk along the shore immediately put me back in my happy place watching children swim, build sand castles, and eat ice cream. A group of teen boys were skate boarding along the edge of the shore, and old people sat in chairs under umbrellas and stared out at the sea. Music played from one of the restaurants on the boardwalk and mixed with the sounds of birds, laughing children, and waves to make the most unique cacophony of sound I'd heard. I took a walk out on the wooden pier to its canopied end and watched in fascination as pelicans flew and dived and filled their beaks with fish. A childhood rhyme popped into my head; *a funny old bird is a pelican, his beak holds more than his belly can.*

I stayed long into the late afternoon. Sandpipers scurried in and out of the tide and children put finishing touches on their sand creations that created an exquisite tableau. The sun began making its gradual decent into the Gulf and everyone but the children stopped to witness it paint the sky ever richer shades of yellow, orange and red before it finally slipped away beneath the water. Then, as if someone had hung a, *The End,* sign in the sky, a round of applause broke out and everyone began the damp, sandy walk back to their cars, stopping to wash their feet in the outdoor showers on the way.

I didn't want it to end so I stayed a bit longer, caught up in the moment thinking I would use this time for deep thought, introspection, and not least of all to figure out how I was going to find out about Dorothy's mystery man.

Remaining in nature's solitude to plan my next move was short lived however, as I felt my ankles being bitten by the aptly named no-see-ums. I trudged back to the lot, washing my own feet on the way, sat in the car and returned the call to Rod from Dharma House.

"Miss Finn, how kind of you to return my call so quickly," he said. "I wanted to thank you again and was hoping I could impose on you for a small favor."

I was grateful he hadn't found embarrassing stuff in the suitcases, but wondered if he was offering them back to me because it would be ridiculous for homeless men to dress in cruise-ship apparel. I was glad I hadn't packed the boating hats.

"I suppose, it depends on what you need," I said.

"Well, I remember you saying you were a reporter, is that correct?"

"I'm a columnist, but I work in Albuquerque, not here." I said.

"Sometimes the universal hand of omnipotence guides us in ways we could never have undertaken, or even planned for ourselves," he said.

"Yes, I agree, I'd like to break that hand's fingers sometimes," I said, waiting for a laugh and getting none, "but that's probably not where you going."

"Our own attempts at comprehension of the circumstances that invade our day to day life can be frustrating," he said," Have you tried meditation?"

"Yes," I said, attempting to move the conversation along, "So what's up Rod?"

"I don't want to take advantage of our brief friendship, but I am in need of some information regarding my newest guest. Since you have a journalistic background, I felt it was a kind of divine intervention that sent you to me."

"You want me to investigate someone?" I asked, incredulously.

"Investigate sounds so formal," he said. "Just look at, casually."

"I thought you were an ex cop," I said. "Surely you must have your own resources."

"I made a vow never to contact anyone from law enforcement in cases involving my guests, unless it was a matter of imminent danger of course."

Again with the making a vow to oneself? I thought. It's a sure bet this guy has never been in politics.

"Well, I don't know that I can be of any help. I don't live here. I don't really know anyone here."

"Maybe if you have some free time tomorrow you wouldn't mind stopping by and I can explain in more detail. I realize you only came by to make a donation, and I greatly appreciate it, and I know this sounds like I am overstepping the bounds of your generosity, but I could sense immediately that you were a person of great heart and mind and your *aura,* if you will, was exceptional."

"All right, I'll call before I come," I told him, "It will be early though, if that's ok."

"That will be perfect. I always rise with the sun."

Of course you do, I thought. *Of course you do*, but said, "See you in the morning."

"Excellent," he said, happily. "Thank you so much. I hope your evening is rich and blessed."

So, I thought, thirty five years languishing at my job of writing insipid newspaper columns, and in less than a week down here I'm Woodward and / or Bernstein, with an aura!

ENGULFED
CHAPTER TWELVE

Living in my parent's nearly empty house was beginning to feel a bit like camping and I hate camping. The few food items I'd purchased were in a box, along with paper plates, paper towels and plastic utensils. I had napkins from Pizza Hut and Subway, straws still in paper and one *to- go* coffee mug.

The morning found me rummaging in my purse for the torn tea bag I remembered seeing in there, nuking some water in a Styrofoam cup, and eating the roll I had stuck in my purse at The Fish House. If I were living in any time in history before packaged food I would have starved to death because, alas, I have zero wilderness skills. I am equally glad I live in a time where transportation does not involve anything I have to get up early to feed; already berating myself for not getting gas on the way home the night before.

I went out without first pre-cooling the car and made my way to Dharma House with a stop first at the 7-11 for gas, coffee and a donut since the stale roll and cup of hot tea leaves were; not surprisingly, unsatisfying.

Pulling into the driveway at Dharma House, I saw Rod by the waterfall doing what looked like slow motion Karate moves in his .pajamas. Since he didn't seem to notice I had driven up, I sat in my car and drank my coffee and watched him go through his routine. After a minute or two of this I saw a much older man come out of the front door and sit on the bench near to where Rod was still exercising. The man began to move his legs and arms out in imitation of Rod, but from a seated position. Then Rod sat on the bench opposite the older man with his legs folded in front of him in Yoga position. They both closed their eyes for some kind of prayer or meditation. I stayed in my car, not wanting to make a sound and intrude on their privacy.

It was the older man who broke the silence. "Are you sure this Jap shit is gonna' help my heart?"

"Shhhh. Focus my brother. Focus on your oasis of peace," Rod told him, without moving or opening his eyes.

"It's too hard. My gut is makin' too much noise from that bird seed shit you fed me this mornin'. I have to go inside and use the crapper. " And with that, he got up and walked back into the house.

Rod sat there a couple of minutes longer and then opened his eyes. He looked directly at me as though he knew I had been there all along, and began walking toward me. I got out and walked to meet him

"Good morning Maggie. Thank you so much for coming to see me today, can I get you anything?"

I thought of the bird seed shit comment and said, "No, thank you."

"No doubt you saw and heard my guest here this morning," he said as we began walking back toward the tree and benches.

"Yes," I said, "I didn't want to intrude. It looked like you two were meditating."

"He calls himself Errol, Errol Flynn. He showed up a couple of nights ago rather wet and disheveled. A friend of mine was driving patrol when he noticed Errol sitting on a riding lawnmower outside of someone's home trying to get it started. Errol told the officer his wife had kicked him out of the house without any money or ID and his heart was too weak to walk any further. My friend brought him here and I agreed to take him in. That was two nights ago."

"You said he was wet," I asked. "That was the night before the hurricane right? It didn't rain at all that day, I remember that."

"He said his wife turned the sprinklers on him when he was leaving."

We were, mercifully, in the shade now, and I was tempted to splash water on my face from the little fountain. Rod didn't appear to have a bead of sweat on him.

"He's obviously lying to you about his name," I said, "Do you believe anything he told you?"

"You don't believe his name is Errol Flynn?" Rod asked me with a big grin and a wink.

"Is he the one you want me to…what was it you said…..look at?"

"Yes, he is. He is a very troubled man and I would like to help him find some serenity in his remaining years."

"Why?" I asked, "I mean, I don't want to seem unkind, but he doesn't exactly sound like he's looking for serenity."

"Maggie, believe it or not, before my accident I sounded much like Errol. My heart, mind and soul were as damaged and broken as my body had become. Someone had been kind enough to set me on the path to peace and enlightenment and I am trying to pay it forward, as it were. That is why I opened Dharma House. Errol is as troubled a soul as I have ever met."

"Maybe he doesn't want to be enlightened," I said. "Some people just like being miserable. It makes them happy."

"Please, come and sit with me." Rod motioned to the benches.

Oh crap, I thought, I'm going to hear a sermon. I suppose he read my expression because he said, "I know you are very busy but this will take only a moment." Seating himself, he patted the spot beside him.

I sat down on the opposite bench. "Look, I appreciate that you want to help this guy but….."

"Mrs. Finn, you…."

"Ms. Finn, not Mrs."

"I'm sorry, Ms. Finn. Have you ever had an incident in your life that profoundly changed the way you not only looked at your own life, but changed the very essence of who you were?"

"No. I don't think so. I'm sure I would have remembered something like that happening to me." I knew that sounded sarcastic but he didn't seem insulted and I felt a bit ashamed of myself. "It sounds like something like that happened to you though, am I right? That's why you quit the force? Came here?" I hoped my new found interest would make up for my earlier snarky remark.

"Yes, Maggie. May I call you Maggie?"

"Of course, Maggie is fine."

"You are right Maggie, I am quite different from the man I was five years ago, and I shall tell you about it sometime if you are interested."

"Sure, that would be great." I told him, weakly.

"But for now, I hope I can share some small part of why I feel the need to help Errol."

"Alright," I said, wishing I had never come.

"I have cultivated within myself a more heightened awareness of people. A more acute sensitivity to what they are feeling and experiencing, and even, to some extent, what they are thinking."

"You're telling me you're a mind reader?"

"No. No. Not at all," he said. "It is possible though, with some training and years of discipline, to acquire a certain awareness of the non-verbal communication of others."

"Alrighty then," I said, standing up. "Well, that's kind of a lot for me to consume at the moment."

"I understand completely. I don't expect you to accept all of this right now, but I told you this to help you better understand why I ask you for this favor. I am certain that Errol is involved in something that may have implications beyond just himself, but since all of this is based on my own psychic connection to him, I have nothing I can present to the authorities."

He was still seated with the sun in his face and was shading his eyes and squinting. The sun made his face look golden and I thought he looked like a skinny Buddah.

"Do you think he is in danger?" I asked.

"That is what I do not know, unfortunately. And that is exactly why I have asked for your help," he said.

"I can see why you don't think the police will get involved, but why not hire a private investigator? I mean, I'm just the About Town columnist from New Mexico."

"I don't want to make you uncomfortable," he said and I immediately felt uncomfortable. "But the moment I met you I sensed you were here for a reason. I am convinced that this is it." He stood and looked directly at me. He kept staring at my eyes like he was trying to look inside them.

"Well, you know," I said, "I really don't think I'm your girl. I mean, I don't want to doubt your sense..ing ability. It's just; I wouldn't even know where to begin. I cannot imagine there aren't at least a hundred people more qualified than me to help you."

I began backing up and stumbled on a Hibiscus plant behind me. Rod caught my arm and gave me that stare again.

"Will you at least consider it?" he asked. "I'll call tomorrow. Maybe after you've had a chance to sleep on it."

"All right, sure," I said, "call me tomorrow. I don't think anything will have changed. I mean, I don't believe...I'm sorry, but if this man is in some kind of danger I am the last person you want to try to help him."

"And I believe you are wrong about that. I will call tomorrow. Have an insightful and rich day Maggie," he said and walked back toward the house.

I got into the car, grabbed my cell, felt it burn my hand and dropped it immediately. Anything you leave in your car here in the tropics turns to the temperature of molten lava in under ten minutes. I was looking down at the floor for it and still backing up when I heard the crackle of pebbles under tires and turned to see a large cloud of dust and a black SUV coming down the street behind me. He honked. I swerved, and nearly drove into the canal on the opposite side of the road.

The man driving the SUV stopped for a minute and looked at me, just stared for a minute, and drove on.

"This day just gets weirder and weirder," I said aloud. "Is everyone down here crazy, or just the ones following me?"

ENGULFED
CHAPTER THIRTEEN

When I was a little girl, before PETA and animal rights, people used to dye the feathers of baby ducklings and chicks pastel pink or blue or lavender and sell them as pets at Easter. When I was about five or six my grandmother gave me one such colorful bird, a sky blue duckling. We lived in the suburbs where our only nearby body of water was a drainage ditch, so I don't know what my grandmother thought I would do with a duck of *any* color, but there he was, on our porch Easter morning. I named him Willy Quack Good Citizen after a book character, and that was as far as I got in my ownership responsibilities. Not being raised on a farm and being five years old and all, I had no opportunity to acquire any duck wrangling skills. I don't suppose I owned Willy more than a day before my mother took him to *a farm.* I imagined that farm as a soft fuzzy pastel utopia, where my little blue Willy could frolic forever with all the other unnaturally hued poultry living there.

That was the vision I was reminded of as I gazed out onto the golf course at The Shell. It was like a farm of pastel blue, lavender, and pink clad people with fuzzy white heads. They were frolicking about with their golf clubs and sipping cold drinks brought to them by a woman in a beverage cart and it did look like a kind of utopia.

Coming back this morning, I expected to find everyone still in a frenzy over the repulsive fate of their doctor, but you would never have known anything at all had happened. No one seemed the least bit daunted by the yellow crime scene tape still wrapped around much of the lake area.

I'm not sure what I hoped to learn by coming back, but it felt like the logical next step; even though it was a certainty I wouldn't find anything the crime scene people hadn't. Detective Gonzales had all kinds of resources at his disposal that I was sure I didn't even know existed. The one thing I had that he didn't was, well, actually,...nothing nothing at all. *Why did I agree to take this case?* I wondered.

"What am I saying, *case?*" I yelled aloud to no one. "I don't have a case. I have a *job* in *New Mexico, I* can't have a *case!*"

I turned my head and noticed a man not far from me looking my way. I put my phone up to my ear in an attempt to look like I was talking to it and not myself. When he began walking toward me I immediately considered the possibility that he was security, or an undercover cop. I raised my voice to my nonexistent caller and said, "OK, well that's about all then, just that one case of root beer and that's it. I'll get back to you as soon as I can."

By now the man was just a few feet from me, waiting for me to end my *call.*

He looked to be somewhere in his late forties or fifties, tall and pretty pale for someone living in Florida. His salt and pepper hair was carefully styled and held in place with lots of wet, shiny stuff. He looked muscular and had a heavy scent of cigarettes. His clothing; dark blue shirt, black pants, black dress shoes, were noticeably out of place.

"Excuse me, I didn't mean to intrude on your call," he said, in an accent straight out of *The Godfather.*

"Oh, that's all right," I told him, "I was done anyway."

He stood there looking at me like it was still my turn to say something, so I did.

"I'm sorry," I said, "but do we know each other?"

"Yes, I mean no," he said, "you don't know *me* but I noticed you were friends with Mrs. Callahan...Dorothy." He lowered his voice when he said that and glanced back over his shoulder as if making sure we weren't overheard.

"How do you know Dorothy?" I asked and found myself lowering my voice and glancing behind me too, "do you live here at the Shell?"

"I'm sorry, where are my manners," he said in a slow, deliberate manner, like he was trying to remember his lines. "I'm Stanley."

Well, I thought, he didn't preface that with *officer* or *special agent* but that may be how they do things.

He stuck his hand forward to shake mine, and smiled broadly at me.

"Getting back to Mrs. Callahan, how long have you known her?" His smile was gone.

Now, of course I knew this was all *way* too suspicious and I should have left, but figured I could learn more from him if I played along, so I did.

"Not too long," I said, "Why?"

The smile was back but this time it looked faked, like a beauty pageant smile, or an appliance salesman's, and he said, "I don't mean to sound foolish, but she is a very attractive woman and I was hoping you would introduce us."

Well, I hadn't seen that coming. "Aren't you a little young for her?" I asked.

"Oh, I'm not as young as you think," he said, creepy smile fixed in place, "but thanks for sayin' that. I like older women anyway.

"She's pretty friendly," I said, "I'm sure if you introduced yourself she wouldn't be offended."

"Oh, I just thought it might be imprudent on my part," he said, emphasizing *imprudent* like it was a word he just learned and was proud of. I stifled a grin; this was starting to be fun for me.

"Imprudent? Why?" I asked.

"Well, she has some very important friends, powerful friends. I'm just a regular guy and ...."

I interrupted, "Powerful? She knows lots of celebrities but I'd hardly call them powerful. Most of them haven't been on the stage for decades."

"Yes," he said, "but none of *them* have limousines with government tags. I saw her leave in one the other night. Someone told me she does that a lot."

"Oh, that," I said, trying to think up a plausible lie at the spur of the moment, and I stink at making up spur of the moment lies.

"She volunteers down at the court house," I said, "sings for the people in jail."

He stared at me, open mouthed.

"They come and get her," I continued, "she doesn't drive anymore and you know Naples; limousines are like taxi cabs here."

He continued to look at me with a mixture of confusion and incredulity and I was not about to go any further with this until I'd talked to Dorothy. I went for the old cell phone ploy again. "Oops! Have to get this." I put my phone to my ear, turned my back and began walking away, then turned to him and said in a whisper, "Sorry, this is important. I have to go now, nice to meet you."

Once out of ear shot, I called Zig and got his voice mail. "Call me as soon as you get this," I said.

Turning back in the direction of the building, I saw Ralph walking out toward Stanley. The two spoke for a few minutes and then turned and looked in my direction. When I looked behind me and saw nothing there, I realized it was me they were watching. I wondered if they were discussing my behavior and whether or not to call the men in the white coats to come get me.

I took the long way around, entered through the front door of The Shell and saw the receptionist whose name I'd forgotten.

"Hello again, remember me?" I asked, "My parents are moving in here, the Carrolls?"

"Yes, I remember you," she said, finishing up a text and putting the phone on her lap, face down. "Can I help you?"

"I need to measure for the drapes. I already have a key."

"Ok," she said and picked her cell phone back up.

I took a few steps toward the elevator and then, on a hunch, I turned back to her, "Do you get many limousine pickups here?"

"Only for Mrs. Callahan," she said, "She has lots of famous friends."

"How exciting, do you know who any of them are?"

"No," she said, "the driver comes in and gets me to call her."

"I'd love to see one on the inside, a limo I mean. Does it come on any specific day or time?"

"It's always at dinner time," she said, pulling her hair out of its elastic band and retying it. "No special day, just, whenever."

I guessed she didn't graduate top of her class at phone answering school because she wasn't at all suspicious of my questioning.

"Does the driver ever hint at *who* he works for or where they go?" I asked her.

"No. Well, except that one time when I think he was trying to flirt with me." She grinned, leaned over her desk and looked around conspiratorially, "He's really cute. He asked me how late I worked because he'd love to see me when he got back. Of course, it was gonna be real, real late, like midnight and I get off at six. He was cute but no way I was gonna wait around seven hours."

I opened my mouth, closed it, and then said. "Midnight? Where could an eighty-something year old woman be going until midnight?"

"I don't know, but I sure don't want to wait around here all night to find out," she said and swiveled in her chair to catch her reflection in the window, "I've got HBO at home."

The phone rang, "Oops, gotta get this. See ya," and she picked up the phone. "Shell Harbor Living, can I help you?"

Dorothy didn't answer my knock right away, so I put my ear to the door to make out if there was any sound from in there. This was necessary due to the loud Polka music coming from the apartment behind me.

I heard the door behind me open and the music flooded the hall. I turned to see a man standing behind me; an elderly man as thin as a rake wearing lederhosen and a green felt cap.

"Do you want a glass?" he asked.

"What?" I asked him, "A glass of what?"

He went inside his apartment and came back with an empty water glass.

"Put this to your ear and you can hear better," he shouted.

"Oh, I'm not eavesdropping," I said.

"Suit yourself," he said, and put the glass to Dorothy's door and placed his ear against it. "Here she comes," he said and moved away, hiding the glass behind his back.

"Maggie!" Dorothy said, opening her door, "how good to see you. Hello Idzy," she said to the polka man, then ushered me inside.

She gestured to her blue and yellow floral sofa and said, "Sit down dear. Would you like a drink? I have a lovely claret."

I looked at my watch; it was just a little after nine. She must have noticed me looking and said, "I don't normally have wine this early but having you here makes it seem like a party."

Boy, I thought, *James Bond's got nothing on this woman.*

"Well, a claret sounds fabulous to me too," I said. "I've been up for hours so this is like cocktail time for me."

She brought our wine out and sat on a chair opposite me. "What brings you here this morning my dear? Don't tell me you have news for me already."

"Not really, no," I said, looking at the design on my glass, which was actually a plastic cup. It had an orange sun design etched onto it along with the name, *The Sun God* and didn't look like anything I would have expected her to own.

"Sorry about these silly things, my wine glasses are in a box. This is easier. I hope you don't mind," she said.

"Oh, not at all, I've been drinking out of Styrofoam for days now. This is actually a step up."

Dorothy set her cup down on the coffee table. "Now then," she said, what shall we talk about this morning?"

She was impeccably dressed in a pale yellow silk blouse with matching necklace and earrings. She looked like she had just stepped out of a salon so I asked her, "Have you already been out this morning? You look beautiful."

"Why thank you dear, and yes. I always take my morning walk early, before it gets too warm."

"You dress like that to exercise? I wear an old Pink Floyd T- shirt with hair dye stains on it and sweat pants."

Dorothy laughed one of those deep throaty laughs that I always associate with Lauren Bacall and said, "Oh dear, you young people."

"Young people?" I said. "Dorothy, if I didn't love you before, I sure do now." I sipped my wine. "Ummmm, I need to ask you something."

"And I shall try to answer," she said.

"Do limousines ever pick you up?"

"That's an odd question," she said.

"I mean, does anyone ever take you out in limousines?"

"I've ridden in hundreds of limousines my dear."

"I mean, recently or, you know, from here…ever," I felt awkward and sounded simple minded but for some reason her smile was making me nervous.

"My, my, people do love to gossip in this place, don't they?" she said and then smiled again.

She's being purposefully vague, I thought, why? If she wants me to find out stuff, then why is she giving me a hard time?

We both reached for our wine at the same time, her smiling enigmatically, me uncomfortably.

My cell phone was vibrating in my purse.

"I hate to be rude Dorothy, but I need to see who's trying to call me. I'll just take a peek."

"You go right ahead dear," she said, "take your time. I'm going to powder my nose." She walked down the hall.

I had missed two calls, one from Zig and the other from my mother. I returned the calls quietly and briefly telling both that I'd call them back in ten minutes.

When Dorothy came back, I decided to change the subject and asked about her lederhosen wearing neighbor.

"Ah, Idzi, he's a darling. He looks like he belongs on a charm bracelet doesn't he? He says he's rehearsing for some kind of talent show, that's why the costume, but that's been two years now. I think he just likes wearing them."

We sat silently again, sipping our wine and then I said, "Dorothy, I'm not sure I can help you without some more information."

"You already have plenty of information dear. I'm confident you'll be able to learn something. Perhaps you can speak to that detective that was here that day, that handsome Hispanic looking man. I hear he is half Jewish and half Cuban, isn't that a delightful combination?" She set her empty cup on the coffee table between us. "I also hear that he has a standing reservation at Saul's Deli every day at 12:30. I bet you can catch him there today."

"Are you sure you're not with the FBI?" I asked, laughing.

She merely smiled at me, and for a moment I was afraid she was going to say *yes*.

"All right," I said, "I'll see what else I can find out."

When I got back into my car and called Zig his phone went straight to voice mail. Then I turned on the radio and realized why; he was on the air. Andy Williams was just finishing up Moon River and Zig's voice came on saying, "It's another perfect day here in paradise. You're listening to the music of your life, WWTF. News and weather coming up after we pay some bills.

"Heyyyyyyy, it's me the Fonz, on my Big Dog....."

I turned the radio off and called to check on my parents who were happily unaware of the tumult here, and were waiting in line for the Country Bear Jamboree. Only small children and old people can enjoy being outdoors in Orlando in summer, God bless their reptilian blood.

My next call was to The Albuquerque Herald.

"Hi Jan, how are things in New Mexico?"

"Maggie. I'm so glad you called. I've been worried about you. Are you done messing around with that dead guy story?"

"In a way. Well, no. Not really. I promised someone I'd check into something."

"Oh. Ok. That's not vague at all. I need you here!" she said, sounding desperate. "I'm getting married and I need my best friend, plus Gail from sales has been filling in for you and I think she's enjoying it too much. You'd better get back here soon."

I felt a mixture of panic and indignation. It was a crummy column but it was *my* crummy column.

"Crap Jan, I still have stuff to do here. Anyway, I thought it was ok for me to be gone these two weeks."

"It *is* ok. I'm just saying, Gail is enjoying writing your column *and* she's a sneaky bitch *and* I don't trust her. Besides, she's acting kind of flirty with Wyatt. "

"Remind me who Wyatt is again?" I asked.

"Wyatt Lynch, editor in chief, the boss over both of us."

"Oh yeah," I said, glumly, "that Wyatt. She's flirting with *him*? She has to be desperate."

Wyatt Lynch is sixty eight and has both acne *and* a comb-over. You couple that with loose fitting dentures that cause him to whistle over any word with the letter S in it, and his daily onion sandwich and you've got one unappealing bit of manhood.

"They can't give her my column, it's MY column." I said, then took a big breath to calm myself. "I'm not worried. Yes I am, but what the hell, I'm staying here till the twenty eighth, that was the deal. And I'll be back in plenty of time to wedding shop with you."

I had a view of the side entrance to the Shell from the parking lot and was staring out the window during this conversation when I saw Brandy, the administrator, talking to that creepy guy Stanley, and watched as they got into a black SUV.

"What the hell?" I shouted

"What?" asked Jan, "Are you OK?"

"Yeah, I'm fine. Can I call you back?"

"No. OK. Fine, but don't forget to call me," she said, and hung up. A sense of fear, panic and confusion came over me.

"Damn," I said aloud, "is that the same SUV that I nearly collided with at Dharma House?" My heart was racing, *This* was getting exciting.

ENGULFED
CHAPTER FOURTEEN

The SUV pulled up to the front of The Shell and idled there long enough for me to get to my car and watch them from the far end of the front parking lot. It was 10:30 which meant I had two hours to see what these guys were up to before Nathan Gonzales would be at Saul's Deli. I was going to have to come up with a plan for how to go about spying on a police detective, but for now, all my focus was on this odd couple. The odd couple turned into a trio when Ralph, the security guard, got into the SUV with them.

Feeling very grateful for my nondescript rental car, I discreetly followed them to, of all places, The Gulf Coast Motor Speedway. After driving past them as they pulled into the lot, I came back to find their car there, but no sign of them. In fact, the only people I saw were two men unloading something from the back of a black pick-up truck with a sign on the side of it that read, *Charley Davidson*. They off-loaded a small motorcycle from the trailer that was attached to the back of the truck. Once they got it down on the pavement, they each took out a cigarette, one sat on the tail of the pick-up, the other on the seat of the cycle, and started talking.

I walked over to them to ask for directions to a shopping mall. While we discussed which one I wanted and they argued over the most direct route to get there, I got a pretty good look at their cargo.

It was a cross between a motorcycle, a mobility device and one of those motorized shopping carts you see at the grocery store. It reminded me of Zig's Indian only in that it was also black with lots of chrome but that was where the similarities ended. This one appeared as though someone had raided a hospital supply closet to outfit it. I spotted a blood pressure cuff on the handle beside a radio that looked better than the one in my car. Attached to the bottom of it though, was a plastic, *days of the week,* pill dispenser, which my own car radio lacked. A silver logo that read "C.D." was attached to the front, and the lettering on the side read *Charley*.

When I asked the pair what it was doing here at a speedway, they laughed and said they were going to run it in the Daytona 500. After they laughed at *that* for a while, they acknowledged they had no idea why it was here, they were only delivering it, and at that moment I heard a loud whistle. When I turned someone was waving at them from the track entrance. The men put their cigarettes out on the pavement and the one sitting on the *Charley* got up and said there was no way he was riding it, so I watched them push, rather than drive it, through the gate that led to the track.

This, I thought, *I've got to see.* I sneaked around under the bleachers to the track area and concealed myself within the deserted concession stand, a perfect hiding spot with a great view of the entire track.

It was obvious the oval track's normal usage was for stock car races and flea markets, but today it looked like an obstacle course. Someone had set up orange cones and barricades, the kind used in car commercials or Drivers Ed courses, and a few other things that I couldn't make out.

From my vantage point though, I was not only able to see everyone clearly, but from where they were standing, to hear them as well.

Brandy was pacing in front of the *Charley* while Stanley kicked at the dirt and wiped the back of his neck with a handkerchief. Ralph was walking toward them from the direction of the men's room zipping his pants.

I hopped up onto the freezer which thankfully, was not turned on, and sat. It was dark in there and the light outside so bright, I was confident I would not be seen but pulled the empty hot dog grill in front of me all the same, and peered through its glass doors.

"Why does that fat slob have to be here?" I heard Stanley say.

"He already knows too much," Brandy answered. "He wanted to come along and I couldn't say no. I don't like him anymore than you do."

"I don't get it. Charlie paid those bastards plenty to get them to pass this thing," said Stanley, nodding to a couple of people in suits who had briefcases at their feet and were scribbling on clipboards. "Now I have to come here and drive around this obstacle course again for what, so they can watch me fall on my face again?"

"What do you mean you don't get it?" asked Brandy. "You have one of these things in the bottom of a lake, not to mention poor Bruce. They're nervous. What did you expect?"

I couldn't imagine what Brandy and Ralph had to do with any of this and why Brandy referred to Doctor Haney as *poor Bruce,* I mean, yeah he's dead but *Bruce?* And did this mean one of these things was somehow involved? I had no idea, but this was getting better by the minute.

The couple wearing suits, a man and a woman, walked toward them and the woman said to Stanley, "So what you've got set up here are ramps, various surface types," she was checking things off her clipboard, "standing water, sand, gravel, ice, rocky and rutted surfaces and a couple of inclines?"

"A half dozen cardboard people are staged behind facades along the track triggered to pop out, unexpectedly, in front of the driver too," her companion told her. She wrote on her clipboard again, turned to Stanley and said, "Ok, we're ready when you are.

Stanley, who looked like he might cry, hopped onto the *Charley* and drove around the first set of cones in figure eights. Next he went through the water, where he slid slightly, but regained, and then went through the rest of the surfaces and came back to where he started.

"We clocked you at three miles per hour," said the clipboard lady. She was a heavy set woman in her late sixties with a down-turned mouth and an expression like she was smelling something unpleasant. "I understand this can travel at much faster speeds than that."

"Yes," said her associate, a man near her age but thin and who blew his nose every few seconds. "I must ask you to repeat the test at the maximum speed please."

Stanley, who by now was clearly agitated, got back on the *Charley,* throwing himself on the seat, and began the course again, this time going much faster. He was having trouble maintaining control on the ice and slid twice, threw up gravel as he drove through it, bounced violently over the rutted surfaces and hydroplaned on the water. He deftly avoided the cardboard people that popped out, although I could have sworn I saw him throw a punch at one of them.

When he completed the course and returned to the group, he was bright red, soaking wet and had gravel stuck to his greasy hair. The *Charley* smelled of something burning.

The woman wrote on her clipboard and said to Brandy, "Now I would like to test it myself, please show me how to use it."

"You'll want to drive it on the straight track ma'am," said Stanley, and rushed over to wipe the cycle's seat.

"Oh yes," said Brandy, "the obstacle course was not designed for regular users."

"The course was designed to simulate normal conditions one might encounter during daily use, correct?" asked the woman.

"Are you sure you want to do this Barbara?" asked her male companion who then blew his nose.

"John, I'm fat. I need to see how well it rides with a fat person on it," she said.

"I'm even fatter than you! I'll drive it" said Ralph.

"Look John, someone even fatter than *me*," said Barbara. "Shall we let him drive it?"

"I'm so sorry," said Brandy, "I'm sure he didn't mean it like that."

"Oh, I know exactly what he meant," said Barbara glaring at Ralph. "Alright, let Orson Wells drive it around."

Brandy was objecting, but to no avail, Ralph hoisted himself onto the scooter and proceeded down the straightaway, in the wrong direction.

He came to the bridge first, crawling slowly up the incline, the *Charley* making a noise that sounded more animal than machine.

"It sounds like it's crying," Barbara said.

"I can't see the back tires anymore," said John.

Ralph had gotten to the top of the bridge and gave the group a thumbs-up. In doing so, he apparently lost control and the scooter veered into the rail of the bridge, turning it around, so that now he was going down the other side, backwards and fast, a look of terror on his face.

"Is he saying something?" asked Barbara

"It sounds like he's singing" John said. "Why is he singing?"

"No, no," said Barbara, "That's Dean Martin. I think the song is, *That's Amore*."

Brandy, who was standing behind John and Barbara, looked at Stanley who shrugged his shoulders, then mopped the back of his neck again.

"It has a very state of the art sound system," said Brandy walking up to stand beside John. "You can hear the quality all the way over here can't you?"

"He's still going backwards," said John. "That's not part of the test," and wrote something on his clipboard.

Once Ralph, moving faster now, got near the wall, a cardboard person popped out in front of him and he swerved slightly to the left while simultaneously reaching his arm out, like he was signaling his turn. In doing so, he struck the cardboard pedestrian causing it to fall on his lap.

Now, at high speed, he was heading for the water.

"Why did he put that woman in there with him?" asked John. "It's not supposed to carry passengers."

"I'm ok," Ralph yelled, throwing the passenger off of his lap.

Barbara was writing furiously on her clipboard now.

Ralph passed by me in the concession stand, a look of determination on his face.

I pushed the hot dog case away and it fell, but it didn't appear anyone heard it over the noise of the *Charley*. I moved to the other end of the concession for a better view of where Ralph was heading. That is when I heard the G.P.S. come on.

"In point two miles turn right, then turn right."

He looked down in surprise when he hit the ice and began sliding sideways, holding onto what looked like a blood pressure cuff.

"Recalculating," said the GPS.

"It's squeezing my hand!" yelled Ralph, "it won't let go!"

"When possible, make a U turn," the GPS said.

Ralph was now bent over trying to remove the cuff from his hand with his teeth when the scooter came to the rutted surface, Ralph's head was hitting the handlebar repeatedly, his tie, it appeared, was caught in the pill dispenser.

Stanley went running across the track toward Ralph, screaming at him to turn the machine off, but was being drowned out by the voice of Dean Martin.

"When the stars make you drool just like pasta fazool, that's amore,"

"In point 3 miles turn right."

Ralph was tugging at his tie and when he finally got it loose, the force of his movement caused him to fall just as Stanley reached him, knocking them both to the ground, the *Charley* still moving.

"When you dance down the street with a cloud at your feet you're in love," sang Dean.

"In one hundred yards, turn right," said the GPS.

"Ralph get off of me you fat bastard," yelled Stanley.

Ralph appeared unconscious, the unmanned scooter now heading to where Stanley was screaming, pinned under the inert man, as he watched the machine make its way directly toward them.

"When possible, make a U turn."

"Scuzza me, but you see, back in old Napoli, that's amore."

ENGULFED
CHAPTER FIFTEEN

I stood inside the doorway of Saul's Deli a few minutes to get my bearings. I had gotten sweaty at the speedway and my shoes were tracking gravel, so I went to the ladies room first to freshen up.

When I came back to the hostess stand, my eyes had adjusted and I scanned the dining room. Everything was bright white; the tables, the floors and the walls which were decorated with black and white photos of people like my old buddy Dean Martin, Frank Sinatra and Marilyn Monroe.

The center of the room was filled with tables for four, every seat filled with either shoppers or retail employees, the former eating their meals over conversations and several cups of coffee; the latter quickly gobbling down their sandwiches while talking on their cell phones.

Detective Nathan Gonzales was seated at one of the booths adjacent to the large picture window and he was not alone. I could see only the back of the person seated across from him.

I gave the hostess my name. "Can I wait for that table over there?" I pointed to the one just behind the detective's. "It's my lucky table."

I meant to say favorite, but the word lucky came out of my mouth. Then I felt the need to explain, so I continued, "I was sitting there one day when I scratched off a winning lottery ticket."

"Sure, fine," she answered, not at all impressed by my story.

The group that was sitting in my *lucky* booth was in no apparent hurry to leave, ordering a slice of cake for dessert that the four of them shared. I was worried my prey would be gone before I was ever seated. When I saw a group leaving the table directly across from Gonzales and his guest I approached the hostess again.

"I'll just take that table there," I pointed to the table I wanted. "It's my second lucky table, the one I scratched off there was only worth ten dol..."

She grabbed a menu and said, "This way," before I had even completed my tale of ticket scratching.

On the way to the table, we had to pass Gonzales and his companion, so I kept my face turned away, although I worried that it looked like my head was attached sideways. Once seated, I put the menu in front of me, reading it nearsightedly.

The woman seated with Gonzales was visible from my peripheral vision. It didn't look like a date since they had separate checks in front of them but she *was* stunning. Her afro stood out about six inches around her movie star features. She had the figure of a fashion model and her uniform was so tightly pressed, it would have made a marine's look sloppy. In fact, I thought she looked like a cop from a movie, or a 1970's TV show.

My menu was so close to my face, I didn't know my server was there until he said, "Are you ready to order?"

"Oh, no, I haven't seen the menu yet," I told him, as quietly as I could, peeking around the corner of it, "can you just bring me a cup of black coffee to start?"

He started to say something else but I hid my face again and he walked away.

Eavesdropping on Detective Gonzales and the woman with him was difficult, to say the least, since every third or fourth word was in Spanish. I have a very rudimentary knowledge of the Spanish language, like the alphabet and three or four colors, but unfortunately, those were not the topic of their conversation. By the time my server had come back with my coffee I had been able to pick up that, either Detective Gonzales' computer was Sunday or had a concussion, although I doubted either of those was accurate, and that *she* wanted to be the Prime Minister, which also seemed unlikely.

When my server set my coffee down, he looked at me expectantly and I realized he wanted me to order food. "Oh, I'll have the number three," I said.

"Our menu items are not numbered," he told me, very slowly.

"Do you have a special?" I asked.

"Yes, it's....," he began.

"That's fine," I told him, "I'll have that." He tried to take my menu.

"No, I want to look at the deserts," I said, and he walked away.

I had my head turned, examining the photo of a young, black and white, 1950s Saul in an apron when I heard a voice behind me say, "You know I'm a detective right?"

I turned to see Nathan Gonzales standing by my table looking down at me. "And you are probably the single worst investigator I have ever seen," he said.

"Oh, I'm not an investigator," I said

"That much is clear," he said, and smiled. "May I sit down?" he motioned to the seat opposite mine at my table.

Nathan Gonzales was tall, dark and...well not so much handsome as, different looking. His eyes were brown to nearly black with enormously long lashes and a nose and chin that were long, angular and pointed toward his feet. His black hair fell in loose, short curls around his head but was also receding from a forehead that sort of protruded. His smile though, was a thing to behold.

If winter could turn to spring with a single bloom, that would be what the transformation was like to the person of Detective Nathan Gonzales and that smile. He turned from plain to dazzling in that flash of a moment and I was speechless.

"Allow me to introduce myself," he said. "I am Nathan Gonzales and I'm a detective with the Fort Myers police department, but I'm certain you already know that, Mrs..."

I extended my hand to him and we shook, "Maggie," I said, "Finn. Well, this is pretty embarrassing."

"Tell me Mrs. Finn," he asked, "what did you expect to learn here today, listening to us from behind your menu?"

"I'm not sure really, it's just that I was there, at The Shell, that day and well..."

"Yes, I saw you. You were counting... let me see, first it was supplies, then, I believe, people."

"You're pretty observant," I said. "I suppose that comes in handy as a detective."

"And you're like watching an episode of *I Love Lucy*," he said. "I've enjoyed the show Mrs. Finn, but I advise you find another hobby."

"Oh, it's not a hobby," I said, "I'm a re..."

Nathan Gonzales's lunch date interrupted, "I'm gonna go cool off the car," she looked at her watch, "I gotta be back by two."

"Go ahead, I'll be there in a minute," he said to her. Then he looked at me and stood, "It was nice to meet you Mrs. Finn."

"Miss," I mumbled as he walked away.

"Excuse me?" he asked, turning.

"Nothing," I said.

I'm pretty sure I saw him smile.

ENGULFED
CHAPTER SIXTEEN

I went home and called Zig after he was off the air to tell him the news about his mother leaving with the limo driver, but before I could say anything, he told me he had gotten a call from detective Gonzales. It seems the detective needed Zig to come down to the Fort Myers police station in the morning to answer some questions.

"You?" I asked, in utter disbelief. "Why you, for Gods' sake?"

"How the hell should I know? Did you say you had lunch with him?"

"Well, not exactly, we barely spoke. I sure as heck didn't mention you though, if that's what you're thinking."

When he didn't say anything I took that as a vote of no confidence.

"Really, your name never came up, Lucille Ball yes, but you, no."

"I'm not even gonna ask," he said.

"That's probably best, anyway, let me tell you what I found out about your mom. She left with the limo driver."

"What about a limo driver?"

"The one that takes your mother to dinner sometimes"

"Mom goes to dinner with a limo driver?" he asked, confusion in his voice.

"Well, I'm sure the driver is not her date, I'm sure who ever her date is sends his driver for her don't you think? You honestly don't know about any of this?"

"No!" he said, sounding annoyed. "How come you do?"

"The girl who answers the phone at The Shell told me."

"What else did she tell you?"

"That was it, except the limo driver was cute and hit on her. You didn't know any of this?"

"No, and would you quit asking me that?"

"Sorry," I said, "you're a very good son. I'm sure after all these years of living on her own, she doesn't feel the need to fill you in on every aspect of her social life. Anyway, her neighbor, Idzy, the little guy across..."

"I know who he is."

"Well," I continued, "he saw the same driver that takes her to dinner come and get her today. He helped her with her luggage. See? That doesn't sound ominous at all does it? I'm telling you, she's off to visit a friend. I bet she did that kind of thing all the time before you moved down here and you just didn't know about it."

"I guess." He was silent for a while. "Are you sure you didn't say anything to that detective?"

"I'm sure. Do you want me to go with you tomorrow?" I asked.

"No!" he said vehemently.

"Wow, sorry. I was only trying to help."

"If you really want to help, you won't try to help."

I laughed, "I get it. Are you going to see if he'll tell you anything about the mysterious friend of your mom?"

"What do you think?"

"Yeah, I don't blame you, one thing at a time. And Zig, about your mom, I'm sure she's fine. She left you a message didn't she? She packed a bag, she took a limo for goodness sakes. She's probably sitting in first class drinking cocktails and keeping everyone in the cabin entertained. No doubt she'll call you as soon as she lands."

"I know," he said, "you're right. "I'll call you as soon as I hear something."

"Thanks, promise me you will."

"I will," he said and hung up.

Since I had nowhere to be at the moment, and was still feeling the pangs of my earlier humiliation with Detective Gonzales, I decided to take a ride over to Dharma House. The little waterfall and wind chimes would be a perfect antidote to my funky mood, and give me the chance to tell Rod I had too much going on right now to spend a lot of time looking into the background of his mystery guest.

I called and told him I was coming by to donate some pizza for their dinner, and, as luck would have it, a Pizza Hut came into view at that very moment.

I went inside, ordered, and sat at one of the tables drinking a diet Coke while I waited for them to make my two large meat lovers, two orders of bread sticks and an order of cinnamon sticks.

I don't have a church I go to, or an orphan in Bangladesh I sponsor or anything, so I do this. It's my way of giving back to the universe, I give it pizza.

Gazing out my window, replaying the horrendous meeting with Nathan Gonzales over and over in my mind, I noticed a familiar car in the lot. No, I thought, it can't be...but it damn sure was, I knew it, it was Stanley.

I walked outside and knocked on the driver's side tinted window of the black SUV. After a minute it rolled down, cigarette smoke pouring out at me.

"Stanley, aren't you going to come inside?" I said. "They don't have car hop service here you know."

"Oh. Hello," he said, "aren't you the lady from The Shell? Well, fancy running into you."

"Yes, fancy that," I said.

Stanley's face was bruised, his eyes were swollen and there was a large bandage across his nose.

"What happened to your face Stanley?" I asked in mock surprise. "You have lots of band aids and...wow, some bruises too. Is your nose broken Stanley?"

"Nah, it's not broken, it got bit."

"Bit?" I asked, this time genuinely surprised.

"Oh yeah, I mean no, I meant *hit*. I was uh...I was uh...bowling. I hurt myself when I went bowling, fell right down on the lane," he said, warming to his lie. "Those lousy shoes they give ya'...laces came undone."

"Bowling huh?" I said. "Ya' know? It doesn't seem like bowling's your game. You should get into, oh, maybe Nascar."

He went pale. "That's funny," he said weakly, "Nascar."

"Well," I said, "You gonna come inside? That's where the food is you know."

"No thanks, I'm good out here," he said.

"Ok, well, I'm going in to get my pizza now, then I'll be leaving again. I guess I'll probably see you around, huh Stanley?"

"Uh yeah, guess I'll see ya' around," he said and rolled his window up.

When I pulled into the drive at Dharma House I didn't see any trace of Stanley but I had no reason to believe he had given up following me either.

After I hollered *hello* a couple of times from the front stoop, a twenty something man in a Bob Marley t-shirt and a hoop earring in one ear opened the screen door.

He yelled over his shoulder, "Who ordered Pizza?"

"No," I said, "it's ok, I'm giving it to you guys."

"Giving us what?" he asked, confused.

"This," I said, raising up the boxes, "in my hands."

He still only stared at me.

"It's already paid for," I said, raising my voice louder still and speaking slowly. "Is Rod here?"

"Yeah, sure, he'll pay you, hang on," and he walked away, letting the screen door slam.

Rod came to the door a couple of minutes later.

"Maggie!" he said, "thank you so much, here, let me take that," and grabbed the pizza boxes while I held onto the bottle of soda and followed him into the dining room.

The seven men seated at the table with dishes of tossed salad in front of them let out a cheer when they saw us walk in. With their white hair and beards I thought they looked like the seven dwarfs.

Rod put one of the men in charge of serving and invited me into the library, saying there was someone there he'd like me to meet.

"Maggie," Rod said, when we entered the room, "I'd like you to meet a friend of mine, Leo, Leo Weinstein."

Like Rod, Leo had a 1960's kind of hippie look. Like Rod, his hair was in a ponytail, although the top of his head was bald and his beard looked like he had just recently started growing it. Unlike Rod, he was shorter, rounder and his denim jeans looked new, with a seam pressed down the front of them, and his shoes looked expensive.

After the pleasantries, and cups of green tea were poured, Rod told me a bit of the history of the men's' friendship.

"Leo is a psychiatrist Maggie," Rod said. "He practices in Manhattan. He's doing a lot of really innovative work, very cutting edge."

"That's interesting," I said, "cutting edge in what way?" thinking I wouldn't even know dull-edged psychiatry if it were explained with pictures, one syllable words and a nap break.

"Leo here was instrumental in saving my emotional, mental and spiritual life," Rod said, "I owe him everything."

"Using cutting edge... sorry, what was it you said about cutting edge something?" I asked, sipping my tea in an attempt to do something with my mouth besides sound stupid.

"Without getting into technicalities that would take text books to explain," Leo said, "I *can* tell you that after Rod's gunshot to the head, his brain was essentially wiped clean. He had to start all over again, like a baby." He paused to take a pipe from his pocket and I wondered if he realized what a caricature that made. He held a lighter up to it, puffed enough times to stink up the room and went on. "Once he learned the basics, he came to me for the more complex stuff; philosophy, theology, relationships, even how to know right from wrong. It was one of the most interesting cases I'd ever worked on. And Rod, well, he took his new life to a level I could never have imagined for him. He studied Taoism, Buddhism, Christianity, Judaism, Zen, you name it, he learned it. No he didn't just learn it, he lived it. He *became* it."

Leo kept talking and talking and what started out as really interesting had now become mind numbing. He was actually quoting from a textbook while I looked out the window. It's not fair, I moaned inwardly, I came here to feel better and listen to wind chimes, now I'm here listening to a bag of hot air. I looked up when I realized someone was talking to me and I hadn't been paying attention.

"...oh yes, Errol." Rod was saying, "I've asked Maggie to see if she wouldn't mind trying to find out anything she can about our newest guest, nothing formal, just any little bits of information that might make our helping him a bit easier."

"Excellent," said Leo, "then we..."

"When did you say he came here?" I asked Rod, interrupting Leo before he went into another ten minute oration.

"Last Friday night," said Rod.

"Well, you know there was some old guy they were looking for at The Shell on the same night. The staff said he called them to say he was staying with his son, and he probably is, but it's just kind of a coincidence, ya know? I want to get a picture of Errol with my cell phone and show it to someone there, just make sure it's not the same guy, would that be ok?"

"It's ok with me," said Rod, "if it's ok with Errol. I'll go ask him."

"So, I said to Leo after Rod had left the room, "you have anything fun planned to do while you're down here?"

"As a matter of fact," he said, "Rod has a friend who captains a fishing boat. We're going out tomorrow with both he and his family."

"That sounds nice, the weather should be perfect for it," I said, having no idea what the weather was supposed to be like.

"That's what I hear. Say Maggie, the boat is pretty big, would you like to join us?" Leo asked

"Oh, thank you so much for the invite," I said, "but I've got some things I have to get done tomorrow."

"We're only going out for a couple of hours in the morning," he said, picking up a cracker and setting some cheese on it. "We'll have you back by lunch. If your errands can wait till the afternoon..."

"Well," I said," I don't know," I waivered, Jan's voice nagging at my brain, *go on a boat, have some fun*, it said.

"Come on," Leo said, sensing my indecision, "the captain will have his wife too and I'm sure she'd love not being the only woman on the boat.

Since I couldn't think of a good reason to say no, I said yes.

Rod came back in and Leo told him that I would be joining them.

"Great news," Rod said, "I'm so glad you'll be able to come. I've got bad news on Errol, though. He said no thanks to the picture."

Yeah, I'm sure that's exactly how he said it too, I thought.

"That's ok," I said, "I'll see if anyone at The Shell has a picture of the guy I was talking about. So, what time should I be here tomorrow?"

"Be here at six thirty," said Rod. "We'll drive to the marina together."

"Alrighty then," I said, thinking Stanley was gonna have a hard time following me around the Gulf of Mexico.

ENGULFED
CHAPTER SEVENTEEN

I rummaged around the refrigerator at Dharma House looking for the jars of fresh basil, sun dried tomatoes and garlic that Rod assured me would be great for cooking up the Snook I managed to reel in today. He was very adamant I not put in too much seasoning when I fried it up since Snook had such a mild flavor I didn't want to overpower it with too much of anything. Since I only had three packets of ketchup in the barren wasteland that was my current kitchen, he offered to let me forage for supplies in his.

"So it's come to this has it?" Leo was gesturing at my stockpile and laughing.

I know, pathetic isn't it, me taking food from a shelter?"

"You're taking some spices Maggie, the fish is yours", Rod said. "You caught it yourself. Are you sure you don't want to take some of the snapper too? I've filleted them both." He handed me my catch, already packaged up.

"Oh, no thank you, this will be great. I had so much fun this morning. Thank you again for everything."

It truly had been fun and I was grateful for Jan's psychic nagging. The weather was perfect and the captain's wife actually was grateful to have me along. She was the same age as one of my daughters and had moved down from Michigan five years ago. We discussed the pros and cons of Florida living as compared to life in what we both termed, *the regular states*. The men had a great time and helped me land a couple of fish myself but I spent most of the time avoiding Rod and Leo since they made my brain feel like it had an itch I couldn't scratch.

I was sticky with sea water on my skin and in my hair and the sunscreen I had applied made a lovely paste for the sweat to adhere to.

Anxious to go home and shower I grabbed my bag of food and was back in the car heading home when my cell rang.

"Maggie, where've you been?"

"Zig, is that you? I was out on a boat all morning. I caught a three foot Snook. I'm going to cook it up for din..."

"Swell, I've been with your detective buddy for nearly two hours," he said.

"Two hours! What in God's name did he want with you for two hours? Two hours? Really?"

"Would you stop saying two hours?"

"Sorry," I said. "I'm on my way home. Well, to my parent's home. Their ex home that is and..."

"Maggie, for Christ's sake, you're babbling, are you drunk again?"

"No, of course I'm not drunk, and what do you mean again?"

"Never mind," he said, sighing. "Can you meet me in an hour?"

"Can we make it two?" I asked.

"Yeah," he said, meet me at the Starbucks at the corner just before you get to The Shell. Do you know the one I mean?"

"Yeah, OK. I'll see you there at what, like two thirty? But if I'm a few minutes late wait for me, I have to...."

"It's ok, I'll wait," he said and hung up.

"...shower first."

I got to the Starbucks before Zig. I ordered an iced Frappuccino and sat out on the patio to wait. In less than a minute I could feel my skin burning, looked down at my bright pink legs, and went back inside and rubbed the condensation from my cup over my sunburned legs and arms.

I heard Zig's voice behind me ordering his coffee so I dried off with my napkin and went up to the counter to join him.

"Wow, you got yourself a nice...."

"Don't start with me," I interrupted, "I know, I'm sunburned."

"I was gonna say great looking Frappuccino," he looked up at the menu. "I think I'll order the same," he said and ordered his drink. He looked at me, "I live here ya' know. I'm used to seeing sunburned tourists. It's no big deal."

While we waited for his drink I stared at the tattoo on his right arm, a classic pin up girl poster type from the thirties. She was seated, wearing short-shorts with one leg stretched upward, her high heel just under the name *Zig* like she was holding it in place, cleavage bursting from a low cut top, and blonde curls framing her smiling face.

He was joking around with the young woman preparing his drink and I wondered if he knew how charming he was.

"Wanna sit and talk for a minute before we drive over?" I asked. "You can fill me in on your meeting with the detective this morning and about your mom and all."

We sat at a table away from the only other customer in there, a young woman seated in front of her laptop, wearing earphones, and oblivious to anyone around her.

Zig looked around the room anyway and leaned in to speak, "Mom called me to say she was staying with some friends in DC."

I looked around the room myself and leaned in toward him, "Is this supposed to be hush-hush?"

"She told me not to tell anyone where she was, except you."

"Me? Why me? She doesn't even know me."

"I don't know Maggie, but I really don't thing that's the issue here."

"There's more?"

"She wouldn't give me the name of the people she's staying with; their number or address, nothing."

"Did she say why?" I asked, scooping whipped cream into my mouth with my straw.

"She said *plausible deniability* again," he said, leaning back in his chair, pushing his drink away.

"Well that's fairly frustrating, don't you think?"

"She was calling me from her cell so I can at least call and check on her. Then this morning the detective asks me where I was last Friday night, the night Haney ended up gator bait. I told him I was at the Lani Kai bar, running into you. Then he said he knew that, but wanted to know what I had to say about the fact that my credit card was used at eleven o'clock that night. Said he'd checked the credit card company and I hadn't reported it stolen."

"Was it stolen?" I asked.

"No, it's here in my wallet, but I've got an extra card that I let mom use. I didn't tell him that naturally. When I talked to mom I asked her if she still had it on her and she said yes."

"Did you tell her about the charges?"

"Yes, and that's when things got weird," he said. "She sounded nervous and I could tell she was talking to someone while her hand was over the phone. Then she came back on and said that yes, her card *was* missing and I should report it lost but that she wanted to pay any charges because it was her own fault for losing the card."

"Well, that sounds overly responsible, but not that weird."

"Maggie, I looked at my credit card statement and the charge that night was for a place called S.G. Entertainment. It's been on there every month for a year now. The first time I saw the charge she told me it was the movie theatre. I never looked at the time of the charges but when I went back they were all for about ten or eleven at night. I checked it out, S.G. Entertainment owns The Sun God, that drag club you were asking me about the other day."

"Your mom served me a drink in a cup from there. Do you think she was trying to tell me something? And if she was, why didn't she come right out and say so. Why the little clues?"

"She's trying to protect us *and* her friend and she thinks that's how to do it. Anyway, that's my read," said Zig

"Why does Gonzales care if you went out and charged things to your card that night? Why is he checking up on you and your work schedule and credit cards? This doesn't make sense," I said, pushing my own drink away.

"I don't know," said Zig. "I asked him that, but he told me it was part of an on-going investigation. Then I asked him if I needed a lawyer. He said that was up to me, but I wasn't being charged with anything, he just needed to ask a few questions to help him with the case."

"So, what do you want to do now?" I asked.

"I'm going to mom's place to look around. I don't care if it's snooping; she may be in over her head on something. It sounds like she's leading some kind of secret life and I need to know what the hell it is."

****

Our search of Dorothy Callahan's room turned up nothing suspicious. It was neat and tidy, and any personal effects that we would be interested in, like address books, calendar, receipts, notes, were not to be found, which we both decided was odd.

On our way out I spotted Idzy peeking out of his door at us.

"Hello Idzi," I said, "you know Dorothy's son Zig don't you?"

He opened the door a little more and looked at us with squinted eyes.

"Yeah, I know Zig," he said. "When are you coming back to do the show? We didn't get to spin the wheel for prizes last time."

"Well," Zig said, "There was that bit about the dead guy and police and I figured it wasn't a good time. We gotta run now Idz, just need to get a few more things for mom."

"She must have forgot to pack a lot of her stuff," Idzi said.

"Why do you say that?" I asked.

"Cause Brandy was just here doing the same thing."

ENGULFED
CHAPTER EIGHTEEN

I've always wondered how people can forget to eat. I've heard people say things like, "This is the first I've had all day, I was so busy I guess I forgot to eat." How is that even possible? Your stomach hurts, it makes noises and your brain tells you it's time to eat. People don't say that about other bodily urges. You never hear anyone say, "Gosh, I'd better go urinate, I was so busy all day today that I forgot to do that." Anyway, *I* have never forgotten to eat and though I should be worrying about Stanley, or Zig's mother, or if I still had a job, or a million other things; I was thinking I should run into Publix and get some wine to go with my fish.

I'd purchased a bottle of white and a York peppermint patty and headed back out of the store to a flash of lightning followed quickly by a large thunderclap. The sky had turned from bright blue to gray-black in the time it took for the senior citizen at the register to tell me I was in the cash only line, for the people waiting behind me to make annoyed sounds, and for me to search for change in the bottom of my purse.

The drive back to the house was harrowing; the rain was coming down in torrents, everyone was driving like they were in a school zone with their emergency flashers on, and the occasional idiot driving past at full speed was causing wakes that made me feel like I was back out in the Gulf.

I couldn't see if Stanley was following me, but was working under the assumption that he was, so I looked over my shoulder as I opened the garage with the remote and pulled inside. The door made its usual grinding noise going down but over that sound, I thought I heard a car with a large engine coming down the street. I jumped out of the car and peeked under the garage door before it closed completely but didn't see anything, and reassured myself that it isn't paranoia if they really *are* following you.

I pulled a few cooking necessities from the box in the garage marked *pots and pans,* entered the kitchen, took the wine out of the shopping bag, and put everything else in the fridge. Taking one sip of the wine and deciding I was more tired than hungry, I lay down for a nap.

My ringing cell phone woke me, and after noting it had only been an hour since I lay down, I decided against answering right away, instead foraging through my purse for the peppermint patty. The phone rang again and I ignored it, ate the chocolate, and wandered back into the kitchen.

I began unpacking the spices procured from Dharma House, basil, garlic, mushrooms and onions, and threw a little of each on my fish, and began pan frying it. My side dish consisted of an apple nabbed from the lobby at The Shell and I threw it in the sink to wash. The fish was frying up nicely and the wine was going down warmly when I looked out the window and saw the familiar black SUV parked across the street. I picked up my cell, turned it back on and dialed 911. Wait, I thought, what was I doing? I wasn't actually *afraid* of Stanley, and at this point was actually feeling a little sorry for him and even admired him a little. There he was, all beaten and battered from being run over by a *Charley* and still he was out there doing his job of following me. I hung up my phone deciding that, (*a*), he might actually be a lead to what's going on, (*b*), that if the police came they'd just chalk him up as a peeping Tom and let him go and, (*c*), he'd be right back here again, only this time, an angry Stanley, and so far, he'd been a harmless source of amusement. I'd decided to call the police *if* he came toward the house, but didn't think that was likely.

And besides all that, the wine had gone to my head so quickly I was already feeling a bit tipsy. Not a good state to be in when one calls the police, I thought.

I put down the glass of wine, turned the television on and tuned into the six o'clock evening news. The local report came on first, the lead being the death of Doctor Bruce Haney. The anchor woman was standing lakeside behind The Shell reporting that the doctor's death was being labeled as suspicious, and evidence at the scene was pointing the investigation toward a possible homicide.

When the name Nathan Gonzales was mentioned, I turned from the stove to look back at the T.V. screen and felt my head spin. My focus was blurred, and the person I saw being interviewed was not the detective, but Lucille Ball.

"Can you tell our viewers why the department is treating this as a homicide?" the reporter asked. "I think you have some splainin' to do."

Lucille Ball answered, "Meshuggah, they're all meshuggah."

A noise from the stove startled me; it was the Snook that I had been frying up in the pan; alive and thrashing about. When I yelled, something came from my mouth that wasn't an actual word. I threw the fish in the sink, filled it with water and watched for a moment as he swam in circles around the apple I had left in there, until he poked his head up and spit at me. Another mysterious word came screaming from my mouth.

My mind felt hazy, my hand had trouble grabbing hold of the kitchen counter. It was difficult to tell if I was the one moving or if the room was spinning around me; stove, table, door, window, coming in and out of view, lights growing brighter and dimmer like a lighthouse beam. The sensation of being soaking wet came over me. Holding my breath, afraid to allow my body any movement, I tried to will my mind into a state of reality.

My body stayed like that, frozen, until my equilibrium returned. In and out of awareness, I knew something was terribly wrong. I wondered if I was going to die, feeling I surely would.

I ran, in slow motion, willing the bottom half of my body to follow the top half until I reached the front door and stepped out onto the lawn. The sight that greeted me there was the most beautiful I'd ever seen. No longer was there a street in front of the house, but a canal filled with hundreds of fish, all of which were illuminated from within with bright multi colored lights. They were swimming in an aquatic parade accompanied by shimmering tiny birds flying above them, the lights somehow illuminating their plumes as they danced in the sky. I became hypnotized; my sense of time lost, watching the fish and birds now swimming and flying in coordinated, synchronized movements.

Suddenly I was struck with an overwhelming feeling of love for them, a love so intense I didn't remember ever feeling it before, not even for my own children, and I began sobbing, without tears. Desperate to share this feeling of sublime joy with someone, I called for Stanley, certain that he would love them too and we could stay here with them forever.

Moving toward Stanley's car, I could see the area around him glowing in a halo of orange and yellow pulsating light, the rhythm matching my own heart beat. I crossed the canal and found him sitting on the ground, leaning against his car, and joined him there, happy to be with a kindred traveler in this new land.

"Stanley," I said, "I've been drugged or something so it's probably just that, but you look very much like Jesus to me."

Stanley said nothing, just stared ahead, looking very wise and God-like despite the band aids.

"If you are, in fact, Jesus," I told him, "and this not a hallucination, then I'm dead right?" I looked at the fish parade; they waved their fins at me as I waved back to them. "I don't mind being dead because it's very pretty and magical, don't you think?"

Stanley - Jesus still didn't answer, so we sat there, silently for a while, until he began singing, oddly enough, without moving his lips, and there was music accompanying him.

"Hey Jude, don't make it bad, take a sad song, and make it better," he sang.

My snook swam up to us and swished his tail in time to the music. I blew him a kiss, relieved and happy that I hadn't cooked and eaten him.

"Stanley- Jesus," I said, "this looks like a dream, but I'm awake so it must be real. I wonder if everything *before* tonight was a dream and I've just now awakened to reality. What do you think?"

"Remember to let her under your skin!" he continued singing, sounding very much like John Lennon.

I began singing along with him and thought I sounded very much like Celine Dion.

Soon Stanley- Jesus -John Lennon and I were joined by the other Beatles who were not singing, but who were wearing their Sergeant Pepper uniforms, grabbing me by my arms and trying to pull me into the water.

"Paul, you're supposed to be the nice Beatle," I yelled as he grabbed my arm. "You're not my favorite anymore."

Then all four of The Beatles made me lie down in a boat, a little swan boat, like the sort they have at Disney but with red lights flashing in time to the song, *"Then you begin to make it better, better, better, better, better, better, better yeah!*

I must have passed out because when I awoke it was in a hospital emergency room. A blood pressure cuff attached to my left arm periodically squeezed and released itself, and an IV was running into my right hand. My jeans were still on me but my shirt and bra were gone, replaced by a hospital gown. A baby was crying loudly somewhere nearby. The privacy curtain opened and a doctor walked in and looked at the chart at the bottom of my bed. He was very young with olive skin, dark hair and eyes, and his white lab coat had the name *Mousique Mann* embroidered in blue above the chest pocket.

"Am I still hallucinating?" I asked.

"Oh good, you're awake," he said in a strong, but unrecognizable accent. "Can you tell me your name?"

"Maggie Finn," I answered him, and then gave him my age, the date and who the current president was when asked those questions.

"You had quite a cornucopia of drugs in your system; from the results I've gotten so far, you must have been on one hell of a trip," he said, looking through his clip board of papers. "What exactly did you take Mrs. Finn?"

"Drugs, me?" I said, "You must be kidding. I don't even like taking aspirin. I don't even trust the stuff my pharmacist gives me. How long have I been here? What happened to me?"

"You've been here for," he looked at the chart, then his watch, "three and half hours. How are you feeling now?" he asked getting right in my face and pointing his pen light in my eyes.

"I have a headache, a really bad one." I pulled my head back and closed my eyes.

"Under the circumstances, we can't give you anything for the pain, I'm sorry, but until we know exactly what is in your system the risk would be too great."

"I don't want anything except to go home and crawl under my covers," I said.

"The police are going to want to know how you got this drug and what exactly it is," he said. "There is a Detective here now who wishes to speak to you. I told him he could come in if you are feeling up to it."

Oh please God, I thought, please don't let it be Detective Gonzales.

"I'll go get him. The nurse will be in later to discharge you and give you some instructions."

He left and was almost immediately replaced by Detective Nathan Gonzales, dressed in jeans and a plain black T- shirt, he had bags under his eyes that told me he hadn't slept for a long time. His curly head of hair was unkempt and his face was long past needing a shave.

"Mrs. Finn," he said, "I would have never taken you for a recreational drug user."

"I told the doctor, I never take drugs," I said, "never. Someone had to have given it to me somehow."

He eyed me suspiciously. "And there is the business of how you ended up in the company of a deceased man."

"Deceased?" I asked, trying to clear my head. "Deceased as in dead? Who? Wait, is Stanley dead?"

"How do you know this man?" he asked me, "what is your relationship with him?"

"Was I with him when he died?" I asked, throwing my head back on the pillow and putting my arm over my eyes. "How did he die? Oh God, I was with a dead guy?"

I started feeling nauseous, panicked and looked for something to be sick in, but it was too late; I threw up on the floor.

Detective Gonzales pulled open the curtain and called, "Nurse!"

ENGULFED
CHAPTER NINETEEN

"Do you think you'll be alright at home tonight if we discharge you?" Doctor Mann asked.

"Yes," I answered, "I feel ok, just tired and headachy."

He began writing on my chart and looked up at me, "You can get dressed now, the nurse will be in with your discharge instructions. I'd like you to follow up tomorrow with this doctor, he pulled a sheet of paper from the chart, gave it to me and walked out. A nurse, or someone in scrubs, it could have been the cleaning lady for all I knew, came in and went over the discharge instructions with me and informed me that someone from the police department would be taking me home.

"He doesn't have handcuffs on him I hope," I said, trying to laugh, not knowing if I were in some kind of trouble. Nathan Gonzales had left after I threw up on him, just one more crime to add to my growing rap sheet, I thought, along with drugs, murder and impersonating a rest- home worker, so I didn't know where I stood suspect wise.

"I'll send him in now," the woman in scrubs said dryly.

"Please God, oh please, oh please, oh please don't let it be Nathan Gonzales," I repeated softly. The privacy curtain opened and there stood, Nathan Gonzales."

The drive home was quiet. No radio, no questions, no attempts at idle chatter. Nathan was driving slowly and cautiously; certainly the vision of my earlier malady was still fresh in his mind and on his shoes. The Gulf breeze was blowing cool air through the open windows of his car and made me shiver as it blew across my sunburned flesh. Nathan turned his head toward me as if to speak but turned his gaze back to the road and closed the window.

My seat was reclined and the view of the stars through the sun roof was reassuring. The car and we were moving, but the heavens remained the same, constant and familiar, the view broken only by a tall palm tree or a street light. Afraid to close my eyes lest the hallucinations were still lingering in my mind, I kept focus on the sky.

We arrived at my parent's home and sat quietly for a moment in the driveway when I reached for the door and said, "Thank you so much for taking me home and for not giving me the third degree. I don't think I would be too coherent anyway."

"No, I don't suppose you would be," he said.

"Am I in any kind of trouble? I didn't do anything wrong you know, just for the record."

"I don't think you did either Mrs. Finn," he said, "but I'm going to need to talk to you in the morning just the same. I should think you might have some questions of your own too."

"Yes," I said and looked over at his feet, "and I'm really sorry about your shoes."

He smiled, got out of the car and came around and opened my door. We walked to the front step where he handed me his card, "please call as soon as you're able tomorrow."

Sleep was pretty much a no-go. Nightmares that I could not recall left my heart pounding. When the sun came up, so did I and made the short drive to the 7-11 for coffee and a doughnut; the parking lot serving as temporary office while I checked my cell phone for missed calls and messages. There were three text messages and five voice mails waiting for me.

I glanced around the lot, wishing to be distracted, wanting to avoid talking to anyone. A landscaping vehicle parked at the gas pump with the name Rain or Shine spray painted on the side caught my attention. Three men tying some piece of lawn equipment to the back of the truck with a rope that was obviously too short for the task were yelling back in forth in rapid Spanish and making large gestures with their arms all of which distracted me for a good ten minutes.

Resigned to completing my task, I placed calls to my mother, my children and to Jan in Albuquerque omitting the previous night's events to all of them. The sounds of their voices were so comforting to me that my own voice trembled with emotion. After assurances that I was fine, just overly tired from too much sun and fun, I returned the call to Zig.

"Any more news from your mom?" I asked.

"She called when I was on the air," he said. "I think she did that on purpose. She left me a voice mail that she was fine and having a great time."

"Did she sound fine?"

"Yeah actually, she sounded great; really up beat. I called her back but her phone went to voice mail. Speaking of which, where were you? I tried calling a couple of times last night."

I didn't have the energy or the inclination to get into so I lied, "Oh, my phone was dead and I couldn't find the charger. I went and got a new one this morning."

"Yeah, ok, I've used that one more than a few times myself," he said. "So, I'm going to The Sun God tonight. I wanna' check it out."

"Have fun. Let me know what you find out," I said, apparently sounding weak because he said, "I was kind of hoping you wanted to come with me but you don't sound too enthused."

"Sorry," I said, "I didn't sleep well last night. Can I call you later and let you know?"

He said ok in a tone meant to guilt- trip me and then hung up.

My next call was the one I was dreading, the one to Nathan Gonzales. Reliving the previous night's experience and hearing about Stanley and how he died was not high on my list of things I wanted to do right now but I had put it off long enough. I was quite relieved when his phone went straight to voice mail and I had only to leave a message.

I watched the landscapers some more, their little logo on the side of the truck looked like it had been painted by one of their children, but it was cute. It pictured a fairy, using a colorful mushroom for an umbrella while rain fell all around her. It made me miss my granddaughter and I started to cry but then stopped mid sob. Mushrooms! Aren't there such things as magic mushrooms?

"Those bastards," I yelled out loud, startling the pigeons that were dining on the assorted debris littering the parking lot. "Those lousy hippie bastards," I yelled again, realizing I sounded like Richard Nixon but not caring. "I spend one morning with tweedle dum and tweedle dee and by night I'm down the rabbit hole. Rod and Leo, I am so coming after your asses! Out of my way pigeons!"

My drive down highway forty-one was infuriating. I was getting every red light and behind every car going twenty miles per hour. My frustration only fueled my anger so that by the time my car turned onto the gravel drive of Dharma House I was furious and took out my hostility on the front screen door. My loud pounding brought several men out, including Rod, who gave me a puzzled look.

"Maggie. Are you alright? You look upset. Come in. Please."

"Upset? No, I was upset thirty minutes ago, I've moved on to enraged. Wait five more minutes and I'll be positively homicidal! No wait, I better not say that in case I really do kill you; I don't want to incriminate myself."

"Kill me?" Rod asked his tone more of mild concern for me rather than himself. "Maggie, please, come out here and have a seat. Let me get you some tea." He guided me into the large windowed room in the back of the house.

"Nohohoho thank you. I don't want anything from this place. Where's your friend Leo?"

"Here I am Maggie." Leo said, coming into the room from one of the doors that led out to the garden. "Rod, have you fixed her some tea?"

"What is with you guys and tea? I asked, my voice becoming shrill even to my own ears. "What's in your tea? Marijuana?"

"Maggie. Please," pleaded Rod, "please sit down and tell us what has happened."

Because my legs were now trembling and I could feel my knees weakening I did as he asked and sat on the chair closest to the door. A small bit of paranoia crept into the back of my mind so it seemed the best spot in the room.

"I'm going to tell the police what you've done but what I want to know is, what did you give me? How did you get me to take it and what the hell was it?" My eyes were fixed on Leo and I could feel my cheeks flush and my heart pound with growing anger as his expression went from concerned to quizzical.

"Don't act like you don't know what I'm talking about." I said to him, pointing my finger in his face.

"I don't know what you're talking about," he said.

Rod walked over to me, bent down, picked up my hand in his and gazed at me with an expression of true worry. "What has happened? You were drugged?"

"It was horrible," I began sobbing, for the first time since the incident. Rod squeezed my hand tighter and looked up at Leo.

"We must get you to the hospital immediately," said Leo, "I'm calling now and letting them know we're coming."

"Yes," Rod said, looking at my eyes with what appeared to be genuine compassion.

"I've already been to the hospital. The police took me there."

"Police?" asked Rod, putting his arm tighter around my shoulder. "Maggie, you must tell us what happened so we can help you through this. But first, is there anything you need from us right now? What can we do to help?"

Leo pulled a footstool near to me and sat down on my other side. "Maggie, I am a doctor. I would never give anyone a drug without their knowledge," he said in a soft tone that was meant to be reassuring. "I am a healer. I would never do anything to harm you, or anyone else. You must believe me and allow me to help you."

My sobbing stopped but my head was still bowed, "I need a tissue."

"Of course," Rod said and left the room. I could hear him speaking calmly in the other room saying that this would be a good time for everyone to do some silent meditation in their rooms, or to nap, which ever they preferred. He came back with a box of tissues and held it in front of me.

I wiped my face dry and looked at him, "You honestly don't know anything about this?"

"You have to know Leo and I had nothing to do with giving you drugs. I don't believe you would have come here today if that is what you truly believed. In your heart you know that is true. I believe you came here because you are frightened and are feeling lost. You have come to the right place Maggie. Leo and I will do whatever we can to help you."

I straightened up and looked at Rod and knew that he was right. I didn't believe they had drugged me, after I thought about it a bit more, I realized I had never even eaten the mushrooms. No, it had something to do with the death of Stanley and I was scared.

I recalled for them everything that had happened the night before while they both sat silently listening to me. Leo would interrupt occasionally to ask me for more details about what I saw and felt while under the influence of the drugs and write in a notebook. Again I noticed glances between the two of them, as though they knew something that I didn't.

"What's with the secret looks?" I asked.

"There's no secret Maggie, I think Leo and I are both thinking the same thing however. It is quite obvious that you were given a very powerful hallucinogenic drug. Is that what they told you at the hospital?"

"Yes, I believe though, that the term used was, a cornucopia of drugs." I said.

Leo stood up and looked down at me with an air of great authority, "I would like you to sign a release of records so that I might view your lab results. I happen to be a bit of an authority in that field. Perhaps I can pick up something that might help you."

"Yes, we need to learn everything we can", Rod added. "This is a very serious crime. I know the police are doing their jobs, and we don't want to interfere, but if we can help in any way...."

"Police! Shit!" I shouted, "I left my phone in the car and a detective is supposed to be calling me back. Let me run out to my car and see if he's tried calling."

I could hear the phone ring when I neared the car and sprinted across the yard to get to it. I tripped over a sprinkler and fell forward on both knees bracing myself with my left hand which hit the gravel drive.

"Ah Damnit!" I yelled. "What else?" I limped to my car, my knees bleeding through my beige Capri pants, brushing pieces of gravel and dirt from my hands. The second series of rings stopped as soon as the hand attached to my painful wrist grabbed the phone.

The send button connected me to Detective Gonzales' voice mail. "Sorry I didn't get to the phone in time detective," I said, "call me back as soon as you can."

Tears ran down my cheeks mingled with the sweat coming from my forehead. I sat in my car and laid my head on the steering wheel.

"God I hate this place, this freaking hot sticky, full of crazy people place. I wanna go home!" I cried for a while, then realized I didn't really have a home which brought forth even more sobs. I had my place in Albuquerque, but that wasn't home. I was a gypsy, rootless, alone in the world. My pity party was going full tilt when the phone rang, startling me, causing me to drop it on the floor. Grabbing it back, my hand hit the steering wheel. "Shit!" I yelled as I hit the green button.

"Sounds like I caught you at a bad time but this can't wait." The detective's voice sounded brusque and short, lacking all the gentleness it had the night before.

"It's always gonna be a bad time as long as I'm stuck here in Dante's inferno. What do you want?" My voice sounded angry when I hadn't meant it to. "Sorry, I mean, what do you need?"

"You need to come in here to answer some questions. Do you want me to send a car for you?"

"No, I can drive. Tell me where and when." I said, in a calmer tone.

"I need you up here at the Fort Myers station in thirty minutes."

Looking down at my bloody knees and pants, scraped hands and sweat filled blouse, I said, "Sure, why not?"

"I know it's not much notice but I've been trying to call all morning. I even sent a patrol car to your house."

"It's OK, I'll be there in thirty minutes," I said

I called Rod from my cell and apologized for not coming back in to say goodbye and promised to get those blood tests from the hospital.

"Leo said to expect some lingering effects," Rod told me, "mood swings, visual disturbances, that kind of thing, for a while. You may have some flashbacks. Are you sure you're OK to drive?"

"Yeah," I said, "they told me all that at the hospital. I'll pull over and call someone if I'm not, talk to ya' later."

I hung up, dried my tears with a Pizza Hut napkin from the glove compartment, washed my knees and hands using it and an old bottled water I found on the floorboard, and drove up to Fort Myers to get arrested for murder.

ENGULFED
CHAPTER TWENTY

I was not arrested for murder. Neither was I arrested for impersonating a retirement- home inventory clerk nor even for spying on a police detective. I did, however, spend five hours talking to everyone at the Fort Myers police department including the lady who poked her head in and said she was going to Burger King and did I want anything; everyone but Nathan Gonzales; I never even saw him.

What I talked about was Stanley, every word he said, every word I said to him until I thought, *this is why people confess to crimes they didn't commit, it's just to have something different to say.*

Fair play is not the motto for those sworn to serve and protect however, as they gave me absotivley nothing, nada, not even what Stanley died from. What was certain, though, is that they didn't suspect me of anything. I was a witness only and not a *person of interest.* I went home by way of Burger King, got a kid's meal and ate it in my driveway, afraid to go in. I called Zig.

"Hey," I said when he answered, "still want some company at *The Sun God?*"

He was picking me up at eight, it was now three; I couldn't go back in the house, I needed to get away, I needed the beach.

The Gulf of Mexico is warm enough to swim in most of the time, which makes it better than any ocean, and since there's never been a Jaws size shark creating havoc on the beaches of Fort Myers, I'd decided to go ahead and buy a bathing suit from one of the dozen or so beach shops within a 50 foot radius of the beach.

You have to pass by all the display shelves of the junk people buy on vacation and then later get rid of at yard sales. Palm tree and dolphin printed salt and pepper shakers, picture frames with sea shells glued to them, and water globes with flamingos in the center. There is nothing created anywhere on the planet that you can't paint a bikini clad woman on and sell in a Florida beach shop.

I spread out my newly acquired beach towel with the image of the state of Florida printed on it. It showed city names along with the oranges and leaping Killer Whales, so I thought it would also serve, quite nicely, as a map. I lay there on my towel for approximately ninety seconds when I became hot, bored and uncomfortable and walked out into the water. I didn't have to suck in my stomach nor stand on tip-toe to brace for the cold because it was warm and delicious. I squeezed my eyes shut and let a wave pass over me.

I lay on my back and floated like that, occasionally bobbed around like a piece of driftwood by the miniscule waves, watching para-sailers and seagulls fly overhead, then closed my eyes and listened to the music of the beach.

"Lovely isn't it?" came a voice beside me. I opened my eyes but there was no one there except a seagull, perched atop a large souvenir ashtray. I stood up, my feet on the sandy bottom; the only part of me above water was my head, which I pivoted in all directions. There was no one else around me, not close enough for me to hear anyway.

"Be careful though, the tides can carry you to places you don't want to go," the voice said again, only this time I knew where it was coming from; it was coming from the seagull. He was bobbing along next to me, standing on his little tin boat with the pictures of Disneyworld on it.

"Who's doing this?" I shouted, looking all around me, "not funny!"

I began walking, then paddling back to shore, the bird in the boat stayed next to me.

"You know," he said, "you don't have to go."

I stopped, "Go where?" I asked, "I don't understand."

"Anywhere," he said. "You should stay. It's lovely, don't you think?" He picked up his little seagull foot and shook water from it. Then, in a voice that sounded just like Nathan Gonzales' he said, "Remember, people loved Lucille Ball," and with that, he flew away, the little ashtray boat disappearing under a wave.

Running in sand when you're chest deep in water is not easy to do, but I did it and got back to my towel. My legs wobbled under me, the sounds of people laughing grew louder then softer in my throbbing head. I sat down, wrapped my arms around my shaking knees and lay my head on them and with eyes closed thought, *that was real, I know it was, but how could it be?*

The longer I sat that way, the clearer my head became until I realized, that was what the doctor warned me about, flashbacks. *Oh Christ,* I thought, *I'm a person who has flashbacks, like a war veteran or someone who went to Woodstock!*

ENGULFED
CHAPTER TWENTY ONE

I was very glad I agreed to go to *The Sun God*. The place had an energy all its own and it fed me with its flashing lights and rhythmic beat of the dance floor mixed with the raucous laughter and immense smiles.

"Stay here, I'll be right back," I told Zig when we seated ourselves in front of the stage.

"No way you're leaving me here alone," he said, tugging at my sleeve pulling me back down to my seat.

"I have to GO!" I said and stood back up. "Besides, this place was your idea, remember?"

"I'll go with you," he said and this time he stood up too and grabbed my arm.

"No, we'll lose our seats. Look around, its standing room only." I started to walk away and he tried to follow.

"OK," he said, "so we'll stand too, I'm not sitting here by myself."

"Stop being a baby," I said pulling my arm away from him. "I'll just be a minute."

"You couldn't take care of this on the way in huh?" Zig threw himself back in his seat and looked straight forward.

"You'll be alright, just don't make eye contact with anyone." I gave him my best reassuring smile.

The bathrooms at the Sun God were near the front, so I had to go back through the bar area we had just come through to get to them. I looked back at Zig who was sitting slumped down in his seat, facing the empty stage.

The Sun God was both lounge and dance club with a drag show every weekend. The theater area was separated from the rest of the club with soundproof walls so the dance music in the lounge could be played at deafening levels and still not be heard in the show area.

The tables were illuminated from underneath with recessed orange lighting. The dance floor itself was in the shape of a large glowing sun and statues of naked men in the style of Greek gods, lined the walls.

The ladies room was painted bright yellow and the two women at the mirror freshening their makeup looked to be in their twenties. They were giggling and talking about a girl named Kelly which caused my mind to snap shut as it always does when confronted with young, drunk girl, babble.

The lights dimmed off and on in a typical theater, *five minutes to show time,* alert.

The abrupt change from the garish bright lights of the ladies room to the subdued mood lighting of the lounge was too much for my pupils and I blindly stumbled into a couple on the dance floor. One man grabbed my hand while his partner, a tall muscular man swung in behind me so that I was sandwiched between them. The music was loud and my attempts to excuse myself with smiles seemed to be interpreted as encouragement because the next minute the three of us were moving, as one, across the dance floor.

Then, as if we had become magnetized, our group of three became five, then six then ten, until we resembled a cell dividing and multiplying, all attached to the one large center of jumping, turning, gyrating mass of tight jeans and expensive cologne.

The change in beat signaled it was time to go back to the bar for refills so I was able to extricate myself. Not before, however, bumping into a man carrying drinks in each hand, some of which spilled onto my new pink dress, the one I had chosen because it covered the scrapes on my knees.

"I'm so sorry," I said attempting to wipe the liquid from my arm and dress.

"That's OK, happens all the time." His smile showed brilliant white teeth on a tanned face. I knew that face, that smile, but couldn't place where.

The bouncer at the theatre entrance opened the door for me and before I could walk to the front where Zig was, I stopped, dead in my tracks. Nothing could have prepared me for what I saw on stage and I gasped.

The woman on stage was dazzling; brilliant light shone on her and from her; she was positively luminous. Her snow white colored gown was covered in no less than a million sequins that radiated throughout every corner of the room. She was a six foot tall, dark skinned, blonde disco ball. The name on a banner behind her read, *Sinna Moan.*

I got to my seat in time to hear her finishing up the old *Lady Marmalade* song *Voulez-vous coucher avec moi ce soir*. She moved off stage, still singing, and began flirting with different men from the audience who showed their appreciation by stuffing bills into Miss Moan's cleavage or, when she raised the slit of her dress, in her sequined garter belt.

"Sorry I was late. I got asked to dance," I said to Zig.

"You're wearing blue Curacao," he said looking at the front of my dress.

"Yeah," I said, "someone spilled a drink on me. I knew the guy but I couldn't place him."

He glanced at me again then back at the performer.

"Isn't she awesome?" I whispered.

"What the hell has mom been doing coming here every week?" he asked, his eyes transfixed on Ms. Moan.

"I can't imagine," I said, and then because you always remember things when you're not trying to, my memory slapped me on my forehead. "Hey, wait a minute. I think I know now where I've seen that…"

That was when Sinna came over and sat on Zig's lap, tousling his hair as she sang, and I could do nothing but stare at her in awe. Her makeup was heavy but masterfully applied, her Adam's apple bounced about in her throat making her necklace move with it. Blonde hair fell in tendrils on her shoulder and her false eyelashes were so long I could feel them fanning me.

She stood back up and looked down at Zig. "What's the matter honey, the wife got your balls, I mean bills?"

The crowd laughed and Zig looked at me with terror in his eyes.

"Oh, I'm not his wife. We're just friends." I smiled at her.

Zig kicked my ankle, hard.

"That's all right honey," she said looking at me, "You make him buy you another drink since you spilt yours all over your pretty dress." Then she looked back at Zig, "You save your money honey, and get that fine lookin' woman nice and toasty, then maybe you can get some of them friend's benefits." More laughs, hoots and applause filled the room and the spot light left us.

She finished up with another chorus of Gitchi Gitchi Ya Ya Da Da Da as she made her way back to the stage and Zig stood up, looked at me and said, "I need a drink."

I followed him to the bar.

"Why are you so freaked out?" I asked Zig, "What did you think you'd find here anyway?"

"Hell, I don't know," he ordered something from the bartender and turned to me, "You want anything?"

"No thanks. Have you been looking around? Do you recognize anyone here?" I asked while craning my head to look around the room. "Anyone you remember seeing your mom with?"

He took his drink, which was a beer, and took a large gulp, and said, "you're kidding, right?"

"Sorry, but I thought that's why we came, so you could figure out why your mom was coming here. I mean, she is a theatre person. You said she did burlesque." I waved my arms around the theater, "Isn't this sort of like what she used to do? I mean, not with men...well not men dressed as women...but you know, singing, dancing...actually, I think they used to have men dressed as women..."

Zig looked at me with his mouth agape. "Maggie!" he hugged me, his beer glass cold and wet on my back. "Of course, that has to be it."

"I agree," I said, "it makes perfect sense, but why would she hide it?"

"I have no idea," he said, "It's not like anything she could tell me would shock me. Her life has been one long cast of characters for as far back as I remember. I don't even think she knows any regular people."

"So," I said, watching him finish his drink, "We just need to go backstage and talk to the performers."

Zig stared at me for a minute like he was going to say something, then turned around and waved his glass at the bartender, "Another please."

"We have to get backstage," I insisted when I could see him wavering. "You know we have to talk to some of the performers. I have a feeling the secret to your mom's visits here has everything to do with them."

"I can't go back there, that's the lady's dressing room," he said.

"They're men Zig. This is all very confusing for you, isn't it?" I asked, trying so hard not to laugh that tears were filling my eyes.

"I was checking out the tits on a guy!" he said. "Yeah, confused is a good word."

"I meant to tell you something," I stopped Zig near the stage curtain. "I remember where I saw that guy, the one I knocked into."

"Which one? I mean, I hate to say it Mags, but you do that a lot."

"Yeah, I know, but I'm talking about the one who spilled the blue cocktail on me. It was the cop who was collecting evidence at The Shell; the one that found the shoe."

"No shit?" Zig asked.

"Yeah, you wanna' see if he's still here?" I asked.

"Good idea," Zig said. "Let's go find him now," he turned and started back toward the bar.

"No. We're going to talk to some of the men here first, see if they remember seeing your mom." I stopped in my tracks. "Hey, I just had a thought. Maybe we should just let him see us here, the cop. That way he can see us seeing him. Then we go find him later, at the police station or something, and ask him to talk to us." I looked at Zig and smiled. "Cool idea huh?"

"I do believe you're starting to think like a real reporter now," he said throwing his arm over my shoulder. "Now, whatever you do, you are not to walk away and leave me, not for any reason," and he tightened his grasp. Then he stopped, looked at me and said, "See us seeing him? You don't write like that do you?"

"Shhh, we're trying to be stealthy," I said.

"You really think we're gonna blend in?" Zig whispered.

The entrance to the dressing room was in front of us. Most of the men still had on their stage makeup but nearly all had removed their wigs and gowns and were wearing bras, tape, pantyhose and underwear that mysteriously made body parts disappear.

"I'm sorry honey, only performers and stage crew back here," said a man with a heavy Hispanic accent. He was short, about five foot six and thin, carrying an evening gown across his arms that I imagined outweighed him by a good ten pounds.

"We were just wondering if anyone here knows a lady by the name of Dorothy Callahan."

"Dorothy? Of course, everyone here knows her, she is awesomacious." He kissed his fingertips and raised them toward the ceiling. "Why do you want to know about Dorothy?" He asked raising his left eyebrow.

"She's my mom," said Zig.

"Get out!" the man said with a huge smile and nudged Zig's shoulder, then reached his hand out from under the gown to shake Zig's. "You're Dottie's son?" he gushed. "I am so happy to meet you. My name is Luis."

"Dottie? She never lets anyone call her that," said Zig

"Well of course she does," he said nudging Zig again. "Look everyone," Luis yelled back into the dressing room, "It's Dottie's son. Isn't he a hottie?" He looked back at Zig, "what did you say your name was?"

"Steve," Zig said.

"It's Dottie's son Steve," Luis yelled back.

I continued standing there in my supporting role as the invisible woman while several of the men came up to shake Zig's hand and express their awe and admiration for his mother.

"She is sooo awesome," a tall man holding what looked like breast implants said to Zig. He saw me staring at them, "we call them chicken cutlets," he said, "for the bra."

"Cool!" I said.

"So…mom just kinda' likes to hang out back here with you guys?" Zig asked the chicken cutlet man.

"She's friends with Carmen. But she always makes time for any of us when we ask," he said, "like with our hair or makeup."

"Carmen?" asked Zig.

"Carmen Electric," another man chimed in behind the chicken cutlet man. This man was completely out of costume, wearing jeans and a tight black t-shirt. He was not wearing makeup or wig but he did have on diamond earrings that dangled down to his shoulders. "Dottie is Carmen's muse."

Zig looked at me, "I can't make any spit in my mouth."

I took over the conversation. "So guys, what can you tell me about Carmen and Dottie?"

"Like what?" asked the earring man.

"Like, what's Carmen's real name?"

"Honey, you tell us, then we'll all know," said Luis. "He's a closet queen; keeps his identity a complete secret from everyone. I'm sure Dottie knows who he is though."

"What does he look like?" I asked to no one in particular.

"Like Carmen Electric," said chicken cutlet man. "She never comes here out of character; leaves the same way."

"She's a total mystery," said earring guy.

"Yes a mystery and very fabulicious," said Luis who was obviously fond of making up adjectives.

"She sure is," said the cutlet guy. "She's a diva but she deserves it."

"She's the headliner here and in DC, so she says," said a guy pulling off his false eyelashes. The glue must have been pretty strong because his eyelid was being pulled out and upwards. "Ouch!" he yelled.

"Honey, I told you not to use that cheap ass shit on your eyes," said Luis.

"So, no one here has any clue who this mystery person is?" asked Zig.

"Not a clue," said Luis, walking to a rack to hang up the gown using large exaggerated movements. "Why don't you ask your mother?"

"Mom never mentioned any of this to me. How long has she…them, been coming here?"

"Oh, I think about two years now, don't you think Hank?" cutlet guy asked eyelash guy.

"Sounds about right," he replied. "I will tell you this much," eyelash guy continued, "They show up in a black town car with a driver."

"I can't believe she didn't tell me this," said Zig.

"Probably thought you couldn't handle the truth," said a guy walking past us wearing a Miami Dolphin jersey and high heels.

"We gotta finish up here," said Luis, "it was nice to meet you Steve."

"Nice to meet you too Luis," I answered for the both of us. "Great show by the way, we loved it."

"Come back next week but not on Sunday, it's amateur night," said chicken cutlet guy. The rest of them groaned in unison.

Zig had his cell to his ear as we left, "I sure wish mom would answer her phone. I've been trying for two hours to get her."

"She's probably sleeping, it's late."

"Apparently not for her, she's Miss Queen of the drag hive. I wonder what else I don't know. Maybe she's taken up bungee jumping, or speed dating."

"Come on, this isn't really such a far stretch for her is it?" I asked.

"She grew up in the business. It's been her whole life. This is really kind of a natural place for her to be when you think about it. Anyway, I think it's very exciting. My mother serves the punch and cookies at church on Sunday. Your mother is someone's muse."

"Would you listen to yourself?" he said. "My mother has friends that hide their testicles with duct tape."

I think you're over reacting. Now come on, let's go find our cop and see if we make him nervous."

ENGULFED
CHAPTER TWENTY TWO

"Did you know that The Gulf of Mexico holds 660 quadrillion gallons of water?" I asked Zig when he called me the next morning. I had gotten up very early and decided to write a travel piece for my column. "I didn't know there even was such a number as quadrillion, it sounds like a Doctor Seuss word. Anyway, a pirate by the name of Jose Gaspar lost 30 million dollars of treasure somewhere on the Peace River; that's near here isn't it? Well, he didn't actually lose it, he got caught by a Navy ship and tied an anchor around himself and jumped into the Gulf, but some of his pirate friends buried the booty."

"His pirate *friends*?" he said

"OK, his pirate *crew,* is that better? Jeeze, who peed in your oatmeal this morning? I had fun last night, didn't you? Even if we missed seeing our cop again, I thought it was a great night."

"I've been called back for questioning by that detective friend of yours. I have to go in as soon as I get off the air. Hey hang on."

I had the radio tuned to his show so I heard him giving the weather, "Expect some showers off and on all day with a high of 86 and the humidity at 40 percent." He came back onto the phone. "What are you doing today?"

"I have a doctor's appointment at nine. It's because of that drug; they want to make sure I'm OK, tell me what they found, that kind of thing. Why?"

"I got a weird call from mom this morning. I was hoping you could go to her place for me and get something."

"I can still do that, The Shell is on the way to the doctor's office. I mapped it out just now. What do you need?"

"She said there's a suitcase in the guest room closet she wanted me to take out of there. It's pretty big but it has wheels. You sure you don't mind getting it?"

"No, of course not; what does she want out of it?"

"Nothing, she just wants it out of her place. Just throw it in your car and I can get if from you later. She said it was important we get it out of there first thing this morning, said she'd call me later and explain."

"How am I supposed to get in there?"

"Ummm, yeah, can you come by the station and pick up the spare key?"

I managed to get in and out of Dorothy's room and get the suitcase without being spotted by any of the usual suspects. Idzy was probably in the dining room having breakfast with his harem and it was too early yet for Brandy and the rest of the day staff. I had just put the suitcase into the trunk and was closing it when I spotted Ralph pulling into the spot marked *Reserved for Security*. A squad car pulled in right behind him and the young cop we had seen at *The Sun God* got out and stopped the guard on his way into the building.

I watched from inside my car and scrunched myself down low enough so as not to be seen. They were out of earshot, so I turned the key over just enough to power the windows down. Still unable to hear them, I crawled over the console into the back seat and landed on *Dolly the Talking Dolphin*. It was something I had picked up for my granddaughter a couple of days ago, thrown in the back, and then forgotten about.

Dolly came alive when my knee hit her, "*Hi, my name is Dolly and I'm a Bottlenose Dolphin. Click click click whistle.*"

The men didn't seem to hear because neither of them looked over. Then, without me touching her, she started talking again.

"*Many people think I am a fish, but I am really a mammal. Click click click whistle.*"

I looked for an off switch and found none. The battery compartment was closed with eight tiny screws.

"This is all your fault Thomas Edison," I whispered to the annoying stuffed creature, "you and your talking dolls."

It appeared neither of the men heard a thing from my car because they were now nose to nose in a heated argument, their voices still indistinct until one of them, the cop, raised his even louder. "Don't get smart with me fat man. You won't be able to drive five feet without a blue light behind you, you got that?"

When I heard a car door slam I peeked out. The cop got into his car and drove off and Ralph gave the retreating vehicle the one finger salute before walking into the building.

With both men and the patrol car gone, I got out, dolphin in hand, and noticed a peppermint patty had melted in the car and stained her. I tried in vain to wipe her clean with my shirt.

Because, it would seem, God no longer loves me, I saw Nathan Gonzales' car pull into the lot. I threw Dolly onto the seat, brushed my hair back into place with my hands and straightened my clothes. It was eight am but sweat was already beginning to form on my upper lip and neck, matting my hair. He spotted me and pulled into the spot next to mine.

"You're out early today, Ms. Finn," he said as he got out of his car.

"Yes, I had to measure the…the bathroom for my mother." I lied.

"You know, you could just call here, the room dimensions are all standard."

"Oh, of course, wish I had thought of that before I drove all the way out here." I said wiping the sweat from my eyebrows and switching the hand I was using to block the sun. "I promise I'm not following you this time. It's just…well…what are the odds, huh? I think I must be working off some bad Karma," I let out a stupid chuckle.

"How are you feeling?" He asked me with what I thought was a warm smile.

"I'm ok. I'm on my way to the doctor now as a matter of fact."

He started to walk away and I said, "My friend Zig said he's seeing you today."

He stopped and looked at me. I could feel a few raindrops fall on my head and shoulders and looked up just in time to allow one to fall in my eye.

"Yes, he is," was all he answered. We stood in an awkward silence for a moment.

"Well, alrighty then," I said, trying to sound cheerful "guess I'd better be going." I wiped away the mascara stained raindrop now running down my face.

"Have a good day Mrs Finn…Maggie."

"Thanks. You too," I said and got into my car.

"*I eat fish and squid and small mammals. I consume thirty pounds of food per day. Click click click whistle.*"

I rolled the window up and he walked away mumbling, I'm pretty sure it was, *meshuggah*.

The doctor's office was small and the waiting room was empty. Thank goodness for early appointments, I thought. I was taken back into the examining room right away.

The nurse left me in the small room to enjoy the art on the wall. I could chose to gaze at the diagram of the inside of a nose or a diagram of a pregnant woman smoking while her fetus clutched a cigarette in its tiny fetal hands, or better still , an out of focus photo of a pink rose signed on the bottom right with the name of my doctor. Good thing you went to med school, I thought, 'cause Ansel Adams you ain't.

There was a brief knock at the door and then it opened.

"Mrs. Finn, hello, I'm Doctor Murphy." He reached his hand out and I reciprocated. "How have you been doing since you left the emergency room, any unusual symptoms?" He asked looking at my chart.

"Well, I'm not sure," I told him, "maybe."

He looked up at me with a raised eyebrow. "Can you elaborate?" he asked and examined my eyes with his little flash light. "What kind of symptoms?"

I answered the best I could with his bacon smelling hand pressed against my nose. "I've been imagining things."

He moved back and said, "Can you be more specific please?"

"Well, a seagull talked to me at the beach."

He leafed through more papers on my chart, "Anything else?" he asked without looking up," any more hallucinations?"

"No, just that one talking bird."

He got up and started checking my reflexes, having me follow his finger with my eyes, close my eyes and touch my nose, stand on one foot and put my arms out.

"Honestly officer, I only had one beer." I joked...no response. "You probably get that a lot, huh?" He made a half smile.

"Catch this," he said, as he threw a small sponge ball at me.

I fumbled a bit but caught it, "What, no mitt?" I asked. "I can juggle too, as long as it's only this one."

Doctor Murphy continued writing and I gave up on humor.

He asked me about headaches, nausea, vision problems, and when I had my last period. This is apparently the single most vital piece of information concerning a woman's body. You are asked this question repeatedly and by every person at every doctor's visit from the time you're twelve until you're given your last rites. "I'm sorry," says the priest, "but before I can absolve you of all sin and allow you to go to heaven, you must first tell me the date of your last menstrual period."

"So, what have you found out about what I got a hold of?" I asked.

"It's a new drug; it's been on the streets for less than six months. We've only seen a couple of cases on this coast but there have been several reported over in Miami. And you don't remember taking it?"

"No, I believe I would remember taking a pill or smoking something or injecting something into my veins. That's not the kind of thing one forgets doing."

"It could have been hidden in food," he said. "Probably not a drink since it's white in color and doesn't dissolve easily. It would really only take a very small amount to produce symptoms, a few milligrams. I doubt you would have even tasted it."

"Can I get a copy of whatever the lab has on the drug? I know another doctor who would like to see it."

"See my nurse about signing a release and she can give you a copy," he said and then left the room after telling me to make an appointment to come back in a week.

I got my paperwork and appointment card, walked out into rain, and drove to a 7-11 to grab a much needed water and some chocolate. Sitting in the parking lot of the convenience store, I watched as the rain falling on the windshield of my car. The drops fell individually, but soon began moving toward each other becoming rivulets of water that ran down toward the rubber of the unmoving wipers. They were alone, falling into an uncertain world, but soon, finding others of their kind, they. Wherever they went they would serve a purpose, not of their choosing as much as their circumstance. But whatever their destination, their ultimate goal would be fulfilled. They were givers of life, and they would succeed in that no matter where chance sent them.

I watched them for a very long time, admiring them, listening to them, becoming one of them, and then a thought jolted my brain. The York Peppermint Patty under my seat! It was a melted blob stuck to Dolly, so, if I didn't eat it that night I hallucinated then what *did* I take out of my purse and eat? The doctor said it would be white and tasteless. The realization hit me so hard it was as though I'd been slapped. Someone drugged some candy and somehow got it in my purse.

"Those bastards! Not you little raindrops, I wasn't yelling at you, but who...and *why* for God's sake...why?"

ENGULFED
CHAPTER TWENTY THREE

After five minutes of knocking on the front door of Dharma House and peering through the windows, the mean old guy I saw talking to Rod a few days ago answered. He was in a sleeveless undershirt and needed a shave. His remaining gray hairs were pointing away from his head at odd angles and he smelled like a combination of body odor and Vicks Vapo Rub.

"Damn lady, you wanna pound a little harder? I think there's still some paint on the door."

"Where's Rod?" I asked him.

"Not here." He started closing the door.

"Wait!" I shouted. "Errol right?" he stopped and looked at me.

"Do you know where he went?" I asked.

The man started walking away. "Do you know when he'll be back?" I shouted at the back of his head.

He was making his way toward the heavily padded chair in front of a small television when he turned and yelled at me over the sounds of audience cheering. "Do you see a goddamned typewriter here? No, and you know why? Cause I ain't a damned secretary, that's why. Him and his Jew boyfriend left, and it ain't my business to tell you anything."

"You could learn a lot from raindrops," I yelled at him and started back out.

"And they say I'm nuts," he said and turned his attention to the television, "Ha ha, I told you youse was bidding too high dumb ass."

Before I made it to the car another elderly gentleman approached me.

"I'm sorry about Errol ma'am. Rod and Leo are trying to help him but personally I think it's a lost cause."

This man was wearing a ball cap over what was certainly a bald head. He was thin and pale and his sunken eyes had a yellow cast to them. His lips were dry and brittle.

He continued, "Rod and Leo were going to have lunch at *Gulfside,* it's on the right, just before you get to the bridge that takes you to Sanibel. They left only a few minutes before you got here.

"Thank you…"

"Hank." He reached out his gnarled hand and I shook it gently.

"Thank you Hank. I appreciate your help. You go get in out of this heat now."

"I will," he said and walked very slowly toward the house, stopping every few steps to rest. I waited until he was inside before I left. Bless Rod's big old hippie heart, I thought.

I put the car window down, turned on the a.c. and drove in the direction of Fort Myers Beach. I love the sensation of driving with the air conditioner on while the hot humid air blows in from outside, it feels sensuous. Additionally it gives you the opportunity to take in all the smells of a coastal town. The closer you get to the beach the stronger they become. The diesel from boat engines, the salt air, and freshly cut bait odors were exhilarating. The sight of the horizon of dark blue water under a cloudless sky, its line broken only by the white trailing wakes of motor boats, was beautiful and made me smile.

I realized right then, that I liked it here. It was crazy, I knew. After being through a hurricane, getting drugged, talking to a dead guy, having women fighting with me over an old guy in lederhosen, and getting ignored by drag queens, it was the most excitement I'd had in…well, in my life. And there is something, something that feels like fun in seeing speed boats and jet skies tied up to old bait shops, hearing seagulls and rushing surf, and getting wet in rain that comes and goes as quickly as a Waffle House waitress.

 Some people compare the geographic look of Florida as the handle to the United States. Others compare it less favorably to a part of male anatomy. I think, though, its shape represents the uniqueness of the place. It doesn't really fit anywhere, like an extra puzzle piece that needed to be put *somewhere,* just like me, I mused.

Gulfside sat right alongside the bridge leading to the Sanibel and Captiva Islands. It was a rustic looking building from the outside with its gravel lot and wooden frame. Apparently hurricane Fanny was not enough of a force to knock this place down, or it was far enough south of the storm to escape her damaging winds.

Inside, however, it was anything but rustic. The tables were covered with linen cloths, and the seats, nearly all of which were occupied, were upholstered. The bar was a rich looking wood that extended the length of the place along one wall. The back of the restaurant was all glass with a view of the gulf. The outdoor patio extended into the water and had a dozen or more tables with large umbrellas for shade. That is where I spotted Rod and Leo. It appeared they had just been served their food and each had a near empty beer glass in front of him when I reached them.

They looked at me and spoke simultaneously, "Maggie."

Rod grabbed a chair from a nearby table and pulled it to theirs.

"What a pleasant surprise," said Leo. "Please join us."

"Yes, please," echoed Rod.

I accepted, and gave the server my order when he appeared.

After the usual pleasantries, small talk, and eating, I reached into my purse and pulled out the lab report I had gotten from Doctor Murphy and handed it to Leo.

"My doctor said he's heard of it being on the streets of Miami, that it's a new drug."

I could see Leo shoot Rod a kind of affirming glance. "OK you two, what's up? I just saw you look at Rod like you guys already know about this, do I need to worry about you again?"

"You don't need to worry about *us*," began Leo, "but you are correct that we have heard of this drug before and were suspicious that it was the one given to you."

"This just confirms it for us, said Rod. "And *we* are worried too, about you. Can you think of how you could have gotten it?"

"I'm pretty sure someone put it into candy, and somehow got it into my purse. The day of the hallucination, the same day we went out fishing, I woke up from my nap and got a candy out of my purse. I thought it was the one I had bought earlier, but today I found *that* one melted under the seat of my car."

"How long after you took the drug did you start to hallucinate?" asked Rod.

"My memory is pretty cloudy about that night, but I think it was less than an hour, maybe only minutes."

The memory of that night was still upsetting and I sipped my wine and looked out into the water watching a pelican dive, submerge his head into the water, and then fly away to perch onto a wooden pylon and swallow his catch.

"Maggie, who in the world would want to do that to you? What about the dead man, could it have been him?" Rod asked.

"I suppose, but I don't know why on earth he would. I just got down here. I don't know anyone except you guys and Zig, and his mother who lives at the Shell. That's it, no one else."

"Tell me about Zig," said Rod. "What's his real name?"

"I'm not really sure. He works at WWTF as a D.J. in the mornings. His mother's name is Dorothy Callahan. I guess that's his last name, Callahan. Oh, wait, she called him Steve. Detective Gonzales has talked to him a couple of times, about the doctor who drowned over at the Shell. Should I be worried?"

"I don't know," said Rod. "I'll check him out."

I turned to Leo, "What do you know about this drug? I've been having weird thoughts since I took it. Not all the time, but sometimes. Will that go away soon?"

"A pharmaceutical company was developing a drug to treat memory and reasoning loss that many times accompany old age," began Leo. "It was pulled during the testing phase because it produced mild hallucinations in the trial subjects. It appears someone got a hold of the formula, probably a chemist from the lab, and found a way to enhance the hallucinogenic properties of the drug. They were able to manufacture it in such a way that only a small quantity was needed to produce some very powerful experiences. There is an investigation into it now, but I honestly can't see how your friend Zig is involved unless he's at the distribution level. I can tell you this though; our dead doctor was on the board of the pharmaceutical company that manufactured the drug."

"Oh... My... God!" I said, "Do you think he was somehow involved?

"That's a big stretch," said Leo, "He was on the board of so many institutions; it's reasonable to imagine he didn't know anything about it."

I thought about that for a minute and decided he was probably right. "You didn't answer my question about the weird thoughts."

Leo was signing the credit card statement our server had placed on the table, while he answered.

"One of the properties of the drug is similar to that of another drug that has been around for decades, LSD. But this new drug is really nothing like LSD. Its effects are closer to what people might experience with mushrooms or peyote than to LSD, but we are still learning about it. It is possible, though I don't know how likely, that you could experience some residual effects indefinitely."

"Indefinitely as in forever?" I asked. "Seagulls are going to talk to me for the rest of my life?" A feeling of panic overcame me and I could tell from the jangling silverware and glasses on the table that my legs were shaking.

"Leo and I are driving over to Miami tomorrow to visit a colleague of his," said Rod, patting my hand. "This doctor is treating someone who has taken the drug several times and is displaying residual symptoms. Leo wants to examine the young man too. I'm sure we'll have more answers for you after that. I have a friend who will be looking after the guests at Dharma House. We'll only be gone for the day, but if you need me, I'll give you my cell number."

"Can I please go with you?" I asked. "If this doctor is a kind of specialist with this drug, maybe I can get an exam. We've already got my medical records right here," I picked up the papers from the table. "Can you call and ask? Please?"

Leo looked at Rod. "Fine by me," said Rod.

Rod said, "Can you be at Dharma House at six?"

ENGULFED
CHAPTER TWENTY FOUR

Alligator Alley is a stretch of road about 80 miles long, connecting the east and west coasts of Florida in the southernmost part of the state. It runs through the Everglades and use to be only two lanes of road and nothing else. Now it's part of the Interstate system with two rest stops, a gas station run by the Seminoles, and nothing else. There is an exit, the one with the gas station, which takes you to Snake Road. Where Snake Road leads I wouldn't even hazard a guess but you can be sure I'm never, ever, going to travel it to find out. A glance out any window affords a panoramic view of swamp, some trees and more swamp. The highway is only seven feet above water and the bridges were built for the wildlife to pass under, which I found really neat.

The three of us, Rod, Leo and I, were making small talk, me from the back seat with my vitamin water and pretzels. Rod and Leo told me a bit about themselves; they had both been married and divorced, Rod for fifteen years, Leo, less than a year. Leo seemed a bit vague about his life, which was the only thing he was vague about, he either knew everything there was to know about everything, or he was the best bullshit artist of all time.

They had a jazz CD playing, but it was not what I considered the good kind of jazz, like Sade or even Louis Armstrong. It was the kind that sounded like all the musicians were playing independently of each other, with no discernible melody. It was nothing you could hum along with, or tap your foot to, it was just noise. That's one big drawback to being a passenger. No one ever plays Journey or Michael Buble, it's always something hip, and I've never been hip, not even close. The other big drawback?...having to ask for a bathroom break.

Miami was disappointing. It looked like one giant import- export business. Warehouses and strip malls were the only things visible from the highway.

"This is not at all what I thought Miami would look like," I complained. "In *The Birdcage* everything looked so pretty."

"That's a great movie," said Rod, "very funny. That movie took place on South Beach. We'll go there and show it to you after we meet with the doctor."

We drove past Miami International Airport on an expressway, and exited shortly into an area called Coral Gables, and then into Coconut Grove. This was definitely *not* the import-export part of Miami, but more of the, *my maid comes in every day*, part of Miami. The homes were set back from the road and partially obscured by large trees, but you could still see the fabulous Spanish and Mediterranean architecture all with the signature orange tiled roofs so common in this city.

We passed Biscayne Bay, its aqua and blue water dotted with white sails, and Dinner Key Marina, where, Leo informed us, Pan American Airlines used to have its sea plane hangars. Now, *this* was the Miami I was expecting.

Rod pointed out the window, "They filmed *Meet the Fockers,* here and that other movie with the dog…"

"*Marley and Me,"* added Leo, who then gave us a lecture on the relationship of humans and dogs, the history of dog domestication and, I think, something about Jennifer Anniston, but by then I had completely tuned him out.

We arrived at Doctor Razi Epstein's office, which was on the top floor of an eight story office building. It turned out Razi is a woman's name. She was stunning in what I'm sure was a designer suit and silk blouse. Her long black hair was pulled back in a braid that touched her small waist. She didn't wear any jewelry and needed little make up over her perfect bone structure and hauntingly beautiful dark eyes. She was elegant and graceful, smart and beautiful, and so naturally I wanted to dislike her, but she was playing Michael Buble on the stereo.

Rod and I went to lunch in a restaurant downstairs while Doctor Epstein and Leo discussed and examined her patient, the one who had taken the same drug that I had. Because of confidentiality we couldn't be there, so we used the time to eat and explore *The Grove.* Two hours later Rod's cell phone rang with Leo asking us to come back upstairs.

When Doctor Epstein examined me, *her* hands didn't smell like bacon, and she was the funny one, making jokes about the exam. Of course, even her jokes were better than mine. My inner voice was reminding me, she likes Michael Buble, she has to be a nice person, and you don't really despise her. She can't help it if she's perfect. Maybe she only has six months to live. Maybe she's in an arranged marriage. That's it; she came here from *the old country.*

I could see her, groveling at the feet of her parents, weeping hysterically. "No," she was pleading, "please don't do this to me. I'm in love with Michael Buble, we want to be married."

Then, her father, throwing her to the man she would have to marry, a man who was unnaturally short and who slept with a teddy bear, and was impotent, and liked bad jazz, was telling her she had to marry him because doing otherwise would disgrace her family and he would drop dead.

Poor, poor, Razi, so unhappy, so lonely, trapped in a loveless marriage. My sympathy for her was becoming so intense my heart began to ache and I could feel my eyes fill with tears until an uncontrollable sob came from my mouth.

"Maggie? Are you alright?" she asked.

I looked at her and was embarrassed, not knowing how long I had been fantasizing. "Sorry, I guess I was daydreaming."

"And how often are you having these types of daydream, the kind that can bring out such strong emotions?"

"Well, they're not really daydreams. They're more like really intense thoughts. Like one time when I had a conversation with a seagull. Another time I was contemplating how much more meaningful the life of a raindrop was than my own."

"What about just now?" she asked. "What were you thinking just now?"

"Now? You mean just now? This past minute? I don't really remember. Well, that's not true, I do remember but I don't want to say."

"Please," she answered, "I'm a psychiatrist. You won't shock or surprise me. I promise."

I stared at her for a moment and she back at me in a kind of game of chicken. "Ok," I said, "I was seeing you in a sad, pitiful, loveless, arranged, marriage with an impotent short guy."

She looked both shocked *and* surprised.

The men took me on my promised tour of South Beach and Leo gave me the bad news. I could expect residual effects from this drug for quite a while. No one knew for certain how long it would continue to affect my brain. I was to be a test subject with follow up trips to Doctor Epstein who was apparently writing a paper on the drug.

"Oh swell," I said to them, "I'm my own little traveling Grateful Dead concert. Groovy."

ENGULFED
CHAPTER TWENTY FIVE

In Florida, something as simple as putting out the trash requires a bit of forethought. You are issued recycling bins; green for paper, red for glass, cans, and I guess anything else that isn't leftover spaghetti. Next, you have to practically hermitically seal them shut because of the wildlife that use them for take out. I was maneuvering all this, and trying to avoid mounds of fire ants, when I spotted the black SUV parked on the street a few doors down. "Oh crap," I said aloud, "I'm having a flashback."

A car door slammed. Footsteps moved in my direction.

"Oh shit!" I said and sprinted to the front door.

"Oh shit, oh shit, oh shit," I said again. I couldn't turn the door knob, "you're not locked you stupid door, you can't be locked."

My hands were shaking. I went to the push button panel near the garage door. My mind went blank. The footsteps were getting closer. "What is the freaking code? Why can't I remember the freaking code?"

I entered some numbers, nothing.

"Goddamnit!" I yelled.

I looked over my shoulder.

He was on the sidewalk, only yards away now.

The back door, I told myself, *you left the back door open.*

I ran around to the side of the house, saw a metal sprinkler on the lawn and picked it up. It was heavy, heavy enough to hurt someone with.

I stepped onto the cement slab outside the patio, put my hand on the door to slide it open and felt someone behind me. An arm wrapped around me. I swung the metal sprinkler over my head and made contact.

"You bitch!" the man yelled and threw me to the ground.

My head hit cement. I saw a pair of boots and smelled something strong and medicinal. A cloth covered my face for a minute, everything got fuzzy, then dark.

141

I couldn't move my arms or legs. I was buried in the sand up to my neck. My head was pounding. A seagull was pecking at it. *My* seagull, the one I met two days ago.

"Come friend and dig me out please!" I begged. "Call your family, everyone you know. Dig me out of this, please!"

He stopped pecking and looked toward the gulf.

The tide was coming in and I knew that drowning was imminent.

My seagull friend looked at me and said, "You're in my spot. This is my spot. I always stand here; you must move."

I asked, "Why this spot? The beach is immense, why this spot?"

"Because the sun sets right in front of me when I'm in that spot."

"But the sun will set in front of you no matter where you are on this beach. I thought you were such a smart bird but you're not; you're as dumb as a pigeon."

"Very good deduction Watson," he answered in a British accent.

I looked closer and saw Nathan Gonzales, pipe in hand. "I was merely testing you, you know. Now I shall leave you."

"No, don't leave. Please, I need help!' I could feel water on my face. The tide was coming in. I didn't want to die now, not like this, all alone, not even my seagull for company.

The sound of a barking dog was getting closer. I'm not going to die, I thought, a dog is coming to dig me out.

The barking became loader. It wouldn't stop. *Bark. Bark Bark.*, over and over.

"Stop dog," I told it. "Please, no more barking; my head, my head."

"I've called 911, someone should be here very soon," the dog said.

I opened my eyes, he was licking my face. I tried to sit up and promptly wretched into the grass, he went over to sniff it.

Sirens in the background were coming closer now. Footsteps appeared all around me. Men in uniforms were examining me, asking questions, putting me on a stretcher and then into the back of the ambulance.

Two men leaned over me from opposite sides of the vehicle.

"Yeah, we were just here Sunday. Same lady, strung out on somethin', sitting by an Escalade with a dead guy."

It was deja vu all over again. Same E.R, same stuff attached to me, even the same doctor: the tall, dark, and handsome Doctor Mousique Mann.

"Mrs. Finn, you're becoming a regular here in our hospital." He looked at my chart. "How are you feeling?" He looked at the gash on my head, and then began the same exam I'd already had twice in as many days. After completing my vaudeville act, a nurse came in and asked if I was ready for a visitor. The curtain was opened before I could respond.

"Detective Gonzales!" I groaned."Perfect, I was hoping for Doctor Kevorkian."

"Are you in pain?"

"The drugs are helping. You probably don't want to get too close; I think I threw up in my hair."

"Mrs Finn, I understand you told the doctors here that you were assaulted."

"Yes, I was. You know, your department of tourism doesn't include any of this in its ads."

"Can you tell me what happened?"

"Another black SUV, down the block. I was taking out the garbage; he came after me. He grabbed me, I hit him with a sprinkler, he knocked me to the ground and put a rag over my face. I'm assuming it was chloroform. Apparently, when my neighbor took his dog out, he found me there, passed out on my patio."

"The front door of your house was unlocked. It's hard to tell if anyone went through it; it's pretty barren in there."

"It can't be unlocked. I tried to get in, it was locked. I'm sure it was."

"It's unlocked now, I've sent a team to dust for prints. It would help if you come back there with me and tell me if anything's missing."

"This all makes no sense. The house is practically vacant. My parents are moving. Why would anyone break into a house that's furnished with little more than a blow-up bed and some napkins?"

"Do you have any enemies?"

"I haven't been here long enough to get a tan."

"How long have you and Mr. Callahan been friends?"

"I'm not sure, what day is it?"

"Is he your boyfriend?"

"My boyfriend? You're joking. I haven't had a boyfriend since tenth grade. No, I just met him, he just moved here too. Neither of us knows anyone here. I like his mother. She lives in the same place my folks are moving into, that about sums up the entirety of our relationship. Wait. You're taking me home?"

"You can't go back the way you came."

"I like your car, it has a sun roof, I can air out."

He smiled at me and I felt that little flutter again.

He was clean shaven this time and wearing a pale blue dress shirt and black slacks and smelled really good. Every time I saw him, he looked less unattractive and was on the verge of actually looking sexy to me. Of course, I had no room to talk about attractiveness. I had a bandage on my head, blood and vomit in my unkempt hair, no shoes, and was wearing a Hello Kitty night gown,

"Come on, they've discharged you, right? You can give me a description of those boots on the way over to your house."

I got in the obligatory wheel chair and he got behind it and pushed.

"Tenth grade?" he asked.

"Tenth grade," I answered.

ENGULFED
CHAPTER TWENTY SIX

Nathan Gonzales had a gun; it was attached to his belt in some sort of leather-looking holder. The sum total of my gun knowledge is that they fire bullets. I stopped staring at it so he wouldn't think I was staring at his crotch and looked back out the window. He had opened the sun roof, but the breeze from it, rather than letting my foul odor out, sent it right back into my nose, making me feel queasy. Acid came up the back of my throat and I gagged.

"Do I need to stop?" Nathan asked, a little panicky.

"Yeah, I think...no, it passed. I'm alright now. You know, I feel like...well...I mean, you must think I'm weird or creepy or...nuts."

"I think you're very charming."

"And you are very polite, thank you. I just wish that you could see me sometime when I'm...well, not this." I looked down at the mess I was.

"We could have dinner sometime, I mean, if you'd like to...that is, if you're feeling..." He turned his head to me and cleared his throat. "Would you like to have dinner with me tomorrow night?"

"I'd love to," I said quickly.

"Pick you up at seven?"

"Seven would be great....Nathan?"

"Yes Maggie?"

"Just to be sure...it would be a date, right?"

"Your first since tenth grade.'

I smiled and felt excited. I had a date, a real honest to goodness date, with a guy who carries a gun.

The excitement faded quickly when my house, my parent's home, came into view with two squad cars and yellow, *CRIME SCENE DO NOT CROSS* , tape all around it. All the lights in the house were on, and we had to duck under the tape to enter. Police, with black booties over their shoes and white gloves, were going through my things, one of them in the kitchen, and another in the bedroom. The acid in my throat came back. I didn't want to be one of those fifties-movies women, who fainted or got the vapors, but this was too much, and stars began appearing before my eyes. I grabbed onto the wall and waited for the dizziness to pass.

"Do you want to wait and do this tomorrow?" asked Nathan.

"Well, if these guys are gonna be here anyway, I might as well do it now." I answered.

The police were leaving things where they were, just examining the few items I had, and putting powder on door knobs, painting them with little brushes, all kinds of thing that would be interesting if it were someone else's house.

We walked together, room by room, me trying to remember what was supposed to be there, Nathan talking to the officers.

"No sign of forced entry." I heard one of them say.

"You can't possibly do this every time someone is robbed." I said to Nathan.

"Not everyone gets picked up in a vehicle with a deceased man, while high on a drug we don't even have a name for yet, and then winds up knocked out and bleeding three days later." Nathan stopped and looked at me, peering at me actually, as though he were trying to see something stuck in my eye. "Maggie, do you know something you're not telling me ?"

"I don't really feel good right now, are they almost done?" I asked.

We walked back to the front door; the officers had already left the house and were in their squad cars. Nathan had made them take the crime scene tape down before they left.

"Do you want to stay somewhere else tonight? Do you have any friends or relatives here?" Nathan asked.

"I don't really have anywhere to go. I'm sure I'll be fine though. I'll leave all the lights on and double check the locks on the doors."

"You have my number," he said. "Don't hesitate to call."

"I'll see you tomorrow at seven?"

"Seven o'clock," he answered.

It was two a.m. but I called Zig anyway and got his voicemail.

"Someone's out to get me. I don't know why, or if it has anything to do with The Shell, or your mom, or if it's this house, but it's scaring the shit out of me, call me as soon as you get this."

I sat on my blow up bed and watched an infomercial for something called The Amazing Bullet, which is a very small blender. The only part of it that intrigued me is why they'd included a woman who looked like a stockyard-whorehouse madam, dangling a cigarette from her lips, as part of the cast.

Watching this mindless nonsense helped to clear my mind and settle my nerves. All the chopping and blending made things feel normal. The old hooker in the house dress was just talking about garlic, which I'm sure lots of people wore around their necks in her presence, when my cell rang and I jumped.

"Zig? What time is it?"

"4:30, why are you up?

"I haven't gone to bed yet, the police just left a couple of hours ago."

"Tell me what happened,"

I told him everything and he was genuinely concerned.

"Why didn't you call me? You could have stayed here. I've slept on the couch before, remember? As a matter of fact I'm thinking of turning the office into a guest room."

"I'm ok, why are *you* up?"

"I'm on the air in ninety minutes. I can't talk much; I have to get ready. I'll call you. No, you might go to sleep, call me when you get up."

"OK, I'll do that."

"Jesus Maggie, I'm glad you're alright. Get some rest and call me."

"Wait! Have you heard from your mom?"

"Not tonight, but I did have an interesting visit with your detective."

"He's not *my* detective." I smiled to myself. "What happened?"

"I had to go in and do a Cinderella number. It was the weirdest day of my life, and I've had some weird freakin' days."

"You're right, I can't hear about any of this right now. I'll call you in a few hours."

I turned off the blending show and tried to sleep, turned the light back on, and grabbed my cell.

"What do you mean Cinderella?" I asked.

"Remember the shoe you said they found at the lake where Haney croaked?"

"What about it?"

"They thought it might have been mine. Said it was bought on my credit card. He made me actually try the damned thing on."

"Did it fit?"

"Hell no, it didn't fit, but a quarter inch bigger and I'd probably be in jail right now. They're giving me the benefit of the doubt for right now that it was credit card fraud, but they still know about my card being used at The Sun God, so I'm guessing this isn't over."

"We're going to dinner tonight."

"We are?"

"No, not *you* and me, the detective and me."

"For the love of God Maggie, whatever you do, don't mention my name. Wait. Why are you going to dinner?"

"It's a date."

"Can you do that?"

"I think so, should I call my father and get permission?"

"I mean, he's a detective and you're...well, you...I don't know, you're part of..."

"Yeah, see? I tried all that too. I'm nothing really, so I guess it's all cool."

"Go to sleep."

"Ok, I'll, talk to ya later." I hung up and went to sleep.

The neighbor's barking dog woke me up close to noon, the first time that I wasn't pissed about it. *Good ole', whatever his name was*, I thought and made a mental note to go next door and thank them, the man and his dog. Maybe I'd even stop by the store and get a bone for the dog and something from the bakery for the man, and introduce myself properly. As far as I could tell, he lived there alone, except for the dog, one of those generic type dogs you see in animal shelters.

My parents had told me what a nice man he was and that he had moved in just a few weeks ago from one of the "I" states, perhaps Illinois. Thank goodness he didn't flee Fanny like everyone else on our block, or I'd probably be out there still, with giant, ugly Florida bugs biting, and stinging me.

Did my parents say he had their cell number? I think so, I think he was supposed to call them in case of emergency before I'd come down, while the house was vacant. My mother's idea of an emergency is advertising fliers accumulating on the lawn or a change in garbage pick up times.

I would have to make sure he didn't call them about all this. If he already had, then surely they would have known about the first incident. No, he couldn't have called them; they would have been here before he'd hung up his phone. The worst thing that could happen now would be for my parents to be here. When I spoke to them yesterday they were planning dinner with Mickey Mouse, with my brother's grandkids pleading for ice cream in the background. They sounded happy, and damn it, they were going to stay that way. There were several voice mail messages waiting for me. Most from my family, one from Zig asking me to call, and one from Nathan, making sure I was alright. The last one made me smile. After returning the calls to my family, I tried Zig, no answer.

A trip to the mall for a date outfit was next on my agenda, which also included lunch in the food court, and a manicure and pedicure at a place called *So Happy Nails*. I was relaxing in the vibrating, massaging pedicure chair when Zig called me.

"I think mom's in trouble."

"Why? What's wrong?"

"I'll tell you later, I'm on-line buying us tickets."

"Tickets? Where? Wait, *us*?"

"Look, something is going on, I'm sure it has something to do with why people keep showing up at your house, it has to. I mean, all this started when you got here."

"What are you talking about? I had nothing to do with anything. Are you saying all of this is my fault?" My voice was getting louder and everyone in the salon turned to look at me.

I lowered my voice, "where am I supposed to be going?"

"Washington, D.C."

"Are you serious? When?"

"Tonight."

"But, I have a date!" My voice got loud again.

"Maggie, this is serious. You're involved in this too, that's why people keep coming after you, I'm sure of it. Don't you want to find out about this before someone actually kills you?"

I thought about that and weighed it against my date tonight for a bit longer than I should have because Zig said, "Maggie, really, you have to think about it?"

"Alright, I'm going with you," I said dejectedly, "but I get the window."

ENGULFED
CHAPTER TWENTY SEVEN

I had the window seat, staring at my beautifully pedicured toes that were going to waste by not poking out of the new turquoise and white sling back sandals I had just bought, to go with the new turquoise and white dress with the plunging back, for which I had bought a very expensive backless bra.

"He's never going to call me again. I really like him and he's never going to call me again."

"Would you get over it? You haven't said anything else since I picked you up. We've got bigger problems than your sex life you know," said Zig.

"I know. It's childish. Everything that's going on and I'm worried about a date, but it was a really big deal to me. I'm not young and pretty anymore, there aren't a lot of men out there who don't want young and pretty and are weirdly attracted to...I don't know, what I am, quirky."

"You're still pretty, in a quirky way."

"Thanks."

"Anyway," he said, "can we leave that subject for a while and concentrate on what's happening?"

"Yeah, ok, sorry. I looked through the suitcase I got from your mom's place like you asked me too. It was all costumes and from what I could tell, way too big for her, probably drag-show stuff huh?"

"She must have thought someone was going to go into her place and see it," said Zig. "She really doesn't want anyone to know about her Carmen Electric friend and I think I know why now, her friend is a sitting senator."

The plane was full. The family in the aisle next to us was all wearing floppy eared Goofy hats. Most of the passengers, in fact, looked like tourists; the men wearing flowered shirts and shorts, and the women wearing sundresses, or tank tops with the names of various Florida beaches printed on them. The older ones, men and women, were wearing golf attire. There were lots of kids, and most of them were either over tired or over stimulated. It was a very noisy plane so we didn't feel the need to talk in whispers.

"I think we should call the police as soon as we get there," I told Zig. "I think you should have told your mother to do that. I mean, she honestly said that her friend was being blackmailed?"

"You don't call the police and accuse a couple of United States senators of bribery and blackmail," he answered, leaning in close to speak.

"Well," I said, "technically, one's being blackmailed; the other one's taking a bribe. I feel better that the one that your mother knows is the good one, the blackmail-ee, and not the creepy one taking the bribe."

"No wonder my dad drank," said Zig. He looked at the ceiling and sighed.

"I still think we're all in way over our heads. Going to a drag show is one thing; flying to D.C. to confront a member of Congress is just crazy."

The father in the Goofy ears looked at me.

"I have to go to the bathroom." I told Zig, and wedged myself out into the aisle.

"I'm sorry, you can't form a line in front of the cockpit," the flight attendant told me. She was my age and kind of plump. I remembered when flight attendants were called airline stewardesses and they had to be young and thin and single and flirt with the male passengers. I supposed this was better, but I still didn't like her.

"It's just me, you can't really call that a line, can you?" I asked.

"I'm sorry, but it's the rule."

I turned and walked to the back of the plane, where apparently you *can* form a line until the attendants want to wheel out the beverage cart, which they did as soon as I arrived there. Before they could send me back to my seat, one of the lavatory doors opened and a man walked out, seemed startled to see me there, and then hurried past.

I got back into my seat and said to Zig, "There's a guy I saw back there that looks familiar to me. I know I've seen him before, but I can't place where."

"What does he look like?"

"An old guy, short, thin."

"That would be a quarter of the population of Florida."

"I guess, but he seemed to recognize me too."

"Wait till we get off the plane, you can point him out to me then."

"Yeah, but it's gonna bug me till I do."

"Everything that we've been through this week and that's what's gonna bug you?"

We sat in silence during the rest of the flight, me starring out the window, Zig listening to his I-pod and pretending to sleep.

"Hey! Hurry! Look!" I grabbed Zig by the arm and pointed out the window at the view of the city laid out below us. The late afternoon sun had painted all her iconic images a warm golden color that made the sight of it breathtaking.

We stood in the taxi line for thirty minutes watching swarthy-faced men from countries I probably couldn't find on a map, pick up their fares. We finally got our turn and jumped into a cab with a driver whose English consisted of *where to* and *cash only please.*

The address Dorothy had given us, 700 New Hampshire Avenue N.W was, as it turned out, the Watergate Complex. The complex overlooking the Potomac River was infamous as the place where Richard Nixon met his Waterloo. The Watergate break-in, and subsequent hearings, filled the TV airways when I was in my late teens. Now, here I was, about to go inside this legendary place of dishonor. Under present circumstances, there seemed nowhere more appropriate.

We buzzed the apartment number from the call box in the lobby

"Who is it?" the voice asked.

"This is Steve Callahan and I'm here to see my mother, Dorothy".

"Mister Callahan. This is Brian Roberts. I'll be right down. Please wait."

Senator Roberts came off the elevator and nearly sprinted toward us. He did, in fact, look as though he had just come from the gym; wearing a sweaty t-shirt, shorts and athletic shoes. He extended his hand to Zig and then to me with a questioning look.

"I'm Maggie Finn. I'm a friend of Zig and Dorothy . . . *Steve* and Dorothy."

"Miss Finn, thank you for coming."

"What's going on? Where's mom?" Zig asked.

"Please, come upstairs," Senator Roberts said.

We rode the elevator to the eighth floor and entered the apartment where I made an involuntary gasp and stood frozen for a moment at the doorway. The view from the large windows across the room caught my eye first before I took in the furnishings of the place. If the senator looked like he was straight out of central casting, then his apartment was from the pages of *Ridiculously Wealthy& Famous People's Homes Digest.*

"Mister Callahan, Miss Finn, please, come in, sit." He gestured to the sofa and we sat synchronously.

"Is mom here?" Zig asked.

"Not just now, but she has been staying here."

"Then where is she?" I asked.

"I'm sorry but I can't answer that."

"And why is that exactly?" Zig looked like he might come off the sofa and punch the senator. I held his arm and he jerked it away.

"She left this morning to run some errands. Frankly, I was expecting her back hours ago. She forgot her cell; it's here in her room. She's done that before, so I wasn't . . ."

The doorbell rang and we both jumped.

"That would be someone with some food and drinks. I ordered them when I knew you were coming," the senator said, walking toward the door.

"I'm sorry, I really am. I know you have lots of questions, but if you could just bear with me a moment, I'd like to change clothes. I'll only be a minute and you can have something to eat and drink."

He left through a bedroom door.

A twenty-something young man came in and began busying himself in the kitchen, while I surveyed the room and Zig stared out at the river.

"If I had to describe this apartment to anyone, I would first need an education in art, antiques and architecture," I said. "Hey, look over here, look at his CD collection; Cher, Brittney Spears, Barbara Streisand, Celine Dion . . . look, there's even Judy Garland."

I walked over to the piano and looked at the sheet music. "*All the Single Ladies*, that's that Beyonce song. . . *if you want it then you have to put a ring on it*, or something like that." I said, singing the chorus.

The young man preparing our food came out into the living room and cleared his throat to get our attention.

"I have some sandwiches and salads for you and there is an assortment of beverages, if you just tell me what you prefer," he said.

"I'm not hungry," said Zig.

"I am," I said, "and I'll have some ginger ale if you have it uhhh. . ."

"Seth, and yes, I do, please, help yourself," he indicated the food on the table.

"Thank you Seth. Do you work here at the Watergate?" I asked.

"I'm a student at the University of Miami, I'm interning with the senator this semester."

"'Oh, what's your major?" I asked.

Before he could answer, Senator Roberts came back out.

"Thank you very much for your patience. I see Seth has taken good care of you. Is there anything else you need?"

His hair was wet but combed nicely and he was wearing a dress shirt and slacks.

"You can start by telling me how you know my mother," said Zig.

"Your mother is a wonderful friend to me and I would never let any harm come to her. You are very lucky Mister Callahan; she is the kind of mother I always wished mine could have been."

He walked to the liquor cabinet and pulled down a bottle of scotch. He held the bottle toward Zig.

"Sure, rocks and water," said Zig

He looked at me next but I declined and he continued to speak.

"She and I have been working together for two years now. I have a little act I do, strictly for fun mind you, but it's been a passion of mine since my Hasty Pudding days at Harvard."

He swallowed his drink and sat down.

"I would send drivers for her once a week, when I was home, and we'd have dinner and then work on different routines. Your mother is the most gifted and talented performer it has ever been my privilege to know. I think she enjoyed out rehearsals even more than I. She wouldn't let me pay her for her time, but she allowed me to fund the little theater there at The Shell. It was the least I could do."

Zig downed his glass and walked to the cabinet for a refill. "Are we getting close to the part of the story where you tell me where my mother is?"

"Yes, of course. Well, as I was saying, your mother would come to my home in Florida, which is where she was when she had a very mild stroke."

"I remember that," said Zig, "she said she was with a friend when that happened."

"Yes, I am the friend she was with. As soon as I suspected she was not feeling well, I called the paramedics and her private physician,

Doctor Haney. I was still in costume when he arrived and he . . . well, let us say he began using confidential information to put pressure on me to . . .

"He was blackmailing you," I said. "You do the drag show at The Sun God"

"Yes, that is true, how did you . . ? Never mind, I didn't tell Dorothy though, about the blackmail. I did not want her involved in any way," he answered. "I'm terribly ashamed I allowed him to...I should have stood up to him, should have..."

"What's he making you do?" asked Zig.

"Was," I reminded him.

"He wanted me to use my influence to get Medicare payments for the company's..."

"And then you killed him," said Zig.

"God no! No, I had nothing to do with that, you must believe me on this point. I can see where you would think that, why the police might think that if they knew. That was what your mother was afraid of. She found out about the blackmailing and she felt somehow responsible. She never let on to me until two days ago when. . . "

He was cut short when his phone rang.

"Yes, this is Brian Roberts, who is this?"

"Where is . . . look here you..."

Senator Roberts looked at Zig, then me, then turned his back to speak.

"I'd like to speak to Miss Callahan now," he said in a more hushed, but very anxious tone.

Zig and I looked at each other and then back at the senator, watched his frame relax a bit and then begin speaking in a more cheerful tone. "Dorothy, it's so good to hear your voice. Yes of course. I understand you're not able to speak freely but can you tell me if you're alright?

Zig grabbed the phone from him.

"Mom, where are you? Are you alright?"

The senator and I were standing close to him now, trying to hear the voice at the other end of the line. Zig was mostly silent, listening intently then said goodbye to her.

The look on his face was one of utter confusion. He handed the phone to the senator who was speaking again.

"Yes, I understand. I've told you already that I would comply. There was absolutely no reason for you to take these measures. I expect her to be returned to me immediately. Then tell me where she is and I will send for her right now."

Zig grabbed the phone from him.

"I don't know who you are but if . . ." He pulled the phone from his ear and looked at it, then at the senator.

"They hung up. Who the hell are these bastards and what the hell is going on?"

"They are the people blackmailing me. I'm to act on behalf of two rather unethical companies this Thursday, to ensure they receive Medicare funding. It's a lot more complex than that, but that is the gist of it. They are holding your mother until then as insurance, in case I change my mind."

"Why mom?" asked Zig.

"Because she was here. I had told them I had changed my mind about cooperating. After the death of the doctor I wanted out. I said I would rather face a scandal than be a part of any of this. She, your mother, was delivering a note to Senator Waldon telling him that I was no longer going to cooperate. He was, I am sorry to say, taking money from Doctor Haney for his cooperation in the same matter."

"I thought it was Haney who was blackmailing you and he's dead," I said. "And this Waldon can't get money from a dead man."

"Apparently Haney was not acting alone," said Roberts.

"Do you know who these people are? Would they hurt her?" asked Zig.

"I have no idea who they are. I am so sorry. After what happened at The Shell, I thought it would be safer for her to be up here. She had confronted Bruce. . . Doctor Haney. I didn't know who he talked to down there. . . I honestly thought she would be better off up here and she agreed."

"You don't think this guy Waldon has anything to do with her being kidnapped do you?" I asked.

"No, he's been around a long time. He's known for his *quid pro quo* but he's not crazy. Your mother called me from his office at eight a.m., she was going to tell him, in person, that I was not going to cooperate. She had taken it upon herself to do this without my knowledge. She called me and told me about it, said Waldon was on the senate floor but expected back in the afternoon. She was going to wait, take a bus tour, have lunch, be a tourist. That's the last time I spoke to her until just now. I tried calling her cell, I went to the Capitol to look for her, then I came back here to see if she'd come home. I went for a workout here in the building, but left strict instructions for the concierge to call me the minute she stepped foot through the door."

"Alright," I said, "we're gonna start from the beginning. I want every detail. But first, write down every word she said to you, both of you. She may have been signaling a clue. Be very specific, every word."

The two men looked at me, then at each other, and then Senator Roberts went to his desk and pulled out two legal pads and some pens.

ENGULFED
CHAPTER TWENTY EIGHT

Zig and the senator may not have had appetites, but I was enjoying a turkey on rye and some potato salad; those six cashews I ate on the plane did not exactly fill me up. We were all sitting at the dining table reading each other's notes and adding some of our own thoughts.

"She told you to tell me this?" I asked Zig, "how very odd."

I pointed to the note that read, '*To love another person is to see the face of God.*'

"I've heard the line before, but I don't remember who said it."

"Les Miserables," said Senator Roberts. "It's from the epilogue, the ending."

He sang the next, "*Take my hand and lead me to salvation, take my love, for love is everlasting, and remember the truth that once was spoken, to love another person is to see the face of God.*"

Zig looked at him, mouth agape. I gave a small, silent applause and said, "Senator, you sing beautifully."

He smiled at me and said, "Thank you, and please, call me Brian," then asked Zig, "Did she ever perform in Les Mis?"

"No, that one I would have remembered."

"You know, I'm going to come right out and say this," Brian told him, "I'm sorry, I hope you won't be offended but your mother sounded very. . . befuddled I guess is a good word. She's normally so sharp, but she seemed to make no sense at times, like she was...confused, what do you think?"

"Gee, ya think?" Zig asked, "Who the hell knows what's going on with her, what they could have given her or done? Shit, I can't... she told me not to forget to feed her bird and to clean his cage for Christ's sake."

"Well, that's not that odd, that she would be worried about her pet," I said. "I'm sorry Zig, but I'm sure she's fine, just really rattled, and who could blame her?"

Zig sat on the sofa, lowered his head in his hands, and then looked up at Brian and me, "I want to call in the police...hell, while we're at it, the FBI, the National Guard, Scotland Yard, The freaking Royal

Canadian Mounties. I want anyone and everyone looking for her, and then I want to get my hands on the bastards who have..."

Brian interrupted him, "Excuse me Zig, I understand what you're saying and I am in complete agreement, but...well... they never actually *said* they were keeping her against her will. They just said she would remain their *guest* until after the vote."

"A guest my ass, they won't tell us where she is and she's not allowed to leave, I'd call that kidnapping," argued Zig.

"Oh yes, of course, I just meant that...listen, the vote is tomorrow, she said she is being treated extremely well, those were her words, *extremely*. And, they made no threat as to what would happen should I not introduce the legislation, no threat at all. I just think, and tell me if you agree, that it might be hard to go to the police with a piece of legislative blackmail and then say that your mother is living as a guest for the next twenty four hours at a place that she refused to give us the address for."

His blackberry made a beeping sound from across the room, and he went to check it.

"That's easy for you to say, she's not your mother," Zig said, following him. "She's not a guest and you and I know it and the police will certainly look at this as kidnapping. I'm not dicking around with my mother's life."

Brian picked up his smart-phone and read it aloud, "A text from Waldon's office that he's still en route and unavailable." He shoved the phone into his pocket and sighed.

"You know, it sounds to me like you're protecting your job, your reputation," Zig told him. "You don't want a scandal, and frankly, I don't care. If the people in Florida don't like their senators wearing evening gowns and singing Doris Day tunes, then that's your problem."

"But don't you see?" Brian explained to Zig, "I'm in complete agreement. That is why they are holding your mother now, because I told them just that. Well, I didn't mention Doris Day but. . ."

"So, you go to the capitol, introduce this legislation allowing this company to get Medicare payments and they send her home, that's it?" Zig asked skeptically.

"Essentially, yes," said Brian, "except that it's two companies, Charley Davidson and Helix Pharma..."

Zig interrupted, "I don't give a flying fu..."

I interrupted, "Senator, *Brian*, I noticed the room where Dorothy is staying. It's lovely and you have gardenias in there, they smell heavenly."

"Oh, yes," he said distractedly. "she loves gardenias."

"And all the framed prints and sheet music, that's quite a collection," I went on. "It would appear they are all autographed by the artists."

"They've been in the family for years. I had them sent down and hung in that room the same time I was arranging for her to fly up; I thought she would enjoy them."

"You really must care for her," I said to him.

His eyes reddened like he was about to cry, then he cleared his throat and looked at Zig, "I would give anything, anything at all, to have your mother home safe with you. There is nothing I won't do. If you want to call the police, if you think that's the best course of action, I won't stop you. I'll cooperate in any way I can, whatever you think."

"She really cares for you, ya' know," Zig said to Brian. "She seemed more worried about you than herself. She didn't want me to do anything that might make things hard on you, hurt your career." He threw himself onto the sofa and stared out of the picture window. "She said you were a very good senator, that you did a lot for everyone in Florida, especially the senior citizens." He looked over at Brian, "She said that I should just do whatever these people want and not cause problems."

"I have waged many an uphill battle to...wait, I'm sorry. Your mother was very kind to say that, but you can't go by what she says, she's. . . well, she's probably saying what they want her to say," said Brian. "I believe we should let you make the decisions here, she is your mother."

Zig and he stared at each other for a few seconds in what seemed like a moment of silent bonding. Then Zig made a small chuckle and added, "She just now told me that if you weren't a senator, you would have been a great song and dance man, like Don Ameche."

"Don Ameche?" asked Brian." Funny she would compare me to him, we're nothing alike. I mean, it's not important I know, I shouldn't even be mentioning it but. . .well, that's hardly a name you'd come up with as famous song and. . ."

"What did I tell you?" I interrupted him. "She's definitely leaving us clues, it's so obvious. She's not at all senile, but she's pretending to be... in front of them."

My mind was racing, it was suddenly all so clear to me. "She figures she can go on about these random names and such and they'll just think she's being. . .oh, I don't know. . .a crazy old lady."

"Well, I must be the senile one because I haven't got the faintest idea what any of it means, do you?" Zig asked me.

"Did you have that on your list, the Don Ameche thing?" I asked, hurrying to the table and shuffling through the papers. "Oh, yes, I see it here now. I overlooked it somehow before. I was kind of taken aback by that love quote. It's really a beautiful one. I've never seen *Les Miserables,* but now I really want to."

"Maggie." Zig snapped his fingers, "focus."

"Oh yes, of course, sorry, alright, so let's assume everything she said is a clue to who these people are. Let's get our papers out again." I was getting excited, we were on a mission, we could figure this out, I was confident of that, I'd never felt so self assured. "We can still call the cops," I said, "but let's see what we can find out from this first. We'll have more to give them. Agreed?" I asked hopefully.

To my astonishment, they both nodded and said, "Agreed."

"Let's start with the Les Mis quote first. Who wrote it?" I asked.

"Victor Hugo," Brian answered.

"OK, write that down," I told Zig. Now, what is the name of the character who said it?"

"Jean Valjean," Roberts answered again using a French accent for it.

"But it could be John?" I asked. "Jean is John in French?"

"Yes, you're right of course, but couldn't she have found a simpler way of communicating the name John to us?" he asked.

"That makes sense," I said. "Ok, what else?"

"The bird, Nathan Lane," Zig said, already writing it as he spoke.

"Her bird's name is Nathan Lane?" I asked Zig.

"Yeah, she has always named her birds after stage actors, the *colorful* ones," he answered.

"Awww, I love your mom," I said. "Oh, and Don Ameche, I know the name, but I'm sure I never saw him in anything. Oh, wait, yes I did, he was in Cocoon right?"

"I don't believe I saw that film," said Brian.

"Nope, me neither," said Zig

"You guys, really?" I asked. "It's a classic. These old people find a swimming pool. . . oh, I forget where, but anyway, the pool has these big cocoons at the bottom of it, and they all start to feel young again, like a fountain of youth. I don't remember a lot else about it but it was pretty good. The lady who played Edith Bunker was in it and the old guy with the big mustache that sells diabetes stuff on TV and. . . ."

"Maggie?" Zig interrupted, snapping his finger.

"Yes?" I answered.

"We were talking about the name Don."

"Oh, yes, sorry. I got carried away again. Alright, what have we got so far?" I asked Zig.

"Nathan, Don, Jean, and Victor," said Zig, "and before you ask, no, none of those names mean anything to me."

"Although she never actually said the names Victor, Nathan or Jean, did she?" said Brian. "I believe the only actual name she said in front of them was Don. I could be wrong but if those names were connected in any way, she would not have felt free to say them to us. What do you think?"

"Yeah, good point," said Zig. "I think your theory has some holes in it," he told me.

"Yes, I agree," I said, a little discouraged. "But I still think she was telling us something in her own language, the language of show business."

I was beginning to feel energized again, I knew I was right.

"We have to start to think like her," I said. "Now, Zig, you grew up with her in the biz, Brian, you like to. . well, you know a lot about it, and I'll . . . I'll Google. Let's start with Don Ameche and work our way backwards, Brian, your computer?"

"Oh yes, of course, good idea" he said, "I'll go get it, it's just in the other room."

When he left, I spoke quietly to Zig, " Do you want me to call Detective Gonzales?"

He was swirling the ice in his glass, staring at the cubes, and took a long moment before answering. "Yeah, go make the call ...no, wait. Right now they aren't making any threats but if they find out we have police involved, it could get ugly. I'm scared of making the wrong call, of screwing this up."

"You've had no sleep, no food and three of those," I pointed to his empty glass. "Let me fix you some food and coffee so you can make a decision with a clear head. I'm not going to give you advice because, frankly, I don't want that kind of responsibility. You're the only one who can make that call, but I think you should do it when you're at a hundred percent."

He looked up at me, weakly, without speaking.

Brian entered the room, stopped and looked at us.

"What are my choices?" asked Zig.

"To see what we can find out on our own," I said. "Or we let Brian do his thing tomorrow with the vote, and we can still call the local police or Gonzales, or any combination thereof."

"No," said Zig, "I meant what kind of sandwiches?"

ENGULFED
CHAPTER TWENTY NINE

Don Ameche had a roll in *Alexander's Ragtime Band* and played Alexander Graham Bell in the movie of the same name, so I jotted down the name Alexander alongside the others we had already listed.

"You know that after Don Ameche played Alexander Graham Bell, people started referring to the phone as the *Ameche*? I'd never heard that before had you?" I asked Zig and Brian. "Like, Hey, you're wanted on the Ameche."

The two men looked at me expressionless.

"Sorry to interrupt, I just thought that was a cool factoid," I said a bit dejectedly.

Their expressionless looks continued, they resumed their conversation and I went back to Google. Ameche was in Vaudeville, but no plays that I could find.

"Zig," I interrupted again, "Your mom was in movies too, right?"

"Yeah, no starring roles but yeah, she was in quite a few," he said without looking up from his notes, his uneaten sandwich, or the glass of scotch that was down to only ice.

"Back in the 40s and 50s probably, right?"

"She was too young for the 40s except maybe late 40s,50s some 60s too, but early 60s, and then she moved back to New York to work Broadway."

"OK, gotcha. I'm going to *Internet Movie Database* now," I mumbled aloud and was ignored. I snacked on carrots and dip from the tray in front of me. Some dip fell onto the keyboard, unnoticed by the men, thank goodness, and I wiped it away with my sleeve.

"Apparently she wasn't in any movies with him," I yelled over to them.

"Him, who?" Brian asked.

"Don Ameche," I said.

"Ok," he mumbled back.

"I'm moving on to Nathan Lane now," I said. 'That's funny, don't you think, two Nathan's in one week. Say, you don't think she was referencing Nathan Gonzales do you? I'm going to write his name down too, it's too uncommon of a name for it to be a coincidence."

Getting no response I continued. "What are you guys up to?"

Brian held his stack of papers off the table to show me, "I'm going over everyone and everything associated with this bill I'm introducing tomorrow. I want to see if I can link any one company, shareholder, or CEO, to anything she told us, so far, no luck."

"And I'm writing down the names of all the plays I remember her in," said Zig. He threw his pen on the table and leaned his head backward.

"I wish I had paid more attention. I was too busy working on my own damned career to pay much attention. Damn it."

Zig's moroseness, though understandable, was beginning to get on my nerves.

"It's OK," I said, in my most cheerful, upbeat tone of voice, "I can get most of that on here. I've already written down any movies she was listed in the credits for, and Google gave me the names of some of the plays, the one's she starred in anyway."

"She was almost never the star, always a supporting role or stand in. There have to be a hundred of them," Zig said. "I think we're wasting our time. It was a good idea Maggie, but she wasn't leaving us clues. She was scared and confused; I'm convinced that's all it was. She was honestly just babbling."

I was not convinced. Even though I'd met her only briefly and this was her son speaking, I still believed she knew exactly what she was saying. He was scared, but I was determined. He was too close to be objective.

I was not, however, convinced that we should not call the police. Despite what they show in the movies, I was pretty sure they could help us and not put her in jeopardy.

"We'll plug away for a while longer, and then we can compare notes and decide where to go from there," I said. "OK?"

The three of us spent the following hours going over every word Dorothy had spoken to any of us over the past days and weeks. We turned over all the events, people and places we could recall in the days leading up to, and since the death of, Doctor Haney and now the abrupt disappearance of Dorothy this morning. The men who were holding her were obviously connected to Haney and probably also to the still silent, Senator Mitch Waldon.

The copious amount of coffee we drank was taking its toll on my digestive system; and a feeling of nausea mixed with fatigue sent me to seek some fresh air out on the penthouse balcony. The night was cool, and the senator had graciously come out to drape a jacket over my shoulders, and then left me to enjoy the quiet my mind so desperately needed.

Voices drifted up from other balconies and open windows below. Washington D.C. is a late night city, I mused, where meetings take place in the dark, over drinks and cigars, in settings that do not include offices with secretaries and computers.

I closed my eyes and tried to concentrate on the voices coming from the apartment directly below me. The smell of pipe tobacco began filling my nostrils and I opened my eyes to see where it was coming from. I turned and saw the glass doors leading to the apartment were closed and there was no sign of either Zig or Brian inside. The pipe smell was getting stronger and the fog of smoke was now so thick I could no longer see the city lights that had been so clear to me just seconds before. I groped my way to the glass doors of the apartment. They were locked shut.

"Hey! You guys! The door's locked. Guys?!"

The voice I heard answer me did not, however, come from inside the apartment but from behind me, from the balcony, from the balcony railing to be precise. The voice was coming from the seagull perched there, pipe in beak, cloth hat over his head and cloth cape covering his feathers.

The smoke began clearing rapidly except for a small circle of the stuff puffing out of the bowl of his pipe. His left wing came forward, somehow grabbed the thing, and he began to speak.

"We had a date, you know."

"Nathan?" I asked "Is that you? In all the smoke you look like…wait…you are a… damnit, I cannot believe this happening again!" I closed my eyes and willed myself to wake up. "He's not real, he's

not really here," I told myself aloud.

"Do you reject that which your own eyes tell you is the truth?" He took another puff on his pipe, and spoke again. "You are not going to solve the puzzle here. The pieces are all down there." He extended his left wing, the stump of the pipe hidden in the feathers, and motioned downward.

The sun was just beginning to rise, coloring the sky with hints of purple light. The landscape was shades of only black and white, except for the orange glow coming from directly beneath us. The desire to see the source of that warm light was tempered by my fear of what I knew to be the hallucinogenic state I was in.

"I don't care if you're a real talking seagull or Sherlock Holmes with feathers, I'm not going near that railing. I've seen enough movies to know that's a bad idea."

"Don't be absurd. Only fools or those inclined to end their lives fall from railings, you are merely seeking answers to a truth that will be plain to see if you just look in the right place."

Aware that I was moving closer, and unable to stop myself from doing so, I was being pulled by the sounds of an ocean…of waves. They were becoming clearer and louder, emanating from the unknown scene below me.

My guide took off his little cloth hat and bowed to me in a grand gesture. "I must go home now, and so must you." He flew upward, circled and then dove, as I had seen gulls do when feeding.

I know what's down there; it's the sea, I thought. That's Sherlock Seagull's home but not mine. What does he mean that I must go home and why am I listening to advice from a seagull detective imposter? Only a crazy woman would imagine a thing like that. I knew it would be crazier still to actually place any relevance to it.

Inching still closer to rail I thought, but he is so wise. I'm certain he wants me to see something important; why else would he fly all the way up here? Dorothy is down there, the sea is down there, Sherlock Seagull is there and all my answers are there.

The sound of waves grew louder. A steel drum was playing, and I began moving my head to the beat. The sun was warming me and the sounds and smell of the sea felt like home.

"You are right Sherlock," I yelled to the sky, "this is home."

The high rise hotels were stacked like dominoes in a straight, unbreakable line, as far as my eyes could see. The blue ocean waters were to my left and a waterway to my right. I know this place, I was just here. This is South Beach, I thought, this is Miami.

"Oh Sherlock," I said again to the sky, "you crazy seagull, you brought us to Miami. Don Ameche was in the movie *Moon Over Miami* and Nathan Lane was in *The Birdcage* here on South Beach. All the clues were leading us to Miami, to South Beach to…"

Sherlock circled and dove again, straight down, just below me.

"I know Sherlock, I know," I said to him, "you're pointing me to the exact spot. I'm going, I'm going."

The sun was gone now, the beach, the steel drum band, the ground beneath my feet, all gone now. In the seconds it took for me to climb over the rail, the dream was gone, only to be replaced by a nightmare. I was dangling over the side of a tenth floor balcony.

"Help!" I screamed out. "Help, help, help!"

My arms hurt, my hands were sweaty and I'd only been holding on for seconds.

"Help! Help!"

Maybe I can pull myself up if I can just get a better grip, I thought. I took one hand off briefly, wiped the sweat onto my shirt, and then repeated that with the other hand.

"OK! One, two, three and...urggghhhh..."

I pulled up, hit my chin on the rail and dropped back down, hanging on by sheer force of will.

"Oh for God's sake, I can't believe I'm going to fall to my death because I can't do a pull up!" I yelled aloud.

"Excuse," came a voice from the balcony below. "I have sleep. You please to make noise less please."

"Help! I'm going to fall," I yelled down to the voice, "Please help me."

I looked below my dangling feet to see a short, round, man wearing a trench coat over bare, hairy, legs and feet, standing on the balcony directly below. The only visible part of him not covered in hair was his head.

"You make quick go away?" he asked in his thick accent.

"A get away? No, I climb by accident," replying reflexively in broken English. "Please call 911. I fall soon."

"You are riding lamb?"

"What? Lamb? No, no, I not on lamb, I make boo boo. Help please!"

"You want I up go?"

"Yes, please," I yelled to him, "Yes Yoda, up go! Hurry!"

He disappeared and I could hear voices, his and a woman's, coming from his apartment. "Oh up go! Please up go" I yelled again.

My hands were growing numb and would soon lose their ability to grip the rail.

A woman's voice came from below now, "Haji is up go stairs to help crazy American lady. Is stupid idea to you do that here."

I noticed the only three words put together in proper sequence were *crazy American lady*.

"Please, tell him to hurry, crazy lady going to fall." I yelled down to her kerchiefed head.

She remained there, staring up at me, making *tsk tsk* noises.

Maybe I won't die, I thought. Maybe I'll just be in one of those body casts with pulleys on my legs and arms, and my head will be bandaged except with openings for my eyes and mouth and I'll drink milkshakes through a straw. I'll be able to say *No, I don't remember anything after I let go. I didn't feel any pain at all.*

Then, just as in every movie, or T.V. show I'd ever seen, just as my hands began to slip and death seemed inevitable, voices called my name and strong hands gripped my wrists and pulled me up to safety.

"Maggie, what..." Brian Roberts was stammering, "wha what happened?"

"It's *The Hotel Victor*," I yelled to him and Zig and little Yoda.

ENGULFED
CHAPTER THIRTY

"What? She's where?" asked Zig.

"The Hotel Victor. It's on South Beach, in Miami." I told them.

After a brief explanation of how I had come to be hanging off the balcony, and assurances that no harm had come to me, other than blind terror, the men bombarded me with questions. Well, Zig and Brian were asking questions, my pal Yoda was just standing there, his head moving quickly from person to person, a portrait of intense concentration."I was there, in South Beach just two days ago, with Rod and Leo."

"But why in God's name do you think she's there?" asked Zig.

"Who are Rod and Leo?" asked Brian.

"Well, for starters, Don Ameche was in Moon Over Miami." I said, and Nathan Lane was in The Birdcage, which took place on South Beach."

"Of course," said Zig, giving himself a forehead slap.

"Who are Rod and Leo?" asked Brian.

"Victor was the name of the guy who wrote that quote," I went on. "The one who wrote Les Miserables, remember? We passed by that hotel, Rod and Leo and me, when we were down there. It came to me when I was hanging out there just now."

"What hotel?" asked Zig

"Who are Rod and Leo?" Brian asked again, in a rather exasperated tone.

"There's a hotel down there, it's called The Hotel Victor," I answered

Zig. "She's got to be there! I know it. That's what she was telling us."

"It makes sense," said Brian, picking up some of the papers on the table and thumbing through them, "It all makes sense now."

"You were right," said Zig. "She was giving us clues. Damn she's sharp. I'm ashamed I doubted her."

" Maggie was the only one who never lost faith," said Brian.

"I'm no hero," I said. "I had a hallucination. It was actually a seagull I call Sherlock Holmes that figured it all out. He showed me everything." The senator's face showed so much incredulity, I realized he didn't know about my recent pharmaceutical adventures. "I keep having these drug flashbacks." I told him. "I was drugged by someone last week. Now, sometimes, I have crazy thoughts. I had one tonight, there's usually this seagull..."

"Oh no Maggie," said Brian, interrupting me "are you alright?" he came over and put an arm around me.

I suppose it was just that small gesture that brought all the events of the past few days together, and I began to cry.

Zig walked over and put an arm around me too; the two of them being supportive, me sobbing softly. We stood there like that for a while, in our little group hug, until a voice broke our moment of bonding. It was Haji standing there in his trench coat over bare legs, looking every bit like a flasher, "Who are Rod and Leo?"

The next scheduled flight to Miami was at 6a.m.. Brian threw a couple of things in a bag while I called for a cab. It was agreed that it would be best to keep the senator's activities secret for the next several hours. We didn't know who we could trust at this point. He left instructions with his intern, Seth, that he was not feeling well and did not want to be disturbed. If there were any calls, he was to take a message.

The critical vote would be that night, he had to be back in D.C. for it, but he insisted on coming to South Beach with us. He felt responsible, and, in fact, he was really. I didn't mention that, there was no need. His level of regret and anguish over Dorothy's kidnapping could not be any worse than it already was.

We landed in Miami at 8:30 and were stepping into a cab fifteen minutes later. The driver was throwing our bags in the trunk when I heard a disturbance coming from behind us. I turned to see a man climbing over a woman and child to get into a cab that the woman had clearly been next in line for. The man's hat was pulled down in such a way as to obscure most of his face but he was familiar to me.

"Hey, I know that guy, the one getting into the cab behind us," I said to my companions.

Zig and Brian turned to look, but our cab was already pulling into traffic and a bus was now between us and him.

"Who was it?" Brian asked

"I'm not sure. I think it's the same guy I saw on the plane on our way up to D.C. He looks so familiar to me, but I just can't place him."

I put the palms of my hands over my eyes in an attempt to block out everything external and to try to focus on remembering where I had seen him. It was a futile effort and I gave it up.

"Well, we are being followed, that's for sure. At least I am," I said, glancing, again, out the back window. The two men did the same but we all pivoted our heads back simultaneously when our driver began yelling something I am certain would translate into an obscenity, out of his window. We were close enough to the airport still, to be surrounded by yellow cabs. Not surprisingly, most of them were carrying men as passengers so I gave up trying to spot the one I suspected of following me.

"This is so creepy," I said. "First it was Stanley following me. He never did anything either, just followed me. Now it's this guy. What the hell are they expecting me to do? Do they expect me to lead them to Dorothy? If they are, then they're not the ones who took her. If they're not the ones who took her than who are they? I feel like Paul Newman in Butch Cassidy and the Sundance Kid."

The men said nothing.

"Don't you guys ever watch movies?"

Again, more blank looks.

"They were being followed by these guys who were really, really good at tracking." I continued. "Paul Newman kept asking, "Who are those guys?""

Zig and Brian just looked at each other, then Brian said, unconvincingly, "Oh yeah, sure, of course."

"Never mind," I said and grabbed up my purse, took out my cell.

There were messages from Jan, my kids, and my mother but nothing from Nathan. Zig looked at me questioningly.

"He's probably really pissed at me." I said.

"Maybe he's just really busy, or he thinks you are. Why don't you call him?" Zig said. "We may need him later anyway."

"I'll wait until we have your mother back with us," I said. "Unless you've changed your mind about doing this without the police."

"No, we've gotten this far without making the kidnappers feel threatened, let's see if we can resolve this with the least amount of interference possible," he answered.

In the time it took us to exit the airport and enter the interstate, the puffy white clouds overhead darkened and grew larger. By the time we got to Biscayne Bay the skies opened up with a fury and rain obscured our visibility to a distance you could measure by inches. The cab's wipers were whipping back and forth at a frantic pace, but not nearly as fast a pace as our driver's hands on the car's horn.

Brian Roberts was good at looking very un-senator-ish. Wearing a ball cap embroidered with the logo for Precious Piglet Barbecue, a faded *Three Stooges* sweat-shirt, and a day's worth of stubble on his face, no one recognized him as the junior senator from Florida. Some people did a double take, but by the time they caught sight of the dancing pig wearing a tutu and crown on the back of his hat, they immediately dismissed the notion. Now that we were about to enter The Hotel Victor, however, we were not confident our kidnappers would be as easily fooled, so we had him wait in the cab, circling the block, cell phone at the ready.

Since I was not able to hallucinate the room number where Dorothy was being held, and since we felt knocking on all 250 doors might arouse suspicion, our plan was to very quietly, show Dorothy's photo around to some of the cleaning women. We had decided not to try any of the front desk staff, since that too, might somehow alert our foes. For all we knew, someone there could be a conspirator. The odds of the cleaning crew being included in that seemed unlikely, at best.

None of the ladies we questioned spoke a word of English, but since our request was simply," have you seen this woman?" A pointed finger, a shoulder shrug and some raised eyebrows were all the pantomime necessary to bridge the communication gap. So far, none of them had, but not knowing how many cleaning ladies there were, we could not be sure we had questioned everyone possible.

"Let's go out by the pool and ask some of the cabana boys," I said.

"Maggie, do you not see the rather large gaping holes in that idea?" Zig asked.

"You mean because it's raining?" I asked "I know, but I'm sure they still hang out there waiting for it to quit."

"Raining? It's not raining," Zig said sardonically. "It's a deluge, a monsoon, a flood, it's like weather from the Bible out there, you're not gonna' find any cabana boys there and even if they were, they're not going to recognize my mother. Do you suppose the kidnappers allowed mom to lie about in a lounge chair requesting towels and bottled water from the pool staff?"

He was right of course, but I didn't want to admit it. I stubbornly said, "Well, you never know until you try. I'll be right back."

Sometimes I behave very stereotypically female. I hate when I do that but since it is probably programmed into my DNA or something, I feel I've been given no choice in the matter. This was one of those times. I stood out by the deserted pool area, my clothes absorbing enough water to fill a wading pool, my shoes becoming size seven canoes, and my hair sending rivulets of water into my eyes. "Yep," I said aloud to no one, "this was pretty stupid."

Now, the odds of the door I walked out of being locked on the inside are pretty good for someone with the week I've been having, so I was actually not even mildly surprised when the handle did not give way for me. Neither was it surprising that there was no one there to see or hear me to let me in. Since it was impossible to get any wetter, I proceeded calmly to find an open door. The next closest one was also locked, naturally.

A very bright bolt of lightning and loud crash of thunder causing me to trip over a lawn sprinkler and bleed from my knee; neither was surprising. There was, however, a surprising lack of gallantry on South Beach. No one offered to come to my aid as I sloshed about from pool area to the open kitchen door where the cook staff was gathered to smoke and converse loudly in Spanish, to the side entrance where I decided to wait for a moment, under a small awning. Zig had been right, there was no end in sight for this storm. The best I could do would be to wait outside for Brian to come circling back in the cab and get in with him, since there was no way to go unnoticed, looking like a five foot drowned rat, dripping my way across the hotel lobby.

Standing in my only sheltered spot, I could hear someone from a window above me. It was a woman's voice singing, It Was a Very Good Year. "Not so much for me," I yelled up.

The cab, with Brian in it, pulled up to the front entrance. I knew it was our cab because I recognized the vulgarities emanating from within. I couldn't understand any of them, but they were familiar nonetheless.

Our driver said something to me that sounded like he was not happy about my getting his lovely cab wet and I was pretty sure he asked Allah to smite me. Next, we picked up Zig, who was waiting under the front door canopy. He was also not happy about me dripping water on him, but he, at least, did not wish me damned, at least I didn't think so. I, however, did not care.

"I take it you didn't get anywhere?" Brian asked us.

I'm not sure," Zig said and then turned to me, "you get any good tips from the pool boy?"

"She's in there. I'd bet all I own that I'm right," I said. "I say it's time to call the cops. We're like The Hardy Boys meet Nancy Drew here. This is too serious for amateurs. We've figured out enough for the cops to be able to go in there and get her now. I'm calling Nathan." I pulled my cell phone out.

"You're right of course Maggie," said Brian, "We can't run around here like teenagers playing cops and robbers, and that's what we're doing. Our time is over now, let the..."

"Wait a minute!" I said more to myself than anyone, "It was a very good year...when I was what? Seventeen?"

"What are you talking about?" asked Zig.

"Maggie. Are you feeling alright?" Brian asked worriedly.

"What are some of the other ages, in the song, the Frank Sinatra song, you know, 'when I was seventeen, it was a very good year,'" I began singing. The voice was Dorothy's, the one I heard singing the song. At least, I'm betting it was. What if the room number was one of those...Shit...come on guys...what are some of those years?"

"Twenty one and....ummm...thirty five I'm pretty sure," said Brian.

"Hey, Mister Ambassador," I said to our driver, tapping his shoulder, "take us back to The Hotel Victor."

ENGULFED
CHAPTER THIRTY ONE

The three of us were walking hunched over, as though we would be less visible somehow in that posture. We took up position behind a row of hibiscus bushes, near the spot I had been standing when I heard Dorothy sing.

"Can you see anything familiar from here?" Brian asked.

"I think one of my contacts washed away when I was looking up," I said. "But I'm pretty sure it was not from the first floor. That only leaves us three floors, times the three years, that's, ah, nine, nine rooms."

"I think we should stay out here for a little longer, see if we can spot her from one of the windows, if that's what you two think," said Brian, "or we could do something else." His Precious Piglet hat was keeping the rain from hitting him directly in the face, so he had the best view. "I mean, she knows we're here, that's obvious from her singing when you were there, don't you think? She saw you and she'll be looking for you now. I'll bet she makes another move."

"As soon as we get her out of there, I'm going to kill the guys who took her," said Zig. "I'm going to beat them to death with my bare hands and I'm gonna' laugh the entire time."

It was difficult to take those words seriously since his face was currently framed in the bright yellow flowers of the bush he was hiding in. He was closest to me, Brian a few yards further still, crouched behind his own bush of bright pink hibiscus.

Having only one contact, I had to close my uncorrected right eye to be able to focus, so I had no depth of field. I looked all around trying to get my eyes to focus when I saw something that looked very much like the thing that ate Doctor Haney. It looked prehistoric and evil and its eye was on me, its malevolent, terrifying eye.

No sound came when I tried to speak; my feet and legs had become petrified. My thoughts turned to Jurassic Park, the man telling the kids to hold still. I opened my mouth again but only gasps came out.

Brian was in my periphery but I couldn't do anything to signal him. The thing moved its head to the side with its demonic eye looking right at me. Sound came from me at last and my wooden limbs animated.

"Oh my God, Oh my God, Oh my God! Run! Run! There's an alligator coming toward us." I screamed as I ran toward the back of the hotel, the two men close behind. I knew gators could move fast, and I was wearing sandals and *it* wasn't. Zig and Brian were next to me and each grabbed an arm and pulled me with them, my feet off the ground.

When we stopped behind a dumpster, out of breath, we turned to see where the gator was.

"Wait, Maggie," Zig said, "Is that what you saw, there, by that short palm tree?"

I craned my neck from my position behind the senator and saw the thing, unmoving, in its same spot.

"That's a friggin' Iguana, Maggie," Zig said, looking heavenward, hands over his eyes, shaking his head. He looked back at me. "Don't you ever leave your house? How can you not know the difference between an alligator and..."

Brian interrupted him. "Zig, that's a very large iguana. Maybe three feet head to tail, and Maggie lost her contact," he was saying as he turned his head from side to side, trying to see me from my position of hiding behind his back.

"Have you guys noticed it stopped raining?" I said eager to change the subject.

"Why don't Zig and I stay here and watch the windows, while you get back in the cab and find a place to buy us some dry clothes," Brian suggested, "you did a great job alerting us to danger by the way. Well done Maggie." He pulled out his soggy wallet and handed me a credit card.

"We passed a lot of shops on our way here," I said. "Some are practically just across the street. I'll be right back."

I ran back to my amiable driver, who, after watching me drip more water on his seat, cursed loudly, spat out his window, and drove me, very quickly, to a beach shop one block down the road. He agreed to wait only when I handed him a twenty. He merely pantomimed spitting this time, and gestured that he would circle the block only one time. I assume that was what he meant with his pointed index figure, unless it meant something altogether different in his culture.

I was able to rejoin the men in less than fifteen minutes with dry clothing for all of us. They had not seen any sign of Dorothy from their look out position and it was decided we would all go to the rest rooms in the ice cream shop next door to change into dry clothes.

It turns out they are rather strict about the restrooms being only for paying customers at Katie's Kreamy Kones. I was not as bothered by this fact as the men seemed to be.

The men changed and rejoined me where I sat enjoying a scoop of Katies's Kokonut with hot fudge topping. Now, I knew that if they had been shopping for themselves, or if I'd had a bit more time to look, they would not be wearing what they presently were, but I had not thought they would be quite as shocked by their new apparel as they seemed to be now.

"It was a tourist beach shop," I protested. "And Ali Baba was not willing to wait very long."

"You know, I don't know what surprises me the most," Zig said, "The fact that there *is* such a thing as a Sponge Bob camouflage t-shirt or that you bought one; no, not one, two of them."

"They were buy one get one free," I said.

"Brian and I look like we're going steady. We look like two simple minded, gay, deer hunters."

"You don't look at all like deer hunters," I said. "Are you guys getting ice cream?"

Brian took my arm as we walked back into the hotel and thanked me for getting the clothes, and for all I had done to help him and Zig and Dorothy. His smile was warm and genuine and I realized that I did not want him to lose his job as senator either. No wonder Dorothy was going to such lengths to protect him.

"I'm certain Zig is very grateful for all you are doing to help us and his mother. He is just deeply worried and it's making him ill tempered," he said to me with a reassuring hug around my shoulder.

"Oh, I know that, but thanks for saying it anyway."

The man at the front desk smiled and nodded at us as we walked through the lobby and then looked back down at whatever he was doing on his computer. That felt like a small relief, his obvious indifference.

We rode the elevator to the fourth floor, the doors opened and a woman with a small child was waiting to enter.

"Sponge Bob!" the little boy exclaimed, pointing to Brian.

The woman muffled a laugh and got on as we got off.

Walking down the hall, the men decided to stay back while I knocked on doors 417, 421, and 435. Putting my ear to the first and hearing children's voices within, I moved on to the next. There was something playing on the television there that sounded like a Spanish language soap opera. I moved on to the last, and knocked. My pounding heart and sweaty palms made me realize how frightened I was. It had just hit me that there could be men with guns on the other side of the door. I could taste Katie's Kokonut making its way back up. I was bent over in case the worst happened, when the door opened to a pair of men's dress shoes. There was a fat, middle age man attached to them. He smelled of cheap cologne and, I thought, pastrami. I could smell something else too, something familiar from inside the room.

"Can I help you?" he asked in an annoyed, Boston sounding accent. When I straightened up he stared at the front of my shirt. It was hot pink with the words, *Beach Blondes Have More Fun,* across the front, it was on sale too. He grinned creepily.

"Wrong room, sorry," I said and quickly walked away, feeling his eyes on my back.

Zig and Brian were waiting around the corner by the elevators.

"She's in there," I said excitedly. "I smelled gardenias."

ENGULFED
CHAPTER THIRTY TWO

"I'm calling Nathan," I said, pulling my cell phone from my pocket.
Zig and Brian turned their heads simultaneously in the direction of the hall I had just come from.

"Someone's coming," Brian said in a stage whisper, frantically pushing the elevator button.

"Act like we're not together," I told them.

The men looked at each other's shirts and then at me.

"Well, act like you're a couple. Hurry!"

Zig put his arm around Brian's waist and took his turn punching the elevator buttons. Brian began humming something indistinct.

"No signal," I whispered loudly, "See? Only one bar, nope, now it's gone," I turned my phone toward them. They sighed in unison.

"I have AT&T," I whispered again, putting the phone back in my pocket.

Footsteps came closer and rounded the corner toward us. It was him, the creep from the door. I smiled at him, "Hello again. Turns out I'm in the wrong hotel" I gave a weak laugh. "You on vacation?"

He looked at me warily, then looked at the men who were both staring at their shoes.

Following the rules of Murphy's Law, my phone rang, just as the elevator door opened. No one made a move to get in.

It was Nathan's name on the caller ID, "I'm at the Hotel Victor, in South Be…" I began, when the Boston Creep turned and began running down the hall.

The three of us took up the chase.

Zig was the first to get to our man just as he opened the door, pushing him in, with Brian and me close behind. We tackled him football style.

"Where's my mother you rotund piece of horse shit?" Zig asked the man who was gasping for breath from beneath the human pyramid we had created.

"I don't think he can talk, or breathe actually," I said. "And I don't know where my arm is. Wait, no, it's here, under your chest, but I can't move it."

"Maggie," Brian said gently, "I'm going to move slightly, please don't take offense if…"

"Oh for Christ's sake Brian, I'm not a nun, just move, you're breaking my ribs." I told him.

"I've got his ankles," said Brian, "but he's quit kicking, is he dead?" Zig grabbed the man's head by his hair, but the head fell back to the floor with the hair remaining in Zig's hand.

"He passed out," said Zig "and before you panic, this is a toupee."

"What are you doing?" I asked Zig. A hand was moving under my knee. My leg touched something hard and metal.

"A gun! He's got a gun!" I shouted and jumped up and then back down on top of Zig, attempting to pin our bad guy more firmly to the floor. Brian was on his knees behind us, looking for the gun. The four of us struggled, arms, legs and heads, all flailing about wildly. My head hit Brian's chin, knocking him backwards with a shout of pain. I turned back and saw the gun again, still attached to a hand, but this time aiming upward, toward the ceiling. I grabbed the hand and bit down hard. The gun fell to the floor and a scream came from Zig followed by a flood of expletives. Our kidnapper rose to his feet and, looking at where the gun had fallen and made a move toward it, but I had grabbed it first and aimed it at him. Zig was on my right.

"Tell me where my mother is," Zig demanded again, blood dripping from his bite wound, "Or we'll…"

"Yeah," I interrupted.

Zig gave me an angry look.

"Well, I have a gun now." I whispered loudly out of the corner of my mouth. I turned back to the man I was aiming at, "Tell us where Dorothy is or…"

"Or what?" our captive asked. "You gonna shoot me, or is the other cheese guy gonna' iron me to death?"

Zig and I turned to look at Brian who was standing behind us with an iron in one hand and a table lamp in the other.

"I figured we could use the cords to tie him up," he said, "if you think that's a good idea."

"Down on your stomach, lard ass," Zig said.

"I don't think so, cheese queer," he responded.

I aimed the gun at the floor next to him and fired, causing my hand to come back and hit me in the forehead right between my eyes. I had never fired a gun before and hadn't expected that it would jolt like that. It also smelled and hurt my ears. Fortunately, however, I didn't drop the gun, and when I was able to focus again our man was now on the floor, on his stomach.

Brian rushed to him and began tying his wrists and ankles with the electric cords making fairly effective sailors' knots.

"Your mother's in the john with Vincent," the kidnapper said. "Now get the gun away from that nut case before she kills one of us."

Zig walked to the bathroom and I followed, but not before I had my say.

"I'm not a nut case," I said over my shoulder, "and those are not cheese...es, they're sponges."

Zig and I stood outside the bathroom door, He tried the knob; it was locked.

"Dorothy? Are you in there? It's me, Maggie."

A loud curse came from the other side of the door; a man's voice was yelling something in Spanish.

"Maggie dear?" It was Dorothy now. "I'm afraid the man here won't allow me to open the door."

"Then duck down Dorothy, I'm going to shoot the lock and if I hit someone I would prefer it not be you."

"Can you do that?" Zig whispered to me.

"Good God no, can you?" I whispered back.

"Hell, I don't even know if that's possible. We don't have a lot of need for artillery down at WTF." He reached for the gun in my hand. "Hand it to me, carefully, I'll give it a try." He cautiously took the gun from me, aimed it at the knob and began squeezing back the trigger when the door opened.

A tall, skinny, young man appeared in the doorway, saw the gun, jumped back, and stood behind Dorothy. His left hand was bleeding, and he was pressing it to his chest.

"She fucking bit me," he yelled out.

183

"Language, Vincent, language," Dorothy scolded him. "Hello Steven, Maggie, I see you were able to unravel the clues I gave you. I knew you would." She smiled broadly. "I'm an excellent judge of character."

She was sitting on a vanity stool, not a hair out of place, wearing a white cotton skirt, blue tailored blouse and large white pearls around the neck that now had the sharp end of a pair of scissors pointed at it.

"I don't believe you bit my hand," He said in his thick accent.

"You shouldn't have had it over my mouth," Dorothy told him. "Besides, it reeks of after shave, you use much too much."

"Uhmmm. You want to move the scissors?" I asked "You're not going to stab Dorothy with them are you? And besides, in case you didn't notice, my pal here has a gun."

"Why you bleeding?" he asked Zig.

"She bit me," Zig nodded toward me.

"What is with you crazy ladies?" He said, still holding the scissors at Dorothy's throat, "You can spread disease like that, you know?"

"Vincent, you're not enunciating properly, no one can understand you," Dorothy scolded, "Now please move the scissors. You know you're not going to hurt me; you'll have to go to prison if you do. I was in a movie once where one of the characters had gone to prison. The other inmates did unspeakable things to him there," she said rising from the stool and smoothing out her skirt. "I'm sure you know what I mean dear. If you give up now, you'll probably get to go to one of those nice facilities instead, where politicians and bankers and television evangelists get themselves incarcerated."

He dropped his weapon and his jaw.

Zig went to Dorothy and moved her away from Vincent, hd had his arm around her shoulder. The sounds of police sirens were getting closer.

"Are you wearing make up?" I asked Vincent, trying to distract him until the police arrived. "You look kind of like a... I'm not sure, what does he look like to you Zig?"

"He looks a little like an old lady in some parts." Brian said, walking up behind us.

Vincent turned to look at himself in the mirror, turning his head side to side and examining his reflection carefully. We stood behind him, all of us staring at his face now.

"Yeah," I continued, "but kind of like a pirate too. Why are you wearing old lady pirate make up?"

Dorothy answered, "I was teaching him the art of disguise when you all burst in. I thought it would be a useful skill in his line of work."

The sirens were outside the windows now.

"Ziggy, put the gun down before the police mistake you for one of the kidnappers and shoot you. Brian dear, give Vincent a damp face cloth and some soap; he can't look like that in his police photos.

ENGULFED
CHAPTER THIRTY THREE

"Wait a minute; you're watching C-Span?" Jan was asking me. "And if you detect a note of incredulity in my tone, it's because," and here she raised her voice very loudly, "that is not what any sane woman would be doing if they had a couple of weeks off and were five minutes from a beach filled with half naked guys lying about on towels!"

"Hang on," I said, "here comes the good part. Ha! Look at that Waldon, crawling away like a cockroach under a baseboard."

"Sorry, I'll have to wait for it to come out on DVD," Jan said, her voice dripping with sarcasm.

Ignoring her, I jumped up and cheered, "The bill failed!"

"I'm excited for you, even though I don't know what the hell you're talking about. Now, are you coming home? I hate to sound selfish, but planning a wedding is no fun when you do it by yourself."

I turned my attention away from the television, "I'm sorry, I've just got a couple more loose ends to tie up, then I promise I'll fly right back home and we'll try on dresses, talk to snooty florists, harass shoe salesmen and drink margaritas on the top of The Sandia; whatever you want, I'm all yours."

We ended with me promising I'd spend at least one hour sipping a Mai Tai in a beach chair with my toes in the Gulf of Mexico.

I was crossing return calls off of my list like a bookie checking off race horses. The last one was to Rod, well, the last one I was going to return. The calls from Nathan would have to wait until a plausible lie made its way into my brain. The standard one used for everyone else was not going to work for him. There were no good answers to the questions he was going to ask.

Rod had news for me that he wanted to share in person, and we arranged to meet at Dharma House at three. I had to drop by the realtor's office to sign a couple more papers, and had promised to meet Dorothy for lunch at The Shell.

When the doorbell rang, I had a sickening feeling I knew who would be on the other side of the door.

"I know you're in there, I see your eye on the peephole." Nathan shouted from the front step.

"Oh Shit," I said, remembering what I looked like; a tangled mass of hair, a nightgown, probably a stray hair in my chin and my eyebrows gone all native.

"Come on Maggie, I feel like an Amway salesman out here."

"I'm not exactly at my best right now, can you come back tomorrow?"

"No, actually, I can't. This isn't a date, this is police business. As you can see from the blind you just lifted, I am not holding flowers."

"You bring flowers to a date?" I asked, quickly dropping the blind down.

"That is something we can discuss at a later time, don't you think? Right now, your neighbors are all tuned to their police scanners trying to find out if there's a drug bust going on here."

"Are you in a police car?" I opened a slit in the blinds and peeked out again. "What happened to your regular car?"

"I'd have come here in the SWAT van if I thought this was going to be this difficult. I'll give you half an hour to change out of the Hello Kitty gown and whatever else you can get done in the remaining twenty nine."

Ah shit, I wasn't getting out of this. "Alright, alright."

"Thirty minutes, exactly," he said, walking back toward the squad car.

The knock came exactly thirty minutes later according the alarm I set. After spending valuable time juggling my afternoon plans, it gave me only fifteen minutes to do something with myself that included a hat and sunglasses. Glancing in the mirror, I saw, reflected back, what looked like one of those people you see on the news avoiding the paparazzi whilst being escorted into a courtroom.

"You want me to find a dark cafe where you can unscrew the light bulb over our table Al Capone?" Nathan asked, grinning at my get up.

"Ha ha," was my witty retort.

I followed his cruiser in my own car, the drive being so brief the gas gauge didn't even have time register all the way.

"Why here?" I asked, after we were seated on a bench in the park less than a block from my home. "We look like we're conducting a drug deal."

"Maggie," Nathan said, obviously not finding any humor in that. "What really happened in Miami? I got the official report, but I want to hear it from you. A couple of witnesses said there was another man with you besides Zig. They all said that he was even wearing the same shirt as Zig, something to do with cheese."

It was hard for me to keep a straight face at that one.

"That sounds a bit absurd, don't you think?"

"I've seen a lot of absurd in my job."

"Look, I gave my statement to the Miami police. I was there with them for nearly seven hours. Surely you've seen the transcripts of that. I really don't have anything else to add."

"We got a match from a hair sample we got from your house; your parent's house. He's a punk, we've picked him up a hundred times for drugs, B&E, stolen goods, domestic violence..."

"Good God, he was in my house? Did he tell you why he was there? Wait, of course; he was the one who put the candy in my purse right? I hope he stays in jail a good long time this time. Did you ask him why he did that? How did he even get in there?" I felt agitated and was alternately standing and then sitting, pulling off my hat and putting it back on. "He is in jail right? Should I go see if I recognize him? Will he be behind one of those two way mirrors with the feet and inches thing behind him?" I sat back down.

Nathan started speaking to me but another idea came to me and I stood up again. "Why me? Did he tell you why me? I mean, I'm nobody. Why would he come into my house and put drugged candy in my purse? It makes no sense." I looked heavenward then back at the detective. "Nathan, you're making no sense."

He looked back at me in a kind of stunned silence, and then shook his head. "Asombroso," he said under his breath.

"What was that?" I asked. "I didn't hear you. Was that some kind..."

"We can't talk to him, he's dead. He jumped from a window; the third floor of an apartment, but he hit...it doesn't matter."

I reached for my sunglasses on the top of my head. "Where are my sunglasses? I had them on when I left the house."

"Your sunglasses are on your face." He stood up and grabbed my shoulders. "Stay with me now, it's ok."

"Oh Christ!" Every drop of saliva dried up in my mouth and a feeling of nausea rolled over me.

"Listen to me," he said looking directly into my eyes, "the coroner said he had found much of the same compound of drugs in him that we found in you."

"Oh Christ!" I pulled my hat off again and the sunglasses fell to the ground. I just stood there staring at them, unable to move.

"I need you to start confiding in me, trust me please. You are in way over your head and so are your friends. I don't want to see any of you hurt. Do you believe me?"

"I wanna go home," I said, beginning to cry. "Really, I'm done; I just want to take the first plane out of here. Why in God's name I ever thought I could..."

"You can. *We* can. You're clever and smart and you have good instincts and people like you. If you'll work with me on this, I promise I can not only protect you, I can protect your friends too. I'm not the enemy."

"Al Franken," I said.

"Who?"

"Al Franken. I'm good enough, I'm smart enough, and dog-gone it, people like me."

Nathan looked at me bewildered. "Is this a drug reaction again?"

"No," I said, "It's Stuart Smalley, from Saturday Night Live. You know, daily affirmations? You just reminded me when you said..." I saw his confused face and gave up with a shrug. "Never mind."

The tinkley sounds of *A Bicycle Built for Two* were getting closer. "Come on," I said, "Buy me some ice cream and I'll tell you everything I know."

ENGULFED
CHAPTER THIRTY FOUR

I drove in and out of two thunderstorms in the twelve or so miles from my parents' house to Dharma House. I mused about opening a store that sold only tropic related necessities like windshield wiper blades, antiperspirants, bug repellant, and maybe guides on how to identify and escape from reptiles, complete with pictures and diagrams. What would I name such a place? *Tarzan and Jane's Jungle Emporium* sounded catchy, but probably too much for a sign or business card. I would continue to contemplate that at another time I told myself.

Rod had not answered when I called to let him know I'd be running a bit late. That was not unusual for him since he was usually having group sessions, meditating, or practicing yoga or one of those other disciplines that require white pajamas with colored sashes. Today, I could see he had his band of merry men sitting in a circle under a tree. In the center of the circle stood a statue about four foot tall representing God only knew who. As I got closer I heard the sound of melodic chanting, the type you associate with monks, coming from a boom box on the ground. One of the men was beating a drum. "That's not how you do it," said the man next to him, wearing a Detroit Tigers ball cap, "give it here."

"No," said the man with the drum, "it's my turn, right Rod?"

"Brothers," said Rod, "let us remember the lesson of the drum, it is to set the rhythm or our bodies, we will be in synch with one another."

191

"Well, he ain't doin' it right, I'm not synchin' with him," said the Detroit Lions guy, and folded his arms across his chest.

Rod certainly makes these guys earn their room and board, I thought, I suppose it thins out the less willing and maybe he actually does rehabilitate the ones that stick it out.

I didn't want to intrude, so I went inside to drop of the boxes of pizza and bread sticks I had brought, and heard the sound of someone laughing heartily from the back room.

In the gathering room I saw Errol Flynn; he was watching *The View*! He saw me in the doorway. "You gotta' come see this," he said, gasping for air and wiping tears from his face. "That Whoopi, she is somethin' else, ain't she? Look how she's lookin' over her glasses at the skinny blonde, like she's…there, see? She's doin' it now." He pointed to the screen and started laughing again which produced a cough and then more laughter. "Pull up a chair, this show is great. Hey, ain't you the lady with the pizza? I don't suppose you got any on ya' now, do ya'?"

"Aren't you Errol?" I asked uncertainly. "I thought you hated pizza, and me, and…ya' know…Whoopi."

He wasn't listening to me. He just stared intently at the ladies of *The View,* and burst out with more laughter.

After serving him a couple of slices of pizza and a bread stick, I went back to the front yard to see if the pow wow was winding up. Rod and Leo were helping a couple of men to their feet, when Rod spotted me and waved me over.

"Maggie!" he shouted, "I'm so happy you came. Can you give me five more minutes? Leo," he said, turning to his friend, "take Maggie to the garden room; I'll join you as soon as everyone is back to full awareness."

"Full awareness?" I asked Leo, when he took my elbow and walked me toward the sun room.

"Yeah, Rod gets them into a transcendental state and needs to make sure they're… *not*, in that state." He looked at me and chuckled. "I know it sounds pretty weird, but he's doing a lot of really great work with the men here."

"I can tell. Errol had been completely transformed. He's like a totally different man than the one I'd seen before."

"Errol?" He asked, stopping in his tracks. "When did you see him?"

"Just a couple of minutes ago, when I brought the pizza in, he was watching *The View*. He was actually not a horse's ass to me, *and* he thought Whoopi was hilarious."

"Yes," he said distractedly, "he is responding quite well."

"That's a ginormous understatement," I said. "Oh look, there's Rod. He's with him now."

Rod was seated next to Errol in front of the television, but the set was turned off. Rod said something I couldn't hear, and it made Errol begin laughing again. He helped the older man out of his chair and walked him out of the sun room, stopping only a moment for Errol to bend over, fart at us, laugh, and walk away.

When Rod joined us, Leo excused himself to make a pot of coffee "That Errol has sure mellowed out. You're a miracle worker or something," I said.

"We are shaped by our thoughts; we become what we think. When the mind is pure, joy follows like a shadow that never leaves," he said in a soft, distant voice. He looked back at me. That is from The Buddha. Have you studied him at all?"

"No, but you got Errol to study Buddhism?"

"I think Errol is responding to the love and peace he is now surrounded by here."

"Ok, that's really swell, I'm happy for him. What did you need to talk to me about? You didn't learn that this drug is really some kind of fountain of youth and my wrinkles will start to go away and my sagging body parts will be all ninteenish again did you? Because frankly, that's the only kind of news I'm prepared to hear right now."

"I'm afraid I asked you here a bit prematurely," Rod said. "Leo has contacts at the federal level and they were supposed to have gotten back to him by now. Would it be alright if we meet later? I don't want to give you half information; that would not be fair to you. We can meet later this afternoon if you'd like. You can choose where."

"That's alright I said, it was worth the trip to see Errol watching *The View*. I'll call you when I'm done at the real estate office."

I walked away chuckling to myself remembering Errol laughing along with Whoopi. I thought I might just have to get myself a Buddha book.

After leaving the real estate office, I drove over to a beach shop to look for more souvenirs for my grandchildren and replace the chocolate covered talking dolphin. I needed some normal time. I turned my phone off and just shopped. There is a term for this called *retail therapy* and it's as real and twice as effective as any hour spent in a psychiatrist's office and if you shop right, a lot less expensive.

I threw my purchases in the car and as soon as I turned my phone on it rang.

"Hi Zig, how's your mom?"

"She's doin' great, I swear, I think the entire thing energized her. I'm on my way back to the D.A.'s office to give them my statement."

"Yeah," I said, "I have an appointment to do that tomorrow. Let me know how it goes. Hey Zig, I talked to Detective Gonzales this morning, I told him everything."

"Good, it makes sense to tell him everything. Mom's out of danger and Brian is no longer an issue. And Mags, I'm sorry I messed things up for you, I hope you get to go on that date."

"Well, in the grand scheme of things a date was the least of our worries, right?"

"You know, when I first met you, I thought you were one of those helpless females, but you damn sure proved me wrong. I can't believe what you were able to do. I don't know what I would have done without you, what mom would have done."

"I'm pretty proud of me too. I honestly didn't know I was capable of doing any of the things I did. I feel like...like the me I always wanted to be. I guess I have your mom to thank for that. She put her faith in me, she saw something in me that I didn't even know was there."

"You are one amazing woman Miss Maggie Finn. Too bad you're going back to New Mexico, I think this could have been the start of a beautiful friendship."

"Me too, Bogey, me too."

ENGULFED
CHAPTER THIRTY FIVE

I made my phone call from the boardwalk on Fort Myers beach. It was late afternoon, so the magicians and jugglers were assembling under the tall pedestal clock on the boardwalk. People coming to watch the sunset and sun bathers and families with children leaving for the day, all passed by the clock. It was an ideal place and time for street performing.

"Hi Jan, I've decided to leave a little earlier than I had originally planned."

"I can't say I'm sorry to hear that, but I hope nothing I said made you ditch what you've got going on there to come here and hold my hand."

"No, not at all," I reassured her.

"Well, it's perfect timing anyway. Your sub was going to attend the Balloon Fest gala and I really wanted you to be there instead. We can shop for your ball dress while we're out shopping for me. You can even expense it if you don't go too crazy. You'll probably have to do the shoes yourself, but I'm sure the paper will spring for the dress. I heard some people from Hollywood will be there too. They're here scouting a location for a new movie. They won't say who's in it, but I've heard rumors that they're going to try for George Clooney. Wouldn't it be great if he was a surprise guest?"

I heard her sigh, "You're not listening to any of this are you? Maggie? Are you?"

"What? No, I mean yes, of course I'm listening." I waited a minute, getting up the courage. "Jan? Do you think I'd make a good investigative reporter?"

"Of course you would, you're brilliant. Is that what you want to do now?"

"I don't know. I'm....well, I'm pushing sixty, a little late for a career change don't you think?"

"I think you should do whatever makes you happy. But, it would be impossible to make that move here at *The Herald*."

"I know, it's just that after everything that's happened here I feel like I'm so much more than..."

"Are you having a *just a tad past mid life crisis* Maggie?"

"Oh God, I think I am...again. How many of these are we allowed?"

"Are you kidding? I have one every time I'm in the grocery store and hear an instrumental version of a Beatles song."

After a long silence she came back with, "so, you sound like maybe I'm not picking you up from the airport?"

"Yeah, I guess maybe not."

"Call me tomorrow."

"Ok...Jan?"

"Yes."

"I love you."

"Of course you do, I love you too. Be careful down there."

I called and arranged to meet Rod here on the boardwalk at 6 p.m. Of course, he showed up with Leo in tow. They both looked like they were headed to a Jimmy Buffet concert, Rod in flip flops, shorts, a leather necklace and bracelets with assorted memorabilia dangling from them; Leo with scraggly beard, leather sandals, hoop earring and a Hawaiian shirt open enough to show gray chest hair.

"People keep wanting to meet me outdoors to talk, I feel like a mobster," I said.

"Under the circumstances," said Leo, "I would find that remark most inappropriate." His brows were furrowed and he stood so close to me I had to turn my head up to see him. "You have no idea the risk you're taking with all of us, shining the spotlight on yourself this way."

"Wait! What?" I asked him, "I really don't..."

"If you care so little about your own safety, that's completely your own concern," Leo interrupted, "however, you have put several innocents in grave danger for no apparent reason that I can discern. How does all of this benefit you? What is your game Maggie, or should I be calling you Sonya?"

"Sonya?" I asked, my voice rising several octaves, "who the hell is Sonya?"

"My goodness Maggie, I must say you are very good. I am a trained psychiatrist and you had me fooled. I can't imagine how..."

"Wait just a moment Leo;" Rod interrupted him, "She looks genuinely distressed, you can most certainly see that." He put a hand on my shoulder and his other on my hand, "I think we should all take a moment to sit quietly and allow the healing power of the sea give us the tranquility necessary to break down our fear-based barriers."

I shook free from him and backed away a few steps, "Ok you two, you better start explaining what the hell Leo is talking about. I've got a detective on speed dial here," I pointed my cell phone at them like a weapon, "Leo, start talking, and Rod, stop breathing, I mean, stop doing that breathing with your arms thing, people are staring at us.

"They think we're performers," Rod said, "come on, let's go sit at one of the tables," He took one last deep cleansing breath and then motioned to the restaurant behind us with tables and chairs set up on the boardwalk.

"Leo?" Rod said looking back over his shoulder as his friend remained in the same spot, texting madly on his cell phone. He finally joined us as we made our way toward a table, but hesitantly, his head swiveling back and forth like a yard sprinkler.

"Maggie," began Rod, "I think this may be a good time to tell you that Leo provides his service as a consultant to the DEA..." his voice trailed off as our young server brought us menus and water. After we said we'd be a few minutes, the server left and Rod continued. "He knows people with the U.S. Marshals Service."

With that, they both stared at me like I was supposed to say or do something, Leo scrutinizing intently before leaning back and saying, "Damn, you are good, really really good."

I stared back at him. "You guys are high, right? I mean stoned or however old hippies get when they smoke pot. Either that or you're both just nuts. In either case, I'm outta here."

"Oh no," Leo said, standing up so abruptly that his chair fell backward. "You're gonna sit right here and tell us everything."

"Come on you two, breathe," said Rod, his arms making large circular motions.

Fortunately, no one was paying any attention to us since an even more interesting show was going on under the clock. A young man, dressed as a pirate, complete with eye patch and stuffed parrot on his shoulder, was juggling, doing magic tricks, telling jokes and singing. The only things lacking, in my opinion, were a pair of cymbals between his knees and a monkey.

Leo looked down at Rod who seemed to be praying, and then to me, "Sit down Maggie, we're gonna talk...right now."

"Rod?" I pleaded. He glanced up at me with one eye, then closed it again and started making some humming noise.

"He's going to his happy place," said Leo. "I taught him to use that at times he feels overwhelmed in stressful situations. That technique is actually based on ancient monastic ritual and it is believed that a part of the brain actually..."

Our server came back, interrupting him, bringing us the wine and hummus with pita bread that Leo had ordered.

Rod was back from where ever his mind goes when he's humming, and was emptying his glass of port while Leo continued his lecture on the brain functions of monks. After his second glass of wine, however, he remembered he was angry, and began questioning me again.

"Who is the WITSEC officer assigned to you?" he asked, "I know some of them that work in Florida."

"I know more about quantum physics than I do whatever the hell it is you're talking about," I said. "Maybe you need to start talking first. You're with the DEA and didn't tell me, even after I took that drug? And you have the nerve to accuse me of something?"

"I'm not *with* the DEA, I consult. As a consultant, I have no legal authority. By definition, actually, the law is set up..."

"Leo," I interrupted, "can we please get to the part where you called me Sonya?"

"You really want to do this Maggie? You really want to have this conversation now?"

"No, I think we should talk about the law as it pertains to monks and drug trafficking," I said in my most sarcastic tone and then realized he might think I meant it. "Of course I want to talk about it!"

I yelled this last part so loudly the juggler missed one of his oranges and it hit a baby in a stroller.

"Oh my God, my baby! Is she dead?" screamed the mother.

"It was an orange lady, not a hand grenade!" said the pirate juggler.

"You better hope she's not hurt."

"You're not a very good juggler," said a small boy with an inflatable duck around his middle.

"You wanna' try doin' this duck boy?"

"Watch your mouth, that's my son," said a sunburned man.

"You're right," said the pirate, "sorry kid. Here, pick a card," he fanned the deck in front of the boy.

"Hey, what about the baby you hurt?" yelled an elderly man. "I didn't hear you apologize."

Several women were gathered around the mother and the baby who was apparently not hurt enough to cry but whose mother was carrying on as though it had been impaled by a spear.

"Hey, I'm sorry the orange fell on the kid. But it's that woman over there screaming and carrying on that started it." He pointed at me.

"Yeah lady," said a really fat woman wearing what appeared to be bedspread. "You don't need to be shouting your business interrupting a show and all."

"Why is everyone yelling at me? I'm not the one who hit the baby, it was the pirate," I said.

"That does it," yelled the pirate. He threw down the deck of cards the duck boy was still pondering over and came stomping over to me.

Duck boy screamed out "asshole," to him and was immediately smacked on the back of his head by his father, who was smacked on the back of his head by his wife who yelled at her husband, "asshole."

I watched the pirate make his way to me, his stuffed parrot slipping from its perch and dangling from his back, falling lower and lower until it was bouncing off his backside.

I heard a bark and saw a dog approach us, pulling its helpless owner behind until it broke free of its leash and attacked the bird. I jumped away just in time to see the dog knock the pirate down in front of my feet.

"Help, I'm being mauled by a dog!" screamed the pirate, scarves and oranges falling from his pockets.

"Precious, come back here this instant," screamed the dog's owner, an elderly woman, making her way to us so slowly she seemed to be standing still.

"Look out!" I hollered as I saw one of the oranges roll into the path of a skateboarder. It was too late. He fell and landed on the same baby who had been hit with the first orange.

"My baby!" screamed the mother. "A pervert is molesting my baby!"

"I'm not a pervert," said the kid. "I fell, look, I'm bleeding and everything."

A young woman in a bikini skateboarded up behind him. "What are you doing talking to her?" She turned to the young mother, "Lady, you need to take your skinny ass and your ugly baby and get away from my boyfriend."

Skinny ass mother and jealous bikini girl began their inevitable dance of destiny, with yelling, cursing and name calling that then escalated to pushing, slapping, and hair pulling. Of course, their respective escorts, in an attempt to end the fight, began one of their own.

The dog had the stuffed parrot in his mouth shaking it violently until the head and body of it were severed, feathers flying through the air. The pirate, his eye patch dislodged and covering his nose, crawled to the dog to retrieve his prop, cursing and spitting blood from his mouth. "God damn you bitch, give me back my bird."

"Are you calling that sweet old woman a bitch? The nerve of you," said bedspread woman hitting the pirate in the face with her straw hat.

The crowd had become an enormous herd, moving toward us, making a group noise that sounded like mooing but was probably more like booing, when a policeman on a bicycle showed up and dispersed them.

I heard a motorcycle revving its engine and saw Zig pulling into the parking lot. He made his way toward me, laughing and shaking his head.

"How did you know where I was?" I asked.

"Your cell phone, it pocket dialed me." He looked around the scene and said, "So just an ordinary day at the beach for you huh?"

"Really, none of this is my fault."

"It never is," he put an arm over my shoulder. "Who are the other two stooges?"

We both looked over at Rod and Leo. Leo was tending to the pirate who appeared to be ok but was being busted by the cop for possession. The parrot, it seemed, was holding pot in his little bird head.

Rod was "counseling" the combating couples. I couldn't hear a lot of what he was saying but I heard him say the name Kierkegaard and something about lovers and destiny. Then the skateboarder punched him.

ENGULFED
CHAPTER THIRTY SIX

An hour later, Rod, Leo, Zig and I were sitting inside a dark corner of The Top 'O Mast, drinking beer and hiding from anyone who might recognize, and have cause to blame us, for the fiasco. We had decided to let a little time pass before we ventured out to our respective vehicles.

This is where, over hushed tones, I finally learned what Leo was getting at.

Zig started to grin, then laugh, and then laugh convulsively. "You think Maggie is a mob wife who turned against her husband and is now in witness protection?" He said, trying to whisper but was more effectively snorting. "This Maggie? The one who can't order a sandwich without causing a scene?" He raised his hand to our server. "Another round please, I think we're gonna be here a while."

"Mick? In the mob? Are you nuts?" I was leaning across the table to be sure they heard me in my panicked whisper tones. "He runs a bar, and he's married to a pair of boobs with an idiot attached to them. He's too scared of her and her mother to even wear his shoes in the house."

"Who is Mick?" Leo asked, seemingly surprised by his own confusion.

"What do you mean, who is Mick? Mick is my cretin of an ex-husband who left me for a twenty three year old rock and roll singer. She actually has a tattoo of a pair of breasts on her breast. What kind of woman does a thing like that? I mean, don't you think that's the craziest thing you've ever heard? Oh, and there are some kind of rings pierced through the nipples of the tattoo boobs. Now, is it just me or is that crazy? Of course I've never actually seen her boobs, but my daughter did when they were at the pool and she lowered her straps to get an even suntan. Why would a grown man want to be with such a classless female?"

They were all staring at me with blank looks.

"Oh never mind, I know what you're thinking, what man wouldn't..."

Zig stopped me. "Maggie, you've wandered off topic a bit. And every time you mention her she gets a few years younger. By next week you'll have him marrying her in a past life.

Rod opened his mouth to say something but I looked at him and said, "don't even start."

He closed his mouth and I continued, "You're right Zig, I'll get back to the topic." I paused a moment.

"You forgot the topic, didn't you?" asked Zig.

"No... Yes... No, I remember now. Am I having one of those drug things? Because, this can't all be real." I laid my head down on the wooden table, heavier than I meant to.

"Ow! Damnit!" It felt cool and smelled like varnish and beer. "I'm just gonna keep my head down here for a few minutes. You all continue without me."

"So, Leo," said Zig, "if you're serious that there are people out there that think Maggie here is some kind of mob informant, then that answers the drug question. I guess they figured they could just make her crazy enough not to be a credible witness. I'm not a cop, or ex cop or part time cop like you guys, but that's the way it looks to me."

My head was resting on my folded arms now, but I couldn't bring myself to sit up. I turned just enough to see Zig from the corner of my eye. He seemed to really be on my side so I thought I'd just let him do the talking.

"That is very sound reasoning...um...Zig, is it?"

"My friends call me Zig, you can call me Steve." Zig leaned back and studied the two men while he waited for Rod to pour another beer. "How is it you two know Maggie? Wasn't she with you guys the day she got drugged?"

"Very interesting, the way you've turned suspicion to us," said Leo. "Although you know we did not drug Maggie nor have anything to do with what has happened to her, you decide to question us in such a way as to force us to give away too much in order to attempt to defend ourselves."

I raised my head and looked at Zig again, "Is that what you're doing? I'm incredibly impressed."

"Don't be, I saw it in a movie."

"Really? Which one? I bet I…"

"Maggie."

"Yeah, I know. Get back to the topic. And yes, I remember what it is."

Leo was looking at us grinning.

"What?" I asked.

"The two of you, you remind me of George Burns and Gracie Allen. And before you get offended my dear, I can assure you I have the highest regard for Gracie. She made more sense than people gave her credit for, and everyone loved her. That is you in a nutshell. And as a psychiatrist, I don't use the word "nut" very often."

"Leo, you made a joke," said Rod. "That's very good; I think you're really loosening up since you've been here. We should do more *laughing Buddha* with you later."

I started to ask what Rod meant when Leo stopped me in my first syllable.

"We're not going to discuss that now. What we are going to discuss is why Maggie has been identified as Sonya Ferrari."

"That's a made up name." I said.

"It could be, but probably not," said Leo. "You see the etymology of the name Ferrari is rather interesting since it means *someone who works with steel*, so it is as common in Italy as the name Smith is here in the…"

"Yeah, this is the conversation we need to be having now," said Zig. "You have any more interesting trivia you want to share while we wait for the mob guys to show up?"

"Yes, of course," said Leo. "You're absolutely right Steve, now to the matter at hand. I know some law enforcement officers who believe Maggie is Sonya Ferrari, who is currently under the protection of WITSEC. That's the abbreviated name for witness protection program."

"Yeah, we got that," said Zig, his eyes wandering to a couple of bikini clad women. I nudged him, hard.

"The question we have to ask ourselves is why?" continued Leo, "and, is the drug incident related? We also have the kidnapping of Steve's mother and the death of Doctor Haney at The Shell. All of these events somehow have ties to Maggie here, and all happened just after she arrived."

"Maggie?" Zig was waiting for me respond to that. I had my head back down on the table, the sweat from the day made my arms smell salty where my nose was resting on them. My head ached and I burped up some beer. I was tired, I didn't want to be Wonder Woman anymore, but I'd be damned if I was going to let this trio of men make my decisions for me. That was the old Maggie.

The new Maggie raised her head and looked at them all one by one. "First of all, I was helping Zig, *Steve*, with his mother, and none of what happened to her was my doing. I was actually instrumental in finding her and getting her back. Next, the fact that the US Government can't keep track of who their witnesses are, can hardly be blamed on me. By the way, you *will* take me to these misinformed acquaintances of yours Leo, and they can answer to *me* how they have been given misleading and dangerous information and just passing it on to anyone wearing leather sandals. Next, Detective Gonzales led me to believe that someone from The Sun God was with Doctor Haney the night he was killed and, oh shit I wasn't supposed to say that."

"That's alright, I knew that already," said Leo.

"Of course you did," said Zig.

"You did?" asked Rod.

Leo just glared at his friend who excused himself to go to the men's room.

"The ladies shoe, right?" Zig asked. "The one they thought was mine."

"Hey, good guess Zig," I said as I opened my purse and got out a pen. "The shoe comes from an online store that sells clothing and other stuff to transvestites and drag queens and all." I started writing on a napkin, but since it was wet, it tore.

"Here, take this," said Leo who pulled a small notepad from his pocket.

"No shit? Really? At the beach, in your shorts, you carry a notepad?" asked Zig.

Leo shrugged and handed me the paper. "What are you doing?"

"If we're gonna solve this puzzle, we need to see the pieces."

ENGULFED
CHAPTER THIRTY SEVEN

Nathan's squad car was in front of my parents' house when I got there, and so were five other police cruisers with blue and red lights flashing. The street in front of the house was blocked with barricades, but I could see some EMTs carrying someone on a stretcher to the waiting ambulance. The fact that they didn't seem to be in much of a hurry led me to assume that the person on the stretcher was beyond medical care.

A uniformed officer walked over and shined a flashlight in my car.

"That's my house," I said.

"Are you Margaret Finn?"

"That's me. Can you tell me what happened?"

"Detective Gonzales asked me to bring you to him. There was an incident inside your home," he answered as he opened my door.

The heat and humidity collided with the cool air from the car's a.c. and fogged the windows so that the flashing lights took on an otherworldly image. I felt dizzy, and when I stood, my knees started to buckle.

"Have you had any alcohol this evening Mrs. Finn?"

"What?" I asked him and stared at what looked like a scene from a movie playing out in front of my home. "Are you asking me something?"

"Are you intoxicated Mrs. Finn?" he asked in a louder voice.

"What? No! I had about a half a beer." I had regained my strength and shook his arm free. "Take me to Nathan."

Nathan met me as I got to the front walkway. "What happened?" I stumbled briefly on nothing at all but caught myself before I fell. Nathan grabbed my arm.

"Have you had any alcohol this evening Maggie?"

"Why does everyone keep asking me that? Can't a person just stumble sometimes?"

He was scrutinizing me when I remembered what I must look like; and smell like.

"Oh, well, I was in the Top O' Mast hiding out from...well, no I wasn't hiding, but...I was with Zig and Rod and Leo and I had about a half a beer and do you want to tell me what the hell happened here?"

"Rodney Lawmore from Dharma House?" he asked.

"Yes."

"And Leo Weinstein, the psychiatrist?" he asked, very deadpan, like he was jotting it all down on mental sticky notes.

"Yes," I said in complete exasperation. "Nathan, please tell me what's going on here."

"A man was shot inside your home. There don't appear to be any witnesses except an anonymous call. We think it must be a neighbor who reported hearing a gunshot, but no number came up on our caller I.D. That was at 9:30," he looked at his watch, "about fifty minutes ago."

"Who was he? Where was he? Was he actually *inside* my house, my parents' house?"

"He was found in the hall that leads to the master bedroom. It looks like he was shot there. The body's on the way to autopsy now. The coroner looked at him here and confirmed the time of death was probably 9:30 which coincides with the phone call. We don't know who it is yet. The guys took prints and they're being run now. Maggie, the victim was carrying a Glock, with a silencer on it."

I felt the beer coming back up my throat and bent over. I was definitely going to have to invest in some Pepto.

"Médico," he yelled to one of the EMTs as he put his arm around my waist and the other under my arm.

A man with a stethoscope came rushing up to us and Nathan spoke hurriedly to him in Spanish.

"What's going on?" I asked when I realized I was not going to vomit and straightened up.

"Sorry, I thought you might be fainting." Nathan said.

"Do you need to lie down?" the other man asked in a Spanish accent. "Do you feel sick?"

"No, no, it's just the beer, it gave me some indigestion, I'll be alright."

"I need you to stay tough Maggie, there's more," said Nathan.

I looked at his face. His eyebrows were furrowed and his jaw was rigid and it scared me.

"The bullet was to the back of his head, at pretty close range. Someone was able to get behind him without him knowing it. This looks professional."

He was staring me in the eyes, looking for my reaction.

"Do you mean like a mob thing? Nathan, for some reason people think I'm someone I'm not. They think I'm someone named Sonya Ferrari who's in witness protection."

"How do you know this?"

"Leo told me, he knows people in the...oh damn, what's the name he said?"

"The U.S. Marshalls?"

"Yes, that's it. He thought I was this Sonya Ferrari with a new identity. God Nathan, someone is trying to kill her...me...us."

"Mishuga," he said, shaking his head back and forth slowly.

"I know what that means now, I looked it up. It's Jewish and it means crazy."

"It's Yiddish, and don't take it the wrong way, please."

"I'm sure it's some kind of compliment," I said. "Thank you, I'm quite flattered."

"I meant the whole idea was crazy, not *you*. You have somehow managed to get yourself involved in an organized crime matter, an illegal drug ring, and possibly the murder of Doctor Haney, and you just got here a week ago. I know this doesn't happen to you all the time so someone..."

"Wait, how do you know this doesn't happen to me all the time?" I eyed him suspiciously. "How do you know I'm not really this Sonia Maserati?"

He laughed. It was the first time I'd heard him do that and it was like a song. I got that kind of lump in my throat that you get when you hear a really beautiful piece of music. I forgot, for a moment, everything that was not him and that laugh. I laughed too. We were at the scene of a murder, in my parents' home, where I was the intended victim, and I could think of nothing but the beauty of that sound.

He stopped laughing, looked around to see some of the other officers looking at us sideways, cleared his throat and said, "I'm assigning someone to be with you at all times. You're not going to argue with me about that are you?"

"Hell no I'm not going to argue. You sure one's enough?"

"Good," he said and smiled that great Nathan Gonzales smile. "You can go about your normal routine, within reason. No picking fights with street performers."

"Hey, how did...?"

"And for right now, the safest place for you is at the department," he was waving over a uniformed officer.

"Please take Mrs. Finn to the station. She's a guest, but I want someone with her all the time. I'm calling Shelton in to take over for you." he told the officer.

"Who is Shelton? I hope he's really big."

"*Rose* Shelton. She's not that big but she's an expert marksman. You saw her with me at Saul's."

"Ok, but she seems awfully small to be a bodyguard."

"She's not a body guard. She is a trained officer who happens to be the best marksman on the force and she has the added benefit of being able to accompany you into places a male officer could not." He turned to the officer next to me, "you can take her to the station, make her comfortable."

"Wait, can't I come inside?" I said, peering through the door. "I need to get some stuff."

"No, forensics is still going over everything. I can get one of the officers to put a bag together for you."

"Thanks, that would be great, and Nathan?"

"Yes?"

"I can still look into the other stuff right? The stuff with Zig's mother and Doctor Haney?"

"Go investigate. You're the press, the law says I can't stop you. Don't go anywhere without Shelton though," he said over his shoulder, and walked back into the house.

I felt much too good for someone who probably had splattered brains in their house.

ENGULFED
CHAPTER THIRTY EIGHT

The phone call to my parents was one of the oddest I've ever had with them, and I've spoken to them from the delivery room. This time they were attending a Disney *character breakfast* and my mother thought it would be fun to hand the phone to whoever was wearing the Goofy costume and cajole the poor kid into breaking character and talking to me.

"Here dear, talk to Goofy; he was always your favorite when you were little."

I could hear her laugh in the background and my dad's voice asking someone for ketchup.

"That's Minnie Mouse," my mother was saying to him, "she's a star, she doesn't bring condiments."

"Oh, they're coming over to get a picture now,' she said to me. "I have to go. Bye bye sweetie, I love you."

"Love you too Mom, kiss daddy for me."

Well, at least I knew that they were not getting any news of the murder and mayhem taking place in their suburban paradise; one less thing to worry about. I slept for a few hours on a plastic sofa in the police station lounge. One of the officers had gotten me my pillow and a small blanket from the house, along with some clean clothes and all the stuff from my bathroom gently thrown into a black trash bag. All I needed was a shopping cart and a cardboard sign to be complete.

It was 7a.m. and I was waiting for my body guard, Rose Shelton, to finish checking in.

"Look here," she said in a Spanish accent, as we got into an unmarked police car, "I'm not interested in eating where you eat or talking to your friends or going shopping or none of that. This isn't some girlfriend day out. I don't even want us to talk to each other, got it? I don't want to hear about your life and I don't share. Now then, all I got to do is make sure no one kills you, so don't do anything stupid 'cause I don't wanna get *my* ass shot trying to save you when you're doing some kind of stupid shit. Are we clear?" She got in and slammed her door. "But I am so ready to waste a dirt bag, it's been one of them mornings, so stay out of my way."

I got into the passenger seat. "Can you please take me to my house, it's 463..."

"I know where you live, that's all you have to say."

She turned the police scanner on and pulled out of the precinct lot and toward my parent's home, Rose yelling at the other drivers in a mixture of Spanish and English. I needed no translation for any of it.

We pulled into the driveway, "I just want to get a couple more things out of the house," I said, "I won't be long."

She got out too. There was yellow crime scene tape across the front door but Rose pulled it off. "Don't worry; I got more in the car."

I looked down the hall toward the master bedroom. A lot of blood and bits of what I assumed were the inside of the man's head were on the walls, floor and even the ceiling. Bloody footprints and thin tire tracks, probably from the stretcher, led from that spot to the front door.

"You need someone to clean that up for you." said Rose. "That's brains and skull and shit, I've seen it before. You don't want to touch that. My sister Jasmine can clean this up, she's good, I'm callin' her now." She started dialing her cell. "Since there's no guts or vomit she can probably do it for a hundred, that's a good deal too, you're not gonna get anyone else to touch that for under three hundred."

I felt kind of helpless, so I just let her keep going, staring at her perfectly manicured blue fingernails with the little silver stars on the tips.

"Jaz, you got time to come down here to Bonita and clean up some brains and shit? This is Rose! How many other people call you and ask you to clean brains up off a floor? Oh, yeah, I forgot about her...ok yeah, them too. Well hush and listen to me, there's a old gringo lady here will pay you a hundred but it's gotta be done today."

She gave her the address and turned to me, "She'll only take cash, come on, I know where there's an ATM."

That taken care of, I called Zig from the car while Rose was inside a 7-11 buying herself something to drink.

"I have a body guard," I told him after relaying the previous night's adventures. "Her name is Rose and she hates me. She's very anxious to *waste a dirt-bag* though, so at least I've got that much going for me. No, you'll love her, she says she's a *Blacksican* and can apparently shoot a gnat off a flea's ass. You get to meet her soon, that's why I'm calling. Can you meet me...us...for lunch? You can't miss us, I'll be the old gringo lady sitting next to Diana Ross in a police uniform.

Rose came back to the car carrying a plastic cup so big it nearly eclipsed her tiny figure. She said nothing of course, just faced front and waited for me to give her my next destination.

"I need to meet a friend for lunch."

"It better not be no Starbucks. I don't do Starbucks."

"No, not Starbucks," I told her, "The Fish House. It's on Bonita..."

"I know where that place is," she said and pulled out of the parking lot.

We had to wait for Zig to get there, so we sat in silence, me looking at the water, Rose looking at the menu. "You're buyin' right? 'Cause this wasn't my idea to come here."

"Don't you get an expense account to do this?"

"Lady, where do you think you are, L freaking A? This is F freaking M, Fort Myers and we barely got a toilet paper budget."

"Then yes, order what you want."

Zig arrived and introduced himself. Rose kept looking at the menu.

"You can only speak when spoken to," I told him, "kind of like the Queen."

I could see Rose's eyes crinkle from a smile behind the menu.

After we ordered beverages, I asked Zig, "Have you talked to Brian since he got back to D.C.?"

"No, haven't you?"

"I've left a couple of messages, but he hasn't returned them. His secretary sounds cagy when you ask her where he is, same with his Florida office."

"Does he have a Facebook page?" asked Rose.

"I don't know, I haven't looked." I answered.

"Don't you know how to stalk a person? I thought you were a reporter."

She walked over to a young man sitting by himself a couple of booths over, using his laptop. "Look here," she said, showing him her badge, "I'm a cop and I'm temporarily confiscating your computer."

"You can't do that, I'm a law student."

"Well, law student, get on Facebook before I suspect you of havin' weed in your car."

He shrugged and started typing.

"What's this guy's name? The one you're lookin' for?" she shouted to us.

I walked over to the booth.

"Brian Roberts," I said, and quickly apologized to the kid.

"Shit, there must be a million guys by that name. I know how to filter to narrow it down. Move over." She sat next to the young man and used her hip to move him over in his booth. Rather than getting angry he seemed to be enjoying this.

"Where does he live? Here in Florida?" She was typing quickly.

"He has a home in Washington D.C. too."

"Are you talking about *Senator* Brian Roberts? What you want with him?"

"Nothing, he's just a friend."

"Maybe he's like that Governor of one of those Carolina states. You know, the one that said he went hiking but he was really with his ho."

"No," I said, "I don't think that's it."

"Well, you should have said he was a senator. Facebook is no good for those guys. They have other people doin' it for them. Here, let me look at my page a minute. I need to see somethin'" The young man just grinned at her stupidly while she checked her page.

I walked back to the table where Zig was talking on his cell. He hung up when I sat down.

"Mom hasn't heard from him either."

"I'm starting to get worried. Have you considered the possibility that it was him with Doctor Haney that night? Could he be lying to us?"

"Yeah, I thought of that too, we need to look into this though, without mom finding out, I don't want any more stress on her. And what about?...hold on, here she comes."

"Everything ok?" Zig asked.

"You know, your voice sounds kinda' familiar," Rose said to him.

"He's a D.J." I told her, but not for a station you listen to I'm sure, it's more for older people."

"Of course, Zig from What the Fu...!

"Waving Through Florida," Zig corrected her quickly.

"I thought you said your name was *Steve*. Shit, I'm sitting here with the Zigster."

She was positively beaming. It was the first time I'd seen her smile.

'You listen to my show?" he asked, forgetting to close his mouth.

"Every morning; I like that shit, it's real soothing. In my line of work, you need to be soothed. I grew up listenin' to that music with my Granny. She loved it all, Louis Armstrong, Billie Holiday, Frank Sinatra, Duke Ellington. You gotta mention me on the air tomorrow. Maybe you could dedicate a song to me."

"Uh, sure, any song in particular?"

"Yep, I know just the one, Sentimental Journey. Send it out to your very good friend Rose Shelton."

"Sentimental Journey, the old one, from the 1940s, is that the one?"

"I don't know no other one do you?"

Our server walked up. "Hey, do you know who this is here?" Rose asked him. "This here is Zig from WTF in the morning. Ain't that somethin'? You all should put his picture on the wall, that way all the other people would know this is where the celebrities come to eat."

"Bring us a pitcher of beer please," Zig said, "just one glass."

ENGULFED
CHAPTER THIRTY NINE

Rose's relief took the form of a fifty something, overweight, balding cop who turned blue sucking in his gut every time I was in the same room with him.

I was on the phone with Zig, "You know, I can't believe I'm saying this, but I wish Rose could stay. Honestly, in an emergency, I can see me having to give this guy CPR."

"You want me to come over?"

"No, you have to be on the air so early tomorrow, I'm sure Officer Ted will be fine. Nathan wouldn't assign someone to guard me who couldn't...well, you know...guard me. I'm just gonna eat some Rocky Road and read until I fall asleep.

"It doesn't bother you too much that someone got shot in your house?"

"Astonishingly no; I have no idea why, it's like I'm becoming numb to all this, weird, but true."

"Alright kiddo, go eat your ice cream and go to sleep."

"Will do, good night. Oh, and, thanks for offering to be my emergency backup body guard." He hung up without saying goodbye, as usual.

I left Officer Ted on the patio with a bowl of ice cream and the little battery operated television. When I walked away I could hear him mumbling about what kind of dumb ass bitch doesn't have a real TV and wasn't it just his luck to be stuck in a house all night with no cable. "Swell," I thought, "someone new hates me. If I do get killed down here, the suspect list is gonna look like the phone book."

A voice woke me up, but not all the way up so I couldn't tell if it was real or a dream.

"Hey, you ok?" the voice asked.

I didn't know where I was, my head felt light but my body felt like lead. When my vision cleared I could see a really large cat and it was the cat that was shaking me, and talking.

"Oh Lord, are you trippin?" the cat asked. "I need you to be straight, we got some serious shit goin' down, now snap out of it.'

The cat swatted at me with its large paw; its blue claws scratched my face.

"Ow!" I yelled. I tried to sit up but fell back on my pillow. "Oh sorry, you're not a cat...are you? Wait! You ARE...you're Diana Ross!"

"Oh Lord, we ain't got time for this shit. *My* phone is broke, *your* phone is broke. We got a passed out fat cop on your back porch. This ain't good. I'm gonna go get some help. I'll be right back. Don't go nowhere."

She started to walk out, "Wait!" I shouted, "Am I a Supreme too?"

"Yeah, that's right, we're the Supremes; I gotta go get the third one..uhhh...Stella..I'll be right back, Don't go nowhere."

"Diana! Wait! Should I be getting ready?"

"No, you don't do anything except just lay there till I get back."

"Ok, my legs don't move anyway, I think I'm drunk, I'm really sorry about that."

"It's ok," she started leaving again, "that's show business."

"Diana!" I yelled to her again.

"What?"

"Take the cat with you."

****

A Supreme can't go on stage looking like they just got out of bed, I thought.

Moving my arms and legs felt funny, like someone else was moving them but I somehow managed to get out of bed and headed to the bathroom. I looked down to make sure that my feet were touching the ground when I stepped; they were heavy, slow steps with giant feet but I made it to the mirror.

"Oh shit, am I a man?"

The person in the mirror was a tall thin man with dark hair. "Is that me?" I asked but the man's lips didn't move.

The man's face said, "Who the hell are you?" Then it yelled back over its shoulder, "Manny, who the hell is this broad?"

Another man appeared in the mirror, this one was bald with a moustache. "Christ Benny, I don't know. This is the house they put Sophia in, but that ain't her."

"No shit you dumb moron, you think I don't know my friggin' wife when I see her?" He walked through the mirror and stood beside me. "You gonna tell me who the hell you are and what you're doin' here?"

"How did you walk through a mirror?"

"Don't fuck with me lady, I'm not messin' around here."

The room started to spin and I felt nauseous. "I'm not feeling well, can we go sit and have some tea?" My arm itched but when I scratched I couldn't feel anything; and the room kept getting dark, then light, then dark again.

"Why you turning the light off and on? You signaling someone?" the tall man asked.

"Jeeze Benny, she's stoned," the bald man said. "Ricky drugged her and the cop. He figured they couldn't be no trouble that way. The cop musta' ate a shit load 'cause he's out good, this one's just high."

"Ricky tried to drug my old lady?" said the tall man.

"Well, he figured since you wanted her dead anyway, you wouldn't mind."

"No one puts any of that shit in my family, you got it?"

"Yeah, sure Benny, I'll spread the word, it won't happen again. Whaddya wanna do with this one?"

"Get rid of her," he turned and started walking out, "and find out where Sophia is or I swear to God, I'm gonna clean house of all of you."

The bald man yelled after him, "Yeah, sure, you got it boss. We'll find her, don't worry," then he grabbed my arm, "Come on lady, we're goin' for a ride."

I jerked my arm away. "No, Diana Ross told me to wait here. She's gone to get Stella." I knocked over a bottle of something blue.

"Well, she told me to bring you to her, now come on."

"No! I have to get ready, I have to rehearse. I grabbed my microphone. "Stop, in the name of love." I sang.

He grabbed my arm. My legs wouldn't move and he pulled against dead weight, slipped on the mouthwash and fell, his head hit the toilet. I fell when he did and couldn't get back up. I was crawling away when I felt him grab my ankle. I kicked him with my other foot but he got it too and flipped me to my back. I grabbed the only thing in reach, a plastic toilet brush, and shoved it into his open mouth. I must have shoved it hard because he started gagging. My hand found the microphone and tried hitting him with it, but my arm felt like it was flying away from my body. It did manage to make contact with his eye. He screamed and I stumbled to my feet, fell again, and realized why I couldn't walk. I'd been drugged...again! Now, instead of fear, I felt rage.

"You friggen drugged me? Again? God damnit!"

I crawled through some kind of fog. "I'm coming Diana Ross!"

I got as far as the patio and pulled myself up using the barbecue grill, when I felt him lunge at me and we both fell to the ground. He was on top of me again.

"You bitch, you stupid whacked - out bitch." He was holding the microphone/curling iron, took the cord, and wrapped it around my neck. My body was pinned under him and I couldn't move. I could see rage in his eyes as he pulled the cord taut, I choked, my lungs gasped for air, the light around me started to fade and tears filled my eyes. I was really going to die, I was scared and sad, *I'm letting down Diana Ross and all our fans,* I thought; and then a voice that seemed to be coming from far away said, "That's *my* backup singer, dirt bag."

There was a loud pop, I gasped for air again and this time it came and filled my lungs. I choked, coughed, felt the weight on my chest leave me, and then everything went dark.

I was lying still, but the room I was in was moving. I could hear loud noises and bright flashing lights penetrated my eyelids. Afraid to open my eyes, thinking I might be dead and not wanting to know, I was aware of a sound, a voice, a *man*'s voice, it was speaking to me.

"God?" I asked.

The voice laughed, "Boy, if I had a nickel for every time someone made that mistake."

"Nathan?"

****

Back at my little home away from home, the Fort Myers Regional Hospital emergency room, I was watching Rose going through drawers and cabinets in her usual agitated manor.

"What are you looking for?" I asked.

"Sanitizers, these places are crawling with all kinds of nasty stuff."

"Well stop it, people will thing you're looking for drugs."

"You really don't know anything about anything, do you? Even little kids know they don't keep drugs in these rooms."

She walked over to get a better look at my neck. "Yep, that was a close one, another few seconds, I'd be lookin' at you in the morgue instead of here."

"That's a cheery thought, thanks. Wait, really...I mean...thank you for real. If you hadn't come when you did...I'm sorry you had to kill someone though."

"Hell, I wish!"

"What do you mean? He's not dead?" I asked, my head swiveling to follow her around the room.

"Oh, he's dead alright, just wasn't me that shot him." She sat down on the stool next to me, "I had him in my sight, gun aimed right at him," she raised her hand like it was a gun and pointed at me, "when, bam!" She spun around on the wheeled stool.

"Bam? What do you mean, bam? What does bam mean?" I asked.

"Would you stop sayin' bam, it sounds ridiculous when you say it. I'm sayin' someone else shot him, right before I got my chance to."

"Who? Who shot him?"

"You think he stopped and handed out business cards? Honey, this here is mob shit. How'd you get mixed up in mob shit anyway?" She stood up and pulled the little eye/ear flashlight from the wall and was examining one of her rings with it.

"They thought someone named Sonya Ferrari was supposed to be living in that house; she's an informant in witness protection." I said, "except these guys were calling her Sophia, at least I think so, I don't know."

"Sonya Ferrari, that's a made up name for sure."

"Anyway," I went on, "I guess they came there to shoot her or kidnap her. I'm not sure."

"You ever hear the saying the enemy of my enemy is my friend?" Rose asked. "Well, those guys got a lot of enemies and one of them just became your best friend."

"It would seem so."

"It would seem so," Rose pantomimed me. "Just listen to yourself. You sound like one of those people who record shit to help people fall asleep, why I just about dozed off myself." She got up and started looking through the cabinets again. "When's that doctor comin' in?" She opened the curtain and looked out.

"Rose?"

"What?"

"Thanks for coming back for me."

"Humph."

****

Doctor Mann, who said he was thinking of naming at least a stretcher after me, said I could leave as long as I had someone to stay with me for the next twenty four hours.

There was no way I was setting foot back in that house, so I called Rod and invited myself to stay the night at Dharma House. The fact that Leo was a doctor was an added bonus.

Rose agreed to go with me to pick up a few things and even went inside to get them, leaving me on the front porch. The morning was a steamy one and I rummaged through my purse to find something to pull my damp hair off of my neck when I heard the familiar bark of the neighbor's dog.

"Hello!" I called to the man walking to his car. He looked to be in his seventies, a few gray hairs covering an otherwise bald head.

I walked across the lawn to him. "I never got the chance to thank you for the other night, when you chased off that burglar."

"I'm glad you're alright," he said in a voice that sounded aged by whiskey and cigarettes. "But if you'll excuse me, I have a flight to catch." He put his dog, who was still barking at me, in the back seat.

"Oh, of course," I said, eyeing his suitcase. "I don't mean to keep you." My voice was raised to be heard over the noise of the dog. "Will you be gone long? I can keep an eye on your house for you."

"Not necessary." He said as he got in the car and slammed the door shut.

"Have a nice flight!" I waved and walked back to my house. I was halfway there when the recognition hit. Airplane, flight, he was the one on the plane, to D.C, the one I recognized, and in the cab, and...

"Rose," I shouted, running back to her and pointing to the old man's house. "The shot, the gun shot that...could it have come from there?"

ENGULFED
CHAPTER FORTY

I don't know how they got the Florida branch of the FBI special crimes unit into Fort Myers as quickly as they did, but here they were, all two of them. One, agent Washington, looked like he was still in high school and the other, agent Burrows, looked like his grandfather, except that agent Washington was black and Burrows white, in the extreme.

Washington spent a lot of time on his blackberry and Burrows had so many twitches he made Barney Fife look calm.

They left the room a lot which made me annoyed and self conscious, wondering if they were in some way watching me. Paranoia did not seem out of place these days.

As lovely as the Fort Myers police department looked on the outside, with its palm trees and colorful hibiscus everywhere, the inside was dull. I was seated in a room completely devoid of any personality other than depressed. The walls were a kind of greenish brownish color and I assumed they sent a blind person to pick out the paint. The floor was a non-descript grayish linoleum and the table was brown with a dozen blue, padded, metal chairs around it.

I called Zig when both agents were out of the room. "I don't think they sent out their A team,"

"You better be careful kiddo, the room may be bugged."

"You know, I don't care. What can they do to me that I haven't already been through in the last ten days?" I leaned back in the chair dramatically.

"That's true."

"I've currently got more drugs in my body than...than...who's that Rolling Stones guy, the one that should be dead by now?"

"Keith Richards."

"Yeah, him.

"You had anymore of those flashback things?" Zig asked.

"No, maybe they're over now, I hope so. I can't always depend on immigrants to be there when I hang off of balconies." I said as I walked over and put my ear to the door.

"You gonna be alright? Want me to come down there?"

"Nah, but thanks. I'm heading over to Dharma House. Rod is an ex cop and Leo's a doctor so I'm feeling good about hiding out there until I fly out Saturday."

As I talked, I amused myself by sitting in each of the chairs and then pushing them away from the table so that the agents would have trouble walking around when they returned. It was petty, but fun.

"OK, I'll stop by later and check in on you." Zig said and hung up.

I looked around the conference room for anything that looked like a camera or two way mirror but found nothing, so I laid my head on the table. I must have fallen asleep because when the door finally opened, I raised my head and saw the need to wipe some drool from the table top.

"Sorry Mrs. Finn," said agent Washington, "We were teleconferencing Washington, no relation," he chuckled. That was the first time I'd heard Washington string more than three words together. He had a manner of speech that sounded more like he was texting than speaking.

Burrows rolled his eyes and squeezed the rubber ball in his hand. I imagined he'd heard that one before. "We have a name for that neighbor of yours," he said. "C-c-constantine Randazzo. He was a hit man back in the late fiftiess. He was still really young then but already had a rep. They c-c-called him C-c-connie the Eye because of his ability to shoot with extreme accuracy."

His left eye twitched so much I could see it from across the room.

"In sixty one, the CIA recruited him and some other...other civilians to go to C-c-...Havana and kill C-c-castro. That never flew, of c-c-course, but they gave him a new identity and he's been living under an assumed name, and assumed life, since then. None of that is top secret; you c-c-can get more than that off of the internet."

He had to push in three different chairs to walk over to the table opposite me. His face twitched, Washington was wiping the table where I drooled and I worked at not laughing.

"What was he doing living next door to my parents and why did he kill the guy that was choking me?"

Agent Washington looked at Burrows with what I think was an attempt at a raised eyebrow, but looked more like he was going to sneeze.

Burrows continued, "He actually was only squatting there the pastc-c-c-few weeks. The owners of that house live in C-c-up north and don't c-c-come down for another week. We're looking into how he managed to get a k-k-key, get the electric turned on, that k-k-kind of thing."

"I kind of don't really care about that, what I want to know is why *that* house and why did he shoot that guy and then just leave?"

Agent Washington said, "On-going investigation," as he went through the room pushing the chairs back in, then spacing them out to be exactly the same distance from each other and the table.

I stared at him, waiting for him to speak another word or letter or sound.

"You talk," he finally said to me, after he had the chairs arranged to his satisfaction.

"Well, until you tell me what's going on, there's a fat chance of that happening." I told him. "I've been drugged, lots of times; I think I might have some trouble remembering stuff. In fact, I'm sure of it."

"Oh for C-c-christ's sake Washington, it's gonna be in the papers by tomorrow," said Burrows.

Washington walked over to Burrows and spoke to him in hushed tones and picked hair off the older man's jacket but I could hear him say, "Your neck, not mine."

I stared at agent Burrows until he shrugged and went on.

"C-c-connie's beef with the Latina family goes back decades, when Sonny Latina ran the family."

"So, Sonny Latina was godfather of the Latina crime family and he and my old- guy neighbor were enemies?

"No...well...yes, in that everyone is an enemy when you're involved in organized c-c-crime, but it was Sonny's son *Benny* that C-c-constantine had a vendetta against. When Benny Latina, the one that put the hit on you so to speak, was just a k-k-kid of twenty- two he ordered a hit on C-c-constantine's brother. He even went behind the rest of the family to do it. When his old man threatened to take away Benny's operation, he got disappeared himself. He turned up in a tuna net off the c-c-coast of San Diego a week later.

"Wow, you think Benny killed his own father?" I asked.

"Or had him killed, yeah, his old man *and* C-c-constatine's brother. Looks like old *C-c-connie the eye* has been waiting for Benny to c-c-come out into the open and last night that's just what happened."

"Came all the way out into the open just to make sure I got killed...well...not me but Sonya, sheesh," I said, a shudder running through me.

"Benny's wife, whose name is actually Sophia, is turning state's witness on him in a plea deal over a drug bust. Somehow they all got word she was c-c-coming out here in WITSEC and the party started. Last night, while Benny and his boys were in the house with you looking for Sonya, C-c-constantine knocked out Benny's driver, removed the distributor c-c-cap on his c-c-car and c-c-called the c-c-cops." By now both his eyes were twitching as well as, I swear, one of his ears.

"Holy Shit!" I said, "excuse my French."

"We figure he shot your attacker just to rub it in to Benny, k-k-kind of stickin' it in his eye.

I involuntarily put my hand to my right eye. "What's gonna happen to him? Constantine, I mean. Are you going to go after him?"

"Nah, we don't c-c-cross the line into agency business, which is what he is. He knew that, that's why he was so bold."

"Wait," I said, "I thought you guys *were* agency. *"*

"Different," said Washington.

"Anyways," said Burrows, "You were pretty lucky. Old C-c-connie the Eye was busy making sure you stayed alive long enough for Benny to get out here. You were like bait on a hook. The party's over now though, you should be safe, but I wouldn't go back to that house if I was you."

"Don't worry; I wouldn't go back in there without a swat team, a guard dog and an exorcist."

"Ha," said Washington.

ENGULFED
CHAPTER FORTY ONE

When I got to Dharma House it was already early evening since I had opted for eating dinner at The Fish House first. I left my things in the car when I got there because Rod was busy with the men in one of their *circles of being.*

It was a perfectly clear night and the stars were so numerous it looked like a planetarium show. The men were all looking up at the sky so I pulled up a chair and sat with them.

Rod was speaking, "If the stars should appear but one night every thousand years, how man would marvel and stare. That is a quote from Ralph Waldo Emerson."

The six aged men were seated in webbed folding chairs. Each would take a turn swatting at something on their body, wiping sweat from their brows with handkerchiefs, belching, coughing and yawning.

"Aristotle," continued Rod, who seemed impervious to both insects and temperature, "said that heavenly bodies are the most perfect realities, because their motions are ruled by principal and not by other heavenly bodies."

"Yeah, but that's wrong, right?" asked a man with red hair.

"Well Gordon, he believed they were made up of the ethereal and therefore not subject to corruption."

"Yeah, but that's wrong too, right?" Gordon asked.

"And," Rod continued looking at everyone *but* Gordon, "their circular motion can last eternally as opposed to our earthly up and down motions."

"Well, that's kind of right, but kind of wrong too, right?" Gordon asked, his voice now raised as he craned his neck to get Rod's attention.

"I can't look up no more," said another man with so many liver spots his skin resembled a topography map. "I'm getting a crick in my neck."

"Yeah, looking up is making me nauseous," said the man next to him, who was wearing only his under shorts and sandals over knee length socks. "I'm gonna' need some Pepto."

"Everything makes you nauseous," said the liver spots man. "You drink up your weight in Pepto. I bet you crap pink turds."

"I can't help it, ever since I took that bullet in Korea, I ain't been the same," said Pepto man, "besides, you need to watch your mouth Bernie, there's a lady here."

"Excuse my language ma'am," he said.

"It's quite alright Bernie," I answered.

"Metal in your body can ruin your system for life, ain't that right Rod?" asked George. "Like, you got shot in the head and don't you get nauseous? Tell these guys Rod."

"You got *shrapnel...* in your *foot* George. You're just an old fart is all, just like the rest of us, right Errol?" Everyone looked at the daydreaming Errol, "You fought in WW2, right?" asked Bernie.

Errol paused for a while and then said, "Rich old bastards are always the ones who start wars and they use the young and poor to fight them for 'em. In the end, no one remembers the ones who died except their families and the one's that watched 'em die." He stopped to rub his eyes. "But the ones who started them wars, well, them assholes are the ones who make the money and then they build entire goddamned empires on those graves."

The men, every one of them, and me too for that matter, sat frozen, mouths agape, holding our collective breaths.

Rod finally spoke, "That was beautiful Errol, it really was. You have come such a long way and now that your spirit is free at last to embrace all the beauty and potential of the life you've long denied yourself...the brotherhood and harmony with your fellow man...well...I'm sorry...please Errol, go on. Is there anything else you want to share?"

Errol looked at each of us, seeming to examine us for a long time and then asked, "Did anyone bring the chips?"

****

Zig showed up after I had gotten my things settled in my room at Dharma House and the four of us, Zig, Rod, Leo and I sat out on those same webbed chairs under the tree. The *guests* were situated in what Rod called *The Gathering Room,* and the men called *The TV Room.*

"Mom wants me to take her to Haney's funeral tomorrow," Zig said. "You wanna' go?"

"Yes indeedy I do," I said. "I'd love to see who shows up. They say the murderer always comes to the funeral. I'll bet the police will be there too, don't you?"

"Hell, I don't know, I'm only going because Mom asked me to."

"I had a long talk with Detective Gonzales the other day," I said. "Stanley, the guy that ended up dead the night I hallucinated, died of a heart attack. When the forensics team went over his car, they analyzed his heartburn meds and found the capsules were tampered with. Someone had replaced whatever stuff is inside them with a heart medicine, digitalis. So, just one more murder to add to my vacation scrapbook."

"Did they ever learn why he was following you?" asked Leo.

"They're working on the theory that he was going to make a play for Zig's mother, try to swindle her. He's done that before with other elderly women. He was probably following me to learn everything he could about her. He arrived in Naples last month and the staff at The Shell remembers seeing him there but they all just figured he was related to one of the residents."

"Are you saying he's been stalking my mother for a month?" asked Zig.

"That's the theory the cops are going on. But why someone wanted him dead is still being investigated. I honestly don't think they have a clue. He's been a real small time con man, never went to prison and has no known criminal associates. He managed to weasel himself into working for the Charley Davidson people once he got here, demo'ing their newest mobility device."

I filled them in on what I saw at the racetrack and said, "That's it, that's all I've learned from Nathan so far."

"You said the administrator for The Shell was there too?" asked Rod.

"Yes, Brandy, I don't know how she fits into all this. I guess maybe she was just acting as hostess for them since they were working with selling that thing to the residents there. I'm guessing The Shell was getting some kind of kick-back on them."

"Well," said Zig, "Brandy's a good gal, I'm sure she's not involved in anything bad, it's got to be all legit."

"I don't know what to think about anything anymore. So many things have happened so quickly, even a cop we saw at the lake that day was yelling at Ralph, the security guard. Ralph is kind of an idiot and I think the cop is gay so it was probably just Ralph saying something bigoted that got under the cops' skin, but, well, do you see what I mean?"

"When you open your mind to the world around you, unpleasantness can find its way in just as easily..."

"I'm still not clear about that mob thing, who were those guys?" asked Zig saving us from another bit of Eastern philosophy.

"Well," I began, "Benny Latina is like the Godfather of a famous crime family. He came out here because his wife was going to testify against him so she could keep herself out of prison for," I searched my memory but drew a blank, "you know, I'm not sure what she was in trouble for, but anyway, she came out here in the witness protection program and those guys, the Federal guys, had bought my parents' old house for her. She was supposed to have moved in there last week but everything got pushed back because of the hurricane. It seems the informants didn't get that piece of information so everyone just thought I was her."

"Christ Mags, you had one hell of a black cloud over your head this week," said Zig.

"Yes, but, I got lucky too. This is the good part. This guy Benny's father, Sonny, who used to be godfather, was like a rival of my neighbor, Connie the Eye's brother, who, get this, was named Sonny too, too as in also not number two."

"Who's name?" Rod asked.

"Connie the Eye's brother." I said.

"And who is Connie the Eye?" Rod asked.

"My neighbor *and* rival of Benny Latina's father Sonny who used to be godfather."

"Ok," said Rod, let me get this straight, "Sonny tried to get you killed because his father Benny was a rival of Connie the Eye."

"Yes... wait, no. S*onny* was the father and *Benny* is the son...who is now godfather. And then Sonny, no wait, *Benny* killed Connie the Eye's brother also named Sonny."

"I'm not sure I've got his," said Leo, "I need an org chart."

"And that's not the end of the story," I said.

"Of course it's not," said Zig rubbing his temples.

"So," I continued, "Sonny's son Benny had him, Sonny, the godfather, killed because he was going to take away his operation for killing Sonny, the other Sonny, Connie the Eye's brother."

"Who killed who just now?" asked Rod.

"Benny, Benny had his father Sonny disappeared and then *he* became the godfather. Oh, and Sonny, the first Sonny that was godfather, turned up in a tuna net in San Diego."

All three men just stared at me.

"You guys, don't you get it? Connie the Eye wanted to get revenge on Benny for killing his brother Sonny so he lived in the house next to me when I was supposed to be Sonya whose name is actually Sophia, Sophia Latina. *Because*, he knew that Sonny would find me, her, and come out here and then he, Connie the Eye, would…would do a revenge thing, which he did. So in order to do that, he had to keep me alive, Connie the Eye did I mean. So he killed whoever was trying to kill me…Sonya… Sophia."

They still just stared so I stayed quiet a moment to let them absorb all that but then I remembered something else. "Oh, and they drugged me with a…with a drug so I would not be a credible witness, well not me really, Sonya…well not really Sonya, Sophia…Latina. That was before some underling decided to take matters into his own hands and kill me, Sonya, but Connie the Eye was looking after me. So you see ,I was really pretty lucky."

Everyone just stared at me, all their mouths hanging open.

"Is anyone hungry?" Zig asked, "I sure am."

Rod and Leo continued to stare at me for few minutes more and then Rod looked at Zig, then back at me, and answered. "There's some chips and spinach dip in there if you can pry them away from Errol."

"I don't want to pry food off of an old guy," said Zig.

"It's ok," said Rod, looking back at Zig, "They have lots of it. Our newest guest, a kid from Texas, makes it up and the two of them will sit in front of the TV and eat the whole thing themselves, but I'm sure they'll share. Just tell them it's for us."

"Will do," said Zig, walking into the house.

"I'm glad we have this opportunity to speak privately," said Rod. "I had your friend Zig there checked out by a friend in the department. He's got a prior for possession, but that was back in the 70s and he got off with some probation time, and that's it. He's a straight arrow, no need to worry about him."

"Thanks Rod, I appreciate that. I think I knew that from the beginning though."

We sat there peacefully for a while listening to the crickets, the breeze through the palms, the tinkling of wind chimes, Leo talking about the salinity of the various bodies of water on the planet when Zig came back carrying a tray.

"Oh good," said Rod, "there's some left."

"How long has your Texas boy been here Rod?" asked Zig.

"Billy?" Rod answered. "He got here two, two and half days ago. He's a lot younger than the rest of them, but he's a veteran of the war in Afghanistan and the rest of the men have a lot of respect for him for that, especially Errol. He calls him Billy the kid."

"Yeah, speaking of Errol," said Zig. "When did you notice him getting a lot nicer? I'm gonna guess it was about the time your kid Billy showed up. Would that be about right?"

"Why yes, it was. I don't know if it was just a coincidence..."

Zig interrupted, "No, not a coincidence, it's not even Billy, it's the dip.

We all looked at the green concoction and said, "Oh noooooo."

Zig looked at us, big grin on his face and said, "Oh yessssss."

ENGULFED
CHAPTER FORTY TWO

Bruce Haney's widow looked as though she should be on the set of *Hello Dolly* and not standing over her husband's flower draped coffin at Everlasting Harbor Cemetery. Her hat could have doubled as an awning and if her black dress had contained even one more feather she could have flown in. Not only did she look as though she hadn't shed a tear in decades, she had so much Botox under her skin I wasn't even sure it would have been possible.

I was there too, also not crying, and although I was standing at a respectable distance beside Zig and Dorothy, I could see there was not a single tear on any of the *mourners*.

"Are those his children standing there with the widow?" I asked Dorothy.

I pointed to the two young men in sunglasses fidgeting with their cell phones and a young woman, probably still a teen, shifting from foot to foot and looking bored.

"They are three of his prodigy from his prior marriage," Dorothy said from the side of her mouth. "That's their mother over there," she pointed to a woman in a black dress and veil, standing surprisingly far back from the gravesite. "She is Bruce's first wife that he left for the wax figure you see by the casket. Those children have turned their backs on their own mother because their fortunes are tied to *Step Mamma*. They are all now major share holders in about a dozen different companies."

"Is she that great of a step-mother that those kids would rather be with her rather than their own mother?"

"On the contrary my dear, they loath each other, but are stuck together because of how Bruce split up his estate; it was quite diabolical of him actually."

"You said three of his children, there are more?" I asked.

"Yes dear and here he is now." She pointed to the uniformed officer making his way to the *first* Mrs. Haney. You could have knocked me over with a feather; it was the cop from the Sun God, the one I saw fighting with Ralph in The Shell parking lot.

"He was disinherited by his father," Dorothy continued, "ostensibly because of his choice of careers but I believe the more plausible explanation would be the young man's choice of romantic interests, the boy being a regular at The Sun God, if you follow my drift."

We stood quietly as the service began. I have no idea what was in the casket, if anything, but the minister said his *ashes to ashes* thing over it as though the deceased man was actually in there and not in the stomach of the rather large reptile being dissected by the coroner. I joined Dorothy in paying respects to the family.

I stood under the shade of the gigantic hat while Dorothy offered her condolences. Dorothy oozed grace and charm but the widow's expression remained frigid, though in all fairness, that may not have been voluntary.

"Come with me dear," Dorothy said and we walked to the first ex Mrs. Haney.

"Elaine," she said and reached her hand to the widow. "I'm so sorry. I can't imagine the difficulty of being here and having to observe this spectacle." They both glanced over toward the graveside.

"They're all going to be very surprised, aren't they?" she said, deadpan and expressionless. "My own children, my spawn; they actually believe that they can win. Not you of course David," she said putting her arm through her son's.

David said nothing; he was staring at his siblings and their father's other widow, wearing the same expressionless mask as his mother, only his had a hint of fire in the eyes. It frightened me and I looked at my feet.

"You're just overwrought," said Dorothy. "You need to get away from this place. Go home, fix yourself a cocktail, have something to eat. There's no need for you to subject yourself to this."

Elaine didn't respond. She looked old and tired; more than what years can do to a face. Dorothy grabbed her hand and patted it, "We must be going now, I'm sorry it took this tragedy for us to meet again after so long. I shall call on you next week, see how you're doing, alright darling? David, take care of your mother dear, she needs to go home, take her there."

We started walking away when the sound of a motorcycle made me turn and I could see David driving away, alone; Elaine was gone.

I heard a familiar voice behind me say *hello* and turned to see Brian Roberts.

"Brian, I'm so happy to see you. I've been trying to get in touch with you. Is everything alright?" I hugged him.

"Yes, all is well, thank you. And how are you? I heard about the break-in at your parent's home. I was very thankful to read that you were unharmed."

"Yes, yes, I'm fine, thanks. But I've been worried about you."

"I appreciate your concern, but there is no need. I'm..."

"Brian, how good of you to come," a voice interrupted.

From the sudden eclipse of sunlight, I knew I was standing under the canopy of the be-feathered widow.

"Elaine, Brian said taking her hand, "I'm so very sorry about Bruce, what a tragedy. This is such a loss to all of us, but my sympathies are with you and your children now. Please let me know if there is anything I can do to help you through this most difficult time."

She air kissed his cheek with as much of a pucker as her rigid face would allow. Seeing that made me glad I couldn't afford a face lift.

"Thank you darling," she said; the smell of beer on her breath so strong that we could just as easily have been at a Packers game. "The past few days have been a nightmare of lawyers and accountants and..."

Her voice trailed off and I saw her stare at something behind me; I turned to see a group of men in dark suits standing under a tree laughing and back slapping.

"I'm sorry, where was I?" she asked Brian. "I'm afraid I've lost my train of thought."

"You're tired Elaine, it's quite alright, please, call my office if there's anything I can do," said Brian.

"Yes, of course, thank you," she said distractedly, still watching the men.

Zig and Dorothy were talking to Haney's daughter and Brian and I joined them. Brian, with his security guard / driver in tow said hello to the group, hugged the daughter, shook hands with the sons and then said his goodbyes. I watched him join the group of men that the widow, Elaine, had been so intently staring at.

"Who are those guys?" I asked Dorothy after we had also said our goodbyes to the family.

"Why that would be the distinguished United States senator from the great state of Arizona, Mitch Waldon," she said, her voice dripping with sarcasm. The rest are a gaggle of cronies and hangers-on I would suppose, though I don't recognize any of them. If you'll excuse the expression dear, they are like flies on a dung heap and little more.

"The widow sure was interested in them." I said.

"Not *them* dear, *him,* Mitch, the one she's having an affair with."

"Ohhhhhh, this is better than a soap opera," I said, "I only saw him on C-span that one time but I didn't recognize him from over here. Why is he in Florida?"

"One need only follow the trail of ooze he leaves behind," she said, "just as you would a slug. He was the perfect associate for our erstwhile doctor, they were business partners."

"So, this is a wild guess, but it sounds like you don't care for either of them much."

"Mitch Waldon is the worst kind of politician and since I have no compunction about speaking ill of the dead I will come right out and tell you that Bruce was also a man of few scruples. He was an absolutely brilliant physician though, I'll give him that much. The list of those whom he has wronged through the years would, I imagine, be monumental by the time of his death. I don't envy Detective Gonzales in his task of narrowing down suspects. I do so hope that extensive list will be shortened by one soon; dear Brian must be cleared of any wrong doing in the matter." She put her arm through mine and said, "let us go find Steven and get ourselves a cocktail, shall we?"

ENGULFED
CHAPTER FORTY THREE

I've never been a big believer in the supernatural or in strange occurrences happening for a reason, but I found it odd that after my visits from a seagull dressed as Sherlock Holmes, the first thing that came on the television screen when I hit the power button was an old, black and white, Sherlock movie.

Rod had let me have his room at Dharma house, which had a television in it. I like the television when I'm alone or anxious, it's somehow comforting to be connected with the rest of the world.

This old movie had Basil Rathbone in it as Holmes, and looked like it was made long before they cared anything about things like acting. In this story, women were being killed and their forefingers removed. There were also hypnotists and lots of screaming and fainting and it all felt somehow too close to home, so I changed the channel to an old episode of The Dick VanDyke Show and fell asleep.

I don't know how long I had been asleep before I was awakened by someone in my room.

"Rod?" I asked the figure at the door, "Do you need something?"

He didn't answer so I turned the bedside lamp on. It was not Rod, it was Sherlock Holmes, of course.

I threw my head back on the bed, closed my eyes tightly and said, "Go away!"

I smelled the familiar pipe and opened my eyes. He was sitting in the chair near the television, which was powered off.

"I do not believe for even a moment that the attempt on your life is not directly related to the death of Doctor Haney and the man Stanley," he said, tapping his pipe on the television. "So is the kidnapping of your friend's mother. They are all related to the same person or group of people."

"But that can't be," I said, "The attempt on my life and the drugging was a mob thing, the kidnapping was about Brian and that vote and that had to do with Doctor Haney so yeah, that's probably related, but the mob... no, it was a weird coincidence I grant you but..."

"Coincidence?" he said, standing, "I think not!"

"Well, then who killed Haney and Stanley, the mob people or the vote people?" I asked.

"They are one and the same."

"But they don't have anything to do with each other."

"Who let it be known that the woman under protection would be in your parent's home?" he said, pacing around the room. "No one was sure what Stanley might have told you, perhaps they thought you knew too much about the doctor's death. Having the mob kill you would take care of everything."

"It would have to be someone who knew about Haney blackmailing Brian *and* the mob thing," I said, "who would know about all of that? It would have to be someone on the inside. The only person who would know all that would be...Nathan? Nathan Gonzales? That can't be, that's crazy. He's a policeman."

"When you eliminate the impossible, whatever is left over, no matter how improbable, must be the truth," he said.

"Yeah, I know, you always say that. But just because you say it all the time doesn't make it true. Nathan's not a bad cop, he's a good one."

"How is it you know his character so fully? Are you one of the greatest detective minds of all time? Because I am, and I say, when you eliminate the imposs..."

"Oh for crying out loud, you're awfully tedious, do you know that mister great detective? And that is the stupidest hat I've ever seen; it's hard to take you seriously in it. I liked you better as a bird."

"I must be off," he said, heading for the door, "for London is a vile cesspool of..."

"Yes, please, go to London, there are women there with missing forefingers."

He turned around before leaving and said, "Gather your data my dear, it is a mistake to theorize before you have all your facts," and walked out of the room, tripping over my suitcase.

At least he didn't try to get me to jump out the window this time, I thought, and turned off the light. I hope I quit having these soon.

ENGULFED
CHAPTER FORTY FOUR

"You can't just keep him, he's not a puppy," I told Rod as Zig and I were waiting to take Errol back to The Shell.

Under the influence, Errol had slipped and revealed that he was indeed the missing Mad Max which came a surprise to no one at all.

"But," I continued, "you may want to encourage Billy to stop by and visit him from time to time and, well, you know, bring snacks."

"Where is he anyway?" asked Zig.

Rod walked back to the TV room and Zig and I followed. Errol was there, frozen in front of the television, a dazed look on his face.

"Hey," I asked, "has he been hitting up the dip already?"

"Errol?" Rod called to him, walking directly in front of the stunned man as he stared at the screen.

I looked at the set just in time to watch an alligator devouring a meal of something unrecognizable surrounded by blood-filled river water.

"Holy crap!" I yelled and turned my face away from the gruesome scene.

"They really do that," Errol said finally, like a man mesmerized, "they just roll and roll till...till it kills him."

"Come on," Rod said, attempting to guide him away. "Maggie and Zig are here, they're going to take you home."

"No wait!" I shouted and stopped them. "Errol, were you...did you see Doctor Haney killed by the alligator?"

He said nothing for a minute, then turned to me and said, "Yeah, I think I did."

****

We called Nathan Gonzales and Errol's doctor and waited in the sun room for them to arrive. We were able to ascertain this much; that Errol, aka Max, was there the night Doctor Haney fell in the lake.

It appeared Max had taken out the scooter for a joy ride, lost control of it, and ran the doctor off the pier and into the water. Max had fallen too, but only into the shallow edge of the lake and was able to get out quickly. At the time he thought Doctor Haney had been able to get out as well.

We also learned there were others with the doctor at the time, but it was too dark and Errol could not tell us anything about them except that he was sure there were more than one, possibly three people there with the doctor at the time. He figured one of them had called for help so he ran, or in Max's case, hobbled away, afraid he'd be charged with stealing the scooter. His back was turned to the lake so he didn't know how it happened, but he heard thrashing sounds, turned back and saw the gator killing its prey. He didn't know what the others were doing, but he ran away.

"So, at least one person, maybe three, saw Haney and Max go into the lake and no one said a word," I said, stating the obvious. "That's got to mean they were up to no good."

Rod and Zig were talking but I didn't hear them, my mind was reeling. I thought of the shoe, the one that had to belong to Brian Roberts found at the scene. Brian and Haney were involved in shady dealings. Brian Roberts had to have been there the night Haney died and he'd done nothing to help. I didn't want to believe it but there seemed to be no doubt of it. My heart was broken, I trusted him, I liked him, Dorothy trusted him enough to jeopardize her life for him and he was, if nothing else, such a coward he wouldn't call for help when a man was being eaten alive.

Then something else popped into my head, someone else's behavior seemed odd to me, someone else had seemed to be everywhere. I looked for Errol, who had excused himself to go to the bathroom. He was gone a long time, even for an octogenarian, so I went looking for him. I saw him through an open bedroom door talking to a shirtless and heavily tattooed young man.

"Billy the Kid I presume?" I asked the younger man.

"Yes ma'am," he stood up and began to salute, then stopped himself.

"Errol," I said to the older man, "or should I call you Max?"

"Max is a schmuk, call me Errol."

"Ok, Errol, tell me something, I know the night you went into the lake is kind of fuzzy to you and you were probably pretty scared, but, could one of the people you saw out by the lake that night be Brandy?"

A chorus of male voices raised at once behind me, I hadn't realized they had followed me.

"Brandy?" shouted Zig. "Are you nuts Maggie?"

"Who is Brandy?" asked Rod.

"Yes Maggie," added Leo, "Are you introducing suspects? Because if you are I think it would be appropriate..."

Everyone turned to Leo and shouted in unison, "Leo!"

"Brandy is the administrator at The Shell," I said. Turning to Zig I continued, "Don't you remember Idzy saying she went into your mom's room just before we did and she referred to Doctor Haney as poor Bruce and..."

"Maggie, you're out of your mind or having a drug relapse or something," Zig said, "Brandy is as much a criminal as The Easter Bunny is."

Rod said, "As a former police officer I would have to agree that those are the least compelling arguments for suspicion I've ever heard."

"I know, but...I don't know," I said, feeling frustrated. "She just *seems* suspicious to me."

"You don't like her, that's why," said Zig. "Just because she's young and beautiful and your ex left you for..."

"Maggie," said Leo, "transferring your feelings of rejection and abandonment onto another person is one thing, but to accuse them of..."

"Are you doing that Maggie?" asked Rod, "because if you are that seems rather petty and mean spirited."

They were ganging up on me. They almost looked like a mob, like a really weird, kind of mellow old- hippie kind of mob, but a mob all the same. My hatred of Brandy grew at that moment because I felt like this was her fault. I got even angrier at myself because I knew they were right, I just *wanted* it to be her.

"Well, excuuuuuuuuse me," I said, Steve Martin style. "I had no idea I was speaking to her fan club, I just wondered, that's all."

At this point I dropped the idea of mentioning Ralph too in case he reminded everyone of some beloved long lost idiot brother of theirs causing them to turn on me again.

Errol was of no use on that score anyway, he had been too busy losing control of the scooter that night to be sure of who else was there.

Nathan arrived just then followed by Errol / Max's physician, so I said nothing else on the subject and just listened. Errol didn't add anything more than what he had told us, and Nathan didn't say anything more than *hello* to me, and left quickly when he got an emergency call. I left, sulking, and let Rod take Errol back to The Shell

I went to one of those frozen yogurt places where you add your own toppings and pay by the weight. When I placed my cup on the scale the cashier looked genuinely surprised. I peeked inside my overburdened cup and said, "I guess I was a little distracted."

I sat and stared and wondered at what I had put into my cup and tentatively spooned in a large mouthful. I got brain freeze, yelled "shit," out loud, and watched two families with children walk out the door and sit at the outside tables. I picked at the toppings, allowing the frozen stuff to become less painful, and tried to come to grips with the fact that I was flying to Albuquerque the next day.

And it was there, at my little round table with the pot of pink silk flowers in the center, that everything started to come together in my mind. All the little things that I had forgotten or pushed into the brain-drawer of unimportant facts were arranging themselves in my mind to make a fairly clear picture. I was proud of myself that I was able to see clues I hadn't before, and felt very clever, like my arch nemesis and closest confident, Sherlock Holmes; in all his guises.

This time I was not under the influence of talking seagulls or fictional detectives, it was just me, with lights illuminating all the previously darkened corners of my brain. Maybe it was some effect of the drug, but maybe it was really me, putting all these pieces together myself.

I put a spoonful in my mouth, felt the brain freeze hit again at the very second I solved the crime and yelled, "Shit! Holy shit!"

ENGULFED
CHAPTER FORTY FIVE

I started to throw my yogurt concoction away, stopped myself, started again and stopped myself again.

Oh hell, it's going to melt out there anyway I thought, attempting to throw it away for the third time and then stopped and asked the young man behind the counter, "do you have straws?"

I slurped and dialed my cell phone from the parking lot of the *Beautiful Bonita Merchant Center*. While I waited for an answer I pondered the redundancy of *Beautiful Bonita* when I got Nathan Gonzales' voice mail.

"Nathan, it's Maggie Finn, I was thinking I knew who...wait...I have an idea about who...well, you probably already know but...."

"You have reached the end of your recording," said the automated voice

I dialed again, "Nathan, Maggie again, you may already know all this but, I was thinking I had some ideas about who might be involved in...well, the drug thing and..."

"You have reached the end of your recording."

"Nathan, this is Maggie, call me please."

Next I called the police station. I said to the male voice at the other end of the line, "Hi, this is Maggie Finn, I need to speak to Detective Gonzales please. Can you tell him this is very important?"

"Detective Gonzales is not in," said the voice.

"Oh, ok. Is Rose Shelton there by chance?"

"She is not," said the voice.

"Ok, well, can you ask her to call me too please?" I gave the voice my number and hung up.

I was so agitated I didn't know what to do with myself. I was almost certain I was right, well almost, pretty sure, had a gut feeling I was right and didn't know what to do with it.

I had arranged to spend my last night in Florida at Dorothy's and since I didn't know where else to go, I went to The Shell.

When I called Dorothy to tell her I was on my way she said, "Wonderful dear, we shall celebrate a bon voyage for you."

I stopped and got some pizza since I was certain *celebrate* meant alcohol and I needed something on my stomach besides liquid yogurt and M&Ms.

In the lobby of The Shell I saw Rod coming toward me, obviously on his way out after dropping off Errol.

"Maggie, how wonderful to see you. I was afraid we wouldn't have a chance for a proper goodbye. You know, I met the woman you spoke of, Brandy. She's delightful and such an asset to this place and the people here. I can't imagine what you were thinking accusing her of being a part of all the misfortune you've had. In the words of Buddah, In the sky, there is no distinction of east and west; people create distinctions out of their own minds and then believe them to be true. "

"Rod, I'm sorry, I don't even know what that means."

"He is telling us that..."

In that moment I stopped listening because I could see, standing in the doorway just behind Rod and in clear earshot of him, Brandy.

"Oh Rod, you didn't know I was just kidding?" I said to him loudly with a fake laugh that sounded ridiculous even to me.

Brandy disappeared back into the room and I felt my armpits grow tingly and sweaty. Damn, I thought, that was not good.

Rod said goodbye in true Rod fashion. "I am blessed to have a found a friend so dear that it makes saying goodbye so difficult," he said as he hugged me. It was a good hug and I forgave him for his inadvertently maybe getting me killed; a good hug can do that.

****

After dinner with Dorothy, mine being pizza and hers, a salad, we sat in the living room and chatted over, of course, cocktails.

"So, here is what I've come up with," I said. "Tell me what you think."

"Of course darling, but first, let us see about making you comfortable. Where are your bags?"

"In the car, I'll go get them." I said.

"Nonsense, have you looked out the window? It's raining cats and dogs. I can give you some nightclothes and we'll send what you're wearing to the laundry. They will have it back here by six tomorrow morning."

"Thank you, but don't you want to hear this first? I've been dying to talk to you about it all, get your thoughts on it."

"Yes, yes dear, I'm very anxious for that as well, but there is no need to hurry. You go get your bath and set your things outside the bathroom door. I'll bring some nightclothes in for you and lay them

246

on the guest bed. Then we'll have a night cap and you can tell me all about your theories."

Since no one ever argues with Dorothy I agreed. In the tub I had time to think some more about my little chaos theory and wondered why I never heard back from Nathan or Rose or even Zig.

"Oh shit," I said aloud. "I left my damn cell phone in the car on the charger, that's why."

I wrapped myself in what felt like the worlds softest towel and made my way to the guest room. There I found, lying across the bed, a full length, bright red, silk gown with matching robe. I looked around to see if there was anything besides this for me to wear but found nothing. I put it on and walked out to where Dorothy was seated on a chair, book in hand.

She looked up when she saw me come in. "Now then, don't you feel much better?"

"I feel like I should be on my honeymoon. It's really beautiful but I wouldn't want to mess it up. Do you have anything less...ummm...fancy?"

"What? Do you mean a flannel something? Heaven forbid. I always sleep in silk."

"Well, thank you, it's lovely really," I said trying to push some of the ruffles away from the sides of my face. "It even has a built in bra."

"Of course it does, a woman should always hold her shape, that's my philosophy anyway."

"Well, it does help not finding your boobs in your armpits in the morning huh?" I said laughing.

Dorothy smiled at me like I was a dull witted child.

"Anyway," I continued, "I need my clothes for a few minutes. I have to go to my car and get my phone."

"I'm sorry dear; I've sent them down to the laundry already. You can wear something of mine but honestly, I don't know if that's a good idea. The storm has now become quite strong with lightening. Can it not wait until the morning?"

"Yes, I suppose so," I said, sitting down and nearly sliding off the chair. I looked for an upholstered one and moved to it, adjusting the gown to cover my leg that was poking out of the thigh high slit."

I had my newest cocktail; something warm with what I thought was Bailey's Irish Cream, and began my narrative.

"So, this is what I've come up with. I think that Brandy was having an affair with Doctor Haney; *A)* because she called him *poor Bruce,* and *B),* it fits into my theory. Next, I think she has become friends with the doctor's estranged son, the cop who, I agree with you, probably got disinherited for being gay. Then from him, learned that the newest Mrs. Haney was having an affair with that senator from Arizona, Mitch Waldon. She told Doctor Haney, and he, instead of challenging Waldon to a duel or something, blackmailed him along with poor Brian. I think Brandy and the cop were both at the lake the night the doctor fell in. By the way, what is the cop's name again? I forgot and I hate to keep calling him *the cop.* "

"His name is David, dear, and please continue, this is fascinating," she set her drink down on the table to focus on me.

"Anyway," I went on, "I think she got Doctor Haney to come out to the lake that night so she could confront him. I'm guessing it has to do with all the money he was leaving to the new wife and not her. I bet he promised to marry her or something and then when he didn't and also cut David out of his will, well, I'm guessing they were there to blackmail *him.*

I stopped to adjust the back of my robe because some of the ruffles were bunched up under my backside.

"Now, I think David actually planted Brian's shoe by the lake to incriminate him in case anyone saw what had happened that night. I figure since he went to The Sun God and as a cop had lots of access, he would have had no problem getting something like that. I bet he knew all along that Brian was Carmen Electric. All he'd have to do would be to run the plates on the limo."

"Very clever my dear, I think you may be right about that. We never thought about concealing the vehicle."

"Thank you," I said. "Now, here's what I think happened after that. I think Brandy and David decided to take the whole blackmail thing over themselves to try to salvage something since it was now too late to get Doctor Haney to change his will, what with him being eaten by an alligator and all."

There was a crack of thunder and we both jumped.

When I recovered I said, "I think that Doctor Haney had his fingers in so many shady deals it would be easy for Brandy and David to make the most of at least a couple of those schemes. The blackmailing senators thing was already in the works. They needed for Medicare to approve that stupid Charley Davidson thing, that's what Brian and Senator Waldon were voting on. And I'm guessing they had their mitts in the drug thing too, since David is a cop and all. I bet Brandy and Doctor Haney had their own little love nest, maybe even here, where she could have access to lots of his stuff."

"Do you think they're the ones who had me kidnapped?" asked Dorothy, appearing like a child being told a very intense bedtime story.

"No, I think it was the Charley Davidson people, they're based out of Miami. But I'm sure Brandy was helping them. She knew when you left and who you left with. I mean, if Idzy knew, Brandy knew. She even went through your room when you were gone."

"But what about you dear, why would they want to harm you? Didn't you say that the man Stanley who was following you was somehow involved with Brandy? Didn't you see them together?"

"Well, this is all just guessing on my part, but I think Brandy found out somehow, and I'm giving her a lot of credit for shrewdness, and if I'm wrong about her then this whole thing unravels. But anyway, I'm wondering if she didn't find out about Stanley's past and make him help her in those schemes. Why she had him follow me, I don't know, other than that I was friends with you and you are friends with Brian. Maybe she thought it was suspicious of me to be hanging around all the time when my parents weren't even here. I don't know. She was worried about me. I have to admit that I, completely by accident, may have acted a little strange."

We both paused to think about that a moment. Dorothy merely smiled, rather enigmatically.

I went on, "Then, maybe Stanley decided to get on the blackmail wagon, and somebody, probably Brandy, might have just put some heart medicine in his antacids. She has to have access to all kinds of stuff like that here. She's always going in and out of these rooms with people's meds out in the open."

"Maggie, you've really weaved a compelling tale. I think you should tell all this to Detective Gonzales. I'm sure he'd want to know."

"You think? It all sounds so farfetched that even *I'm* having trouble believing it. Nathan will probably think I'm nuts, and maybe I am, I'm starting to wonder myself. But honestly, after what I've been through since getting into town, nothing seems too weird. *And,* I think that David somehow, in some sort of cop circle-of-friends or something, knew about that mob wife coming to live in my parent's old home and told the right, or wrong person, depending on your point of view, that I was her, the mob wife. That is the only way I can see how all of this ties together. The same person, or in my theory, *people*, Brandy and David, were behind all of it."

Again, another loud crack of thunder followed a bright flash of lightening and the power went off.

"Ok," I said, "now that's just creepy. I don't mind telling you, I'm making myself scared. Let's call someone, let's call Nathan, or Zig or even Leo."

"I'm sorry dear, but when the power goes off, so do the phones, they're all connected to the cable television," said Dorothy in a calm tone, "I wonder what I've done with my cell phone."

I could hear her patting at the sofa. "Well, it's no use my looking," she said, I can't see a thing. Why don't we go to sleep for now, and by dawn, if the power is not restored, we'll at least have daylight to help us?"

"Yes, alright," I said, thinking the last thing I was going to be able to do was sleep.

ENGULFED
CHAPTER FORTY SIX

I lay there in Dorothy's guest room in the silk gown with the built in bra waiting for the lights to come on, waiting for it to stop storming, waiting for morning. The thunder was so loud it sounded like gun shots and the lightening made jagged sideways bolts across the sky. I said my prayers, recited the pledge of allegiance, and tried to remember all the words to *American Pie*.

"I met a girl who sang the blues," I whispered to myself, "and asked her for some happy news...but." I couldn't remember the next line and lay there silently trying to remember when I heard voices. They sounded as though they were coming from across the hall.

This place is full of eighty year olds, I thought *and it has to be past midnight.*

I got out of bed and felt my way out of the room, along the walls, and to the front door. I saw light coming from under the Idzy's door across the hall, a golden flickering light as if from a candle. I was going to go knock on the door when I remembered what I was wearing and went back for the robe. After managing to find the arm holes through all the fru-fru, I headed back to the hall. I had just poked my head out when I saw a flashlight coming toward me from the end of the hall. I couldn't see who was behind the light so I hollered out, "Hello!"

The light got closer until I was blinded by it.

"I said, go inside," said the voice, hushed and angry.

I pushed past her, down the hall, knocking her arm with mine, and heading for the stairway. Just as I reached the stairway door I tripped over something large and fell. As I scrambled to get back to my feet, the flashlight came toward me and illuminated the area. The large object on the floor was Brandy. Her head, and now me, were covered in blood. I couldn't make a sound, just like in a dream. I looked up to see a gun next to the flashlight, it was aiming at me. I tried to flee, slipped on the bloody floor and fell again.

"Now, I'm certain you will want to do as I say, go back to Mrs. Callahan's room, I'll be right behind you," said the voice that I now realized was too deep, too old, to have been Brandy's.

I staggered back down the hall, my legs like rubber. I felt faint and had to keep placing my hands on the walls. When I was just outside Idzy's door, I threw myself against it as though I were falling.

"Shhhhh," she whispered loudly, grabbed my arm, pulled me back into Dorothy's apartment, and closed the door.

"Maggie dear, are you alright?" asked Dorothy as she came out of her room, "it sounds like Marley's ghost out..."

"Dorothy, go back to your..." I began.

"Good heavens!" she said when she saw me and my captor and made her way toward me. "Maggie, you're covered in blood, are you...?"

"Stay where you are you ridiculous old woman," said the woman with the gun.

"Good Lord!" said Dorothy, "is that you Elaine?"

"Elaine? The widow?" I asked and turned to look at her.

That's when she hit me in the head with the gun. Unlike in the movies, the hit did not knock me out, it didn't even knock me down, it just hurt a lot and now the blood on me was my own.

"My God woman, have you lost your mind? What is that you've got there, a gun?" asked Dorothy. "You're not really going to shoot anyone."

"I think she already did," I told Dorothy, "I think Brandy is dead in the hall."

"Are you two going to sit down or shall I just kill you both now and be done with it?" asked Elaine.

I grabbed Dorothy by the arm and we moved to the sofa, me clinging to her. I could feel her trembling and the fact that she was afraid made me even more terrified.

"Now then," she said to us when we were both seated, "tell me what you know, or what you think you know."

"You're the first Mrs. Haney? Why are you after me? I never..."

"Second," the woman said, "there was another one before me, the idiot that paid to put him through med school. He was having an affair with me while he was married to her and the stupid bitch never found out."

That really got to me and I blurted out, "probably because she was working two or three jobs to pay for him to go to school and whore around with you."

Another hit with the gun; only this time I saw it coming and raised my arm. The barrel of it hit my wrist and made a cracking sound that sent waves of pain up my arm that hurt so badly, for a moment I couldn't breathe. Dorothy cradled me in her arms and this time I did not feel her tremble but I could hear her heart and it was beating wildly.

"You're a real spitfire aren't ya?" she asked, "a real stupid one too."

"Are you alright?" I whispered to Dorothy. "Are you feeling ok?" Her breathing was too shallow and she was gulping as though she couldn't swallow.

"I'm fine darling," she whispered, but I knew she was not.

I stood up, "Elaine, before you kill me, or interrogate me or whatever your plans are, can we get Dorothy an aspirin?"

"An aspirin? You really are stupid aren't you? How could Brandy and David ever have believed you were on to them?" She shoved me back on the sofa.

A flash of lightening illuminated her face. There were spots of blood covering her and I knew it was probably Brandy's. I had heard the shot and thought it was thunder. But it was her, shooting that girl in cold blood. She was insane, I could see it in her eyes and I knew right then she was going to kill both of us.

"I thought Brandy was the one behind all of this," I said, trying to stall for time, waiting for the cavalry to come, but knowing none would.

"She thought she was too, she thought she was using David when all along it was the other way around. David and I had it all worked out, we had a plan. That little moron Brandy actually believed Bruce was going to divorce Linda and marry her. She thought Bruce would be so outraged about Linda's affair he'd divorce her on the spot. When that didn't happen, she tried to use my son to get what she wanted. What she didn't count on was how loyal dear David is to his mother, me." She smiled with satisfaction and sat on the chair opposite us, still holding the gun, still aiming it right at me.

"What has that got to do with me, with us?" I asked.

"You two know too much, all your snooping around and then coming back and telling everyone. Brandy heard your conversation with that hippie who was here earlier. I listened in when she called David. I had my ear to the phone too. David tried to tell her that it was all over, that things had gotten out of hand. He told me that too.

253

I said, no! I would not turn back now. We had already gone so far, we were so close to having it all. David wouldn't listen; he pushed me away and was actually going to walk out on me." Her voice became louder and hysterical.

"He was going to leave, leave the force, leave Florida, leave me. Don't you see? Then I would have had nothing. And that whore Linda was going to get everything. I ran after him. He got on his motorcycle and I got in my car and drove after him. He wouldn't stop. "

She was sobbing heavily. "I didn't mean to..to..I only wanted to make him stop...I would have never killed my own son!" She stood up and glowered down at us.

Now she panted and paced like a wild animal. "When I saw him in the road I knew he was dead, I knew that someone would come and see me there and that I..."

I got up from the sofa as quietly as I could when her back was turned. A flash of lightening momentarily lit the room. I grabbed the bottle of Baileys Irish Cream and held it behind me.

Elaine was still ranting, "It was Brandy's fault. I told David we didn't need her. It's her fault David is dead. You're lucky I got here when I did, she was coming to your room; I was following her. Stupid woman never even saw me until it was too late. I wasn't going to kill her but she frightened me. She had no business frightening me like that."

I could hear Dorothy's breathing becoming more erratic and feared she was going to have a heart attack. I held the bottle over my head and lunged for Elaine. That's when she turned, and in a flash of lightening saw me coming toward her, raised her gun and fired.

I didn't know if I had been hit but I didn't feel anything, so I kept going and knocked her to the ground and hit her in head with the liqueur bottle. The glass didn't break but it knocked her unconscious. Even so, I couldn't stop myself and I hit her again and again until I heard Dorothy say, "Maggie!"

I jumped off the inert body and ran to Dorothy.

"Are you alright? Where is your medicine?" She felt limp and her pulse was weak. "Hang on Dorothy, I'm getting help"

I stumbled to the door. Just as I put my hand on the knob it opened and I fell into the hall. There in front of me were two little hairy, lederhosen covered legs.

"Idzy," I said, "get help, please. It's Dorothy, she needs an ambulance."

"We sent for help already," I heard a familiar woman's voice from behind Idzy say.

"Pearl, is that you?" I asked, trying to see into the open door of Idzy's room.

"You didn't take her gun?" Pearl asked, looking behind me.

I turned and saw Elaine, gun in hand, making her way toward us. The flashes of lightening outside the window acted like a strobe and gave the whole scene a slow motion feel. Blood ran down her face and she was screaming.

Someone came from behind me and knocked me back to the floor. I looked up to see Errol storming in, brandishing a sword in his right hand and holding what looked like a hand grenade in his left. He threw the object at the charging woman. A light as bright as the sun came from the doorway. Reflexively, I turned to look behind me and was momentarily blinded. When I looked back I could see Elaine, now blinded herself still coming at us. The gun fired as she fell to the floor and I heard her scream a loud, agonizing wail.

"Dorothy!" I yelled, "Dorothy, are you ok?"

I still couldn't see and was feeling my way toward where I thought she was and tripped over the fallen Elaine. A sword pierced her arm, the gun lay harmlessly, inches from her outstretched hand, I put my head near hers and could hear her soft moaning.

"See?" I heard Errol say, "I told youse guys that old Jap sword would come in handy one day."

The sound of police sirens and the flash of the blue and red lights got louder and brighter and I sat with Dorothy who was so still and quiet I kept my fingers on her wrist to make sure she still had a pulse. It was weak, but it was there. I didn't let go until the paramedics took her away.

I heard them say they found an unconscious woman in the hall with a gun-shot wound to the shoulder and a fractured skull. Oh, Brandy, I thought, you're not dead, thank God.

I sat on a chair trying to concentrate on what was happening, but everything was blurry and soundless except the blood pounding in my head People moved in slow motion. Someone was examining me and asking me things but I couldn't hear them. It was like I was underwater and voices were only distant noise until I heard the one that sounded safe; Nathan's.

"This is quite a step up from the Hello Kitty, I like it." He smiled at me. It was tender and sympathetic and I thought I might cry, but stopped myself.

"I look like I should have a room over a saloon. Well, except for the blood and this thing." I held up my arm to show him the sling the paramedic had just applied, red silk ruffles draping it over it.

"We'll get you to your favorite ER in a minute, can you take a call?" He handed me his cell.

It was Zig. "Maggie? Are you ok?"

"Zig," was all I managed to say before I started sobbing.

"I got a call," he said, "the ambulance is bringing mom in. I'm meeting them at the hospital. I'll call you from there. Are you ok?"

"I tried to..." I said through sobs. "Is she…will she be ok?"

"I don't…I mean, it doesn't…look, I'll call you from the hospital."

The room was frantic with police and paramedics. The officers were taking statements from Pearl and Idzy.

"Look here," I heard Rose saying, "It's the little guy that makes cookies."

****

This is how it all happened. Idzy, with his glass to the door, heard our voices in Dorothy's room. He couldn't phone for help because all the phones were out. Pearl, however, who was his *guest* for the evening, happened to have been in the signal corps in World War II. She used her mega-flashlight to send out code through the bedroom window. Errol, whose room was in the next building and who was familiar with the code, saw it. Apparently keeping watch on Pearl and Idzy was a hobby of his. He grabbed his war souvenirs and somehow made it to us just in the nick of time. The grenade he threw was not loaded, but I suspect he was.

 And that is how I came to be saved by Idzy, Pearl, and Errol Flynn.

ENGULFED
EPILOUGE

It was dark, but not so dark that I couldn't see Zig from the corner of my eye trying to hide behind a curtain. Fear and dread made my head pound and all the noise of the place became a muffled drone. Oh God, I thought, I have to pee, this can't be happening to me, what have I gotten myself into now? My knees were shaking and my throat closed up.

Rose, who apparently never felt fear in her life, looked as calm as if she were in her own living room.

I'm going to die right here on the spot, I thought, and I have to pee. What if I pass out and pee in my pants? What a way to go.

Suddenly, light shone in my face; light so bright I thought it must look like what people see in the moment right before they die. "Don't go toward the light," I whispered over and over to myself.

A loud, God-like voice that seemed to come from everywhere said, "Ladies and Gentlemen, the Shell Harbor Talent Jamboree is proud to present to you, Carmen Electric and the Supremes!"

I walked forward and stood behind Brian, then glanced behind me to see Zig and Dorothy smiling and applauding. With Rose at my side, I raised my right hand and sang out, "Stop, in the name of love."

The crowd went wild; Nathan Gonzales sat in a front row center seat clapping, a bouquet of roses on his lap. Behind him I could make out Rod, Leo, my parents and...was that a seagull?

Kathleen is currently writing the second novel in the series. Entangled will have even more adventure, danger and maybe, finally, a bit of romance for Maggie.
She is also writing a drama with the working title *The Mule* about a woman being forced into crime to protect the lives of her family.

17912754R00142

Made in the USA
Lexington, KY
04 October 2012